Ella Gyland grew up in Norther[...]
with books, and this library [...]
entertainment in the long, da[...]
imagined that she might one day write a book herself, but
instead moved to England after she graduated from
University of Copenhagen to look for a job involving her
language skills.

Aside from a stint in the Danish civil service, she has
worked for a UK travel agent, a consultancy company, in
banking, hospital administration, and for a county court
before setting herself up as a freelance translator and
linguist. When she began to pursue her writing in earnest,
she won the New Talent Award in 2011 from the Festival of
Romance and received a Commended from the Yeovil
Literary Prize.

Ella lives in London, happily surrounded by books in all
genres.

henriettegyland.wordpress.com

twitter.com/henrigyland

THE DAY THE GERMANS CAME

ELLA GYLAND

One More Chapter
a division of HarperCollins*Publishers*
1 London Bridge Street
London SE1 9GF
www.harpercollins.co.uk
HarperCollins*Publishers*
Macken House, 39/40 Mayor Street Upper,
Dublin 1, D01 C9W8
This paperback edition 2023
1
First published in Great Britain in ebook format
by HarperCollins*Publishers* 2022

A catalogue record of this book is available from the British Library

ISBN: 9780008591748

Printed and bound in the UK using 100% Renewable Electricity
by CPI Group (UK) Ltd

Prologue

Copenhagen, Denmark

29th September 1943

Golden trees flanked the streets around Rosenborg Castle Gardens, also known simply as the King's Garden, in the centre of Copenhagen. A fresh September morning, the sun high in the sky and the air crisp, it was the perfect day for cycling, to work or to the shops, and something David always enjoyed.

But today he was troubled. It was the final year of his Law degree, and he hadn't done well in his last exam. Truth be told, he'd probably enjoyed student life a little too much; the late nights in the jazz club dancing with pretty girls, or debating politics with his fellow students in dingy, smoke-filled taverns till the early hours. He hadn't focused enough on the actual work and was feeling the effects of that now.

A convoy of German troop transport vehicles thundered down Gothersgade, and David stopped and watched as they drove past. Despite being under German occupation, Denmark had more or less been able to carry on as normal, with their own government and their own laws. Except lately the Germans had tightened their grip, and after increased pressure the Danish government had resigned.

He wondered what the consequences of that might be for himself and others like him.

This morning, a special service was to be held at the Great Synagogue in Krystalgade, on the occasion of Rosh Hashanah, the Jewish New Year, and it was the first time he was celebrating the holidays without his mother who was in hospital. He would visit her, of course, as he did every day, but she tired easily, and it wouldn't be the same.

A man was singing in the street, as if he hadn't a care in the world, his rich baritone joyful and hearty, and normally David would have smiled and nodded in recognition, but today neither the singing nor the glorious sunshine could dispel his worries and the strange sense that clouds were brewing.

What happened if he didn't do well in his next exams? It had been his late father's dearest wish that his only child received an education, and he had scrimped and saved to give David that opportunity. An opportunity David welcomed with immense gratitude, but it also came with the responsibility not to disappoint.

A greater worry was his mother. What if she didn't recover from her illness? It didn't bear thinking about.

Turning right into Landemærket, which led into Krystalgade, he parked his bike outside the synagogue. When he spotted the rabbi and his fourteen-year-old son about to wheel their bicycles behind the building, he realised that he was early.

'Good morning, herr Melchior,' he said. 'I trust all is well with you and your family.'

Frowning, the rabbi gave a curt nod. 'As well as can be expected under the circumstances. I had a visit last night.'

David raised his eyebrows. 'Oh?'

'I may as well tell you. It's been on my mind all night.' The rabbi lowered his voice and placed a comforting hand on his son's shoulder, worry etched on his face. The boy looked set to cry.

'As we were getting ready for bed, a lady turned up. An elegant lady, soberly dressed, but with an urgency about her. Turns out to be Hans Hedtoft's secretary.'

'The politician?' David felt a sliver of unease.

'The very same. She was relaying a message, through Hans Hedtoft, which had come from none other than Georg Duckwitz. You're familiar with the name, I take it. The German naval attaché?'

'Yes, of course.'

The rabbi drew a deep sigh. 'Well, here's what the secretary had to say…' He motioned for David to come closer.

When he'd finished, David felt the blood leave his face. This was what he'd both expected and hoped would never happen.

'And now it rests on my shoulders to pass the message on to our community,' said the rabbi, 'but I worry that people will not listen. I'm not the official rabbi. This is what's been keeping me awake. That and whether we can reach everyone in time. It seems almost impossible.'

David understood his concern. The chief rabbi had been arrested the same day the government had resigned, along with some of the leading figures in Danish society. Suddenly Melchior, who was relatively young, was faced with a heavy task.

'Of course people will listen to you, herr Melchior,' he reassured the rabbi. 'If there's anything I can do to help…'

The rabbi smiled for the first time. 'You can stay and hear my full message to the congregation; I would find that reassuring. But – and I apologise – I plain forgot to ask after your mother. How is she?'

'A touch of pneumonia. She suffers regularly, but the doctors assure me that she'll be out of hospital soon.'

'I'm relieved to hear it. As for my own burden, may God forgive me if I'm too late.'

Later, David sat amongst the congregation, listening to herr Melchior again. The rabbi had changed into his robe, hat, and black and white *tallit*, the Jewish prayer shawl, and there was no sign of the doubting and worried man he had been earlier. Standing before the Torah, he gave out nothing but authority as he looked out over the wooden pews flanked by a two-tiered gallery on either side.

More than one hundred people had gathered in the early morning hour. Some of the men, not all, wore *kippahs* and some of them prayer shawls; the women had donned sombre dresses with a modest hemline. There were young children too, restless with youthful energy, innocent and unsuspecting.

Clearing his throat, the rabbi began. 'My friends, we have no time now to continue prayers. What we have long feared is now upon us. There has been news that this coming Friday night, the night between the first and the second of October, the Gestapo will come. They will come and arrest all Danish Jews.'

David felt the mood change immediately, from one of expectancy to horror, as he'd known it would from the moment the rabbi had confided in him.

Eyes widened with fear stared back at the rabbi, and several of the women put their hands over their mouths to stifle their cries of distress. Even the children stopped fidgeting, sensing a change in their elders. One old man, his body bent with age, sobbed openly, and the sound of his despair cut right through David.

We believed ourselves safe in Denmark, in Hitler's so-called model protectorate, he thought. *But no longer*.

Rabbi Melchior continued. 'They have a list of addresses, and they will come to every home on the list and take us all to two big ships waiting in Copenhagen harbour. Then, from what we know, on to camps further east. We must warn as many of our community as we can.'

They'd all heard stories from German and Austrian refugees who had joined their congregation earlier on in the war. The unspeakable horrors of the camps. The unimaginable fear and persecution. Now, for the people in this synagogue and those all over the country, these weren't just rumours or stories anymore. This was their reality.

As people recovered from their initial shock, they began to mutter urgently, too many voices at the same time for David to make anything out.

'There are two things you should do,' the rabbi went on, more firmly. 'Number one, you should stay away from your homes on Friday night. What will happen after that we don't know, but on Friday night, in any case, don't be at home.'

Several of the congregation rose, shuffling and talking urgently as they began to leave the pews.

'Number two,' he said, raising his voice to drown out the commotion, 'tell everyone. Pass this news on to as many friends, family, whoever you can, so that they also know to leave home by Friday. We must look after each other. We must protect as many as we can.'

Those about to leave stopped and looked back at him, and he delivered the final part of what he had planned to say.

'The synagogue will be closed for the New Year. This will be another way of telling people something is going on.'

As the congregation left, as quickly as they could without causing suspicion or panic, many of them nervous and tight-lipped, heading home to pack or pick up their children from school, David caught Melchior's eyes.

The rabbi had delivered the message. People had

believed him, and it was now up to them all to get themselves to safety.

And I must go to my mother, David thought.

How on earth do I explain to her that, once again, she has to flee for her life?

Chapter One

Helsingør, Denmark

August 2018

The smell of old carpets and empty rooms greeted Cecilie Lund as she unlocked the door to her grandmother's ground-floor flat in a quiet neighbourhood of Elsinore. The flat was in a low-rise red-brick tenement block, flanked by several other similar blocks and all built in the 1940s, and was only five minutes' walk to the centre of the large town if you walked at a quick pace. The train station, the ferry, the beach, and a lively pedestrianised shopping street were all within reach, and her grandparents had loved living here.

Like most tenement buildings in Denmark, the ground floor was actually a sort of mezzanine, one short flight of stairs above the ground, with the area next to the steps set aside for prams and pushchairs, or other items too cumbersome for the tenants to carry up and down the stairs each time they were going out or returning home.

And as in many tenement buildings in similar neighbourhoods, these items would be left largely undisturbed by the other occupants; in Denmark you could trust your neighbours. There was faith in the community. Stealing someone else's pram was the lowest of the low.

A deep sigh escaped Cecilie as she pushed the door to the flat shut behind her whilst clutching a large cardboard box, and she tried to close her mind to the idea of prams. In spite of the area designated for prams and the like, there were no babies amongst the tenants who used the same stairs, as the five other flats were occupied by older people like her grandmother, Inger.

Just as there would be no babies in Cecilie's life.

Balancing the box in front of her, she leaned back against the door as the feeling she vaguely recognised as grief and loss came over her, that giant emptiness she faced every morning as she woke and which caught her unawares several times during the day. A sense of having failed, of having flunked an important test with no chance of a re-take. It was an obsessive thought she would spend the first half hour of every day contemplating.

Unexplained infertility, the doctors told them. Sometimes they used the words 'biologically incompatible' too. At any rate, it was clearly her fault. Her husband, who had looked deep into her eyes when they vowed 'for better or for worse', wasted no time in finding a woman who could give him children, and the happy couple were already expecting.

'We had a good thing, Cici,' he'd said as he turned in the doorway and smiled sadly at her, which somehow made everything ten times more unbearable. 'But I want children, and we're wearing each other down over it.'

She'd flinched at the casual cruelty of his words, even as she understood that at thirty-eight and forty respectively, time was running out for them both.

Her mother had been one of five, and the rest of her family had been similarly blessed. Of the twelve cousins, she was the only one who hadn't had children, fit for nothing except a full refund.

Stop it.

Angry with herself for dwelling on what she couldn't change, she shrugged off her summer jacket and hung it on the fitted coat rack beside the door, one of the few items of furniture left in the almost empty flat. It would soon be taken over by the next council tenant. The death of her grandmother, Inger, had provided Cecilie with an opportunity to focus on something other than her own self-pity, and today she would make a start on clearing out the cellar room as she'd promised.

Two months ago, the fiercely independent ninety-six-year-old Inger Jensen, who had refused to wear an alarm around her neck or stop living on her own, had fallen on her way to the bathroom in the night and had lain on the floor with a broken hip for a few hours, listening out for the sounds of her neighbours waking. Always resourceful, she'd managed to use a coat hanger to pull her duvet over her to keep warm, and when she'd heard people stirring next door, had used the same coat hanger to bang loudly on her wardrobe, shouting for help, until the neighbours realised something was wrong and called the fire brigade.

A few weeks later, Cecilie's funny and affectionate grandmother, who knew how to wolf-whistle better than any builder, had unbelievably succumbed to pneumonia in hospital.

Afterwards, the family discovered that she'd suffered from stage-four cancer, which she hadn't told anyone about. Her death, and not being taken into her confidence, had devastated her children, in particular Cecilie's mother.

Cecilie wondered why her grandmother had chosen not to say anything, but perhaps it was a matter of pride, of not wanting to worry them. Or maybe not wanting any fuss.

'An old person's best friend', people would say, referring to the pneumonia and shaking their heads as they made their condolences. 'A blessing, really.'

A blessing…?

Cecilie wanted to spit whenever someone said that. She'd never known anyone to embrace life as wholeheartedly as Inger Jensen had. Her grandmother had lived for the present and taken things as they came, tackling life's ups and downs with common sense and a willingness to roll up her sleeves if required.

I could learn something from that, she thought. *Maybe we all could.*

On the doormat of her beloved grandmother's flat lay the post. Inger had been a keen correspondent of the old-fashioned letter-writing kind, and had acquaintances in several countries. Briefly, Cecilie glanced at the postmarks – Santa Barbara, Tel Aviv, Rotterdam. Full of admiration for her well-travelled grandmother and suddenly overwhelmed by the thought that Inger was truly gone, she swiped angrily at the tears welling up in her eyes. She had grieved like the rest of them – oh, she had grieved – but had hoped she was over the worst by now.

'Grief doesn't come with a sell-by date,' she remembered her grandmother saying when Cecilie had asked if she was getting over it, following the death of Cecilie's grandfather almost twenty years ago.

Stupid question, really. Of course it didn't. To this day her own immature comment made her flush with embarrassment.

Sighing deeply, she put the letters in the box. She'd take them round to her mother later. Together they would open them and decide on the best way to respond.

In the narrow kitchen with its blue-painted cupboard doors – a colour that had never changed for as long as she could remember – she plugged in the electric kettle she'd brought. Tea made, she grabbed a packet of biscuits and a roll of bin liners, lifted the keys to the cellar off a hook by the door, and went outside again and round to the gable end of the building to the cellarway.

The concrete steps were still wet from a shower earlier, but the cellar was dry and warm, the small windows having recently been replaced by double glazing by the Housing Department in a token nod to renovation. A quiet hum came from the locked boiler room to her left, dust motes danced in the air, and the familiar smell of wood, laundry powder, and bicycle oil assailed her. Cecilie stopped for a moment on the doorstep in the sudden realisation that this was the last time she'd ever come here. The last connection to her childhood.

She smiled as a memory intruded, of playing down here with her cousins. How they used to have races down the corridor, from one end of the building to the other, or playing tag running in and out of the connected rooms; laundry room, wood workshop, bike storage, ducking under sheets and pillow cases or dodging the older kids souping up their mopeds away from prying eyes.

Occasionally they would skip rope or play hopscotch, outlining a pattern of rectangles on the floor with chalk. If she closed her eyes, she could almost hear the sound of banging doors, the slapping of sandals against concrete, and the muted echo of high-pitched voices.

She unlocked the door to her grandmother's private cellar room and propped the door open with an old tin bucket in case a draft from the main door caused it to slam.

The room was about two by three metres with a high cobweb-covered window at the end, an old wardrobe to the right of the narrow door, and a shelf rack on the left, stacked high with cardboard boxes, faded ink indicating their content. Because of the open door to the laundry room opposite, it was surprisingly bright in there. Even so, Cecilie switched on the ceiling light – a single fly-specked bulb – if only to provide a sense of comfort, and put her mug on a space on the shelf where she was unlikely to knock it over.

'You deal with it, please,' her mother had said of the

cellar. 'There's nothing down there I want. Nothing any of us want, I think.'

Her face tightened in irritation that none of her cousins had offered to help, excusing themselves with kids-this-and-kids-that, but in hindsight there was hardly room for more than one person, and she preferred tackling it on her own anyway. She began the seemingly monumental task by going through the labelled boxes that been stored there for years, blowing away the fur of dust on top and discovering, to her horror, the corpses of all manner of creepy-crawlies that had become trapped inside.

Most of it was junk, like old newspapers and magazines she didn't think would be of use to anyone, and a box of yellowed tablecloths made of fine, old-fashioned linen. They were too big for a normal-sized dining table, but one of the aunts might want to sell them to an antique shop. There were old children's shoes and several pairs of rusty ice-skates, the kind designed to be strapped onto the wearer's own boots, two boxes of empty jam jars, old-fashioned crockery too ugly to be retro, moth-eaten jumpers from her mother's childhood, tarnished picture frames without the glass, and a stack of children's books with old-fashioned spellings which were disintegrating at the spine.

A box of Christmas decorations made her go, 'Ooh,' and having picked out the few broken baubles, careful not to cut herself, she put the rest aside for the eldest of her aunts who liked to make a real fuss of her Christmas tree.

After having replenished her mug of tea twice, the shelves were devoid of boxes. Some of the junk went straight in the communal bins, the rest Cecilie carried to her car.

She'd saved the old wardrobe till last. Inside it, which she knew from last time she was down here with her grandmother, was a selection of old dresses which had fascinated her as a child, and that she and her cousins, both boys and girls, had used for dressing up on the rare occasions they were allowed.

The dresses were still there, each wrapped in a protective cover. When Cecilie had started in her current position as English and Drama teacher at Old Hellerup High School, and been tasked with revamping the props for the Drama Department, she'd asked her grandmother if she could make use of the dresses. The answer had been a resounding no.

Ten years later, in hindsight, Inger's refusal made perfect sense. Dating back to the 1940s and 1950s, with a few from the swinging 60s thrown in, the dresses were probably valuable and belonged in a museum rather than in the hands of stroppy high-school kids who didn't appreciate their cultural significance.

Except Cecilie wanted them for herself.

Briefly, a guilty colour rose in her cheeks over her selfishness. This was the main reason she was glad none of her cousins were helping clearing out the cellar. They had their families, their supportive husbands/wives and their blonde, perky-nosed, and confident children. What did *she* have? The dresses from their grandmother's youth seemed like a fair exchange, and in her own head she'd managed to persuade herself this was what her grandmother would have wanted anyway.

There were fifteen in total, ranging from elegant ladies' suits to evening dresses, some so glamorous it was hard to imagine the kind of occasion her practical grandmother would have worn them. Reverently she lifted them out one by one and folded them neatly into an IKEA bag she'd brought for the purpose. Another day she'd see what could be salvaged and worn again, perhaps with a few adjustments.

Then she started on the shoes, flattening the shoe boxes as she went along, but these were too worn and scuffed to be of interest to anyone, and they went straight in a black bin liner. One of the shoe boxes contained an old wooden cigar box instead. Puzzled by this parcel-within-a-parcel, she flicked the lid open, then sat back on her haunches in surprise.

Even in the fading afternoon light the tarnished jewellery shone with a dull glow – broches inlaid with what looked like amber, gems and semi-precious stones in several colours, rows of pearls held together by elaborate clasps, heavy bracelets too chunky for her grandmother's delicate wrists. Despite their tarnish the pieces were stunning but probably fake, otherwise why else would they be in the cellar?

That's odd, she thought. She'd never seen her grandmother wear anything other than her wedding ring and her gold *Dagmarkors*, the Danish crucifix traditionally given to a baby girl at birth or to a young woman on her confirmation.

Yet the discovery charmed her. Had Inger Jensen been into amateur dramatics in her youth, or had she simply been a closet magpie, attracted to shiny objects? It was as if a window had opened into a part of her life, the kind you never imagined your grandparents to have had because to you they were just, well, old.

Cecilie wondered if her mother knew anything about this and resolved to ask her later when she dropped by.

A slip of paper was tucked in underneath one of the larger pieces, and she unfolded it. On it, in her bold and distinctive hand, her grandmother had written:

Property of Mrs Nathan & Mr David Nathan

The little hairs at the back of her neck stood on end as she considered those words. Was the jewellery stolen? And had Inger's bad conscience compelled her to hide it in the cellar? Cecilie couldn't imagine her grandmother as a thief, but how else could it have come to be in her possession? Again the question came back to her why these pieces were in the cellar. If the jewellery had been given to her grandmother as a gift, wouldn't she have worn it? Or if it was genuine, sold some of it when money was tight, which it had been sometimes when Cecilie's mother was growing up? Given the note in the box, it was more likely her grandmother, or maybe both her grandparents, had kept it safe on behalf of someone else and forgotten about it. Surely there could be no other explanation.

But what do we really know about other people when it comes down to it? Just look at her husband, Peter.

Wishing she could un-see her find, she snapped the lid shut, and put the cigar box in the bag with the dresses. Her mother was fragile at the moment; perhaps it would be best to run this by her father first.

She locked the cellar door behind her and headed towards the outer door, laden down by the last two bags. Then she stopped, returned to the room and unlocked it again, thinking of the note she'd found with the jewellery. Something was niggling at the back of her mind.

Had she forgotten anything?

No. The room was completely empty except for the shelf rack and the old wardrobe and ready for the house clearance company next week. Shaking her head, she locked it again and went back upstairs to the flat to collect her things. Then, as she said her final goodbye, she walked around the abandoned rooms, touching the woodwork, the textured wallpaper, which was darker in places where pictures had hung, and the pencil marks measuring the grandchildren's height as they grew. This flat was the last link to her childhood, to a time of fewer complications, and the loss was two-fold.

'I'll miss you, *Mormor*,' she whispered to the silent room.

Leaving the old tenement building, she stopped by the recycling centre and dropped off the rubbish, then rearranged the IKEA bag and the few boxes in the boot of the car, breathing in a curious mix of cellar odours and a faint hint of her grandmother's perfume. She was about to close the hatch when her eyes fell on one of the letters she'd found on the doormat.

Sender, D. Nathan, Tel Aviv

That was it. She knew she'd seen the name Nathan before.

Frowning, she snatched it up. It had to be *the* David Nathan who owned the jewellery, surely? It would be too much of a coincidence otherwise. But why had Inger never spoken of a David Nathan before? She had been a born storyteller and had loved regaling her grandchildren and anyone else who would listen with wonderful tales from her many years.

Inger Jensen had had a few secrets, had perhaps hidden more from her family than her illness and the cigar box in the cellar. What they were, Cecilie couldn't even begin to fathom, and her grandmother couldn't tell her now.

But perhaps this David Nathan had some answers.

Chapter Two

Helsingør

September 1943

The train stopped with a jolt, and I adjusted my travel suit, which consisted of a plain grey pencil skirt and one of my father's old dinner jackets that a tailor had turned inside out and repurposed to fit a woman's figure. I'd perched a red felted wool hat on my head at a rakish angle to give the impression of a young woman about town, yet inside my stomach roiled with nervous tension.

This was my first time in Helsingør since before the Nazis invaded and it was also the first time I'd travelled by train without my parents. My last train journey had been a trip to Rungsted Beach four years ago, and I'd sat on a blanket with my mother and father and drunk coffee from a flask. I'd been seventeen at the time, and it had been real

21

coffee. Slowing my breath, I allowed my memory to take over. Waves breaking gently, seagulls squawking, the tang of sundried bladderwrack littering the sand. It seemed like a lifetime ago, and the substitute coffee, which was all you could get these days, was just that; a substitute.

Today the train was packed with German soldiers, young men, some of them still only boys, and I found myself surrounded by them, my red hat a single splash of colour amongst the grey-green of the Wehrmacht. One of them had been trying to catch my eye throughout the journey, but I'd kept my gaze firmly fixed on the landscape rolling by, ignoring his disappointment.

I'd never been much of a flirt, and even if I'd occasionally wished that I knew how to, especially when passing the neighbour's handsome son on the stairs, I did not possess that skill.

'Hello, Inger Bredahl,' he would say in a sing-song voice and with a teasing glint in his eyes, and I'd go red and tongue-tied and hate myself for feeling so awkward in his company.

But I would *never* flirt with a German, no matter how attractive and attentive he was. That sort of behaviour earned you a bad reputation.

As I rose to retrieve my suitcase from the luggage rack, the flirtatious soldier jumped to his feet, and I felt a moment of alarm.

'*Erlaube mich,*' he said and lifted it down for me. *Allow me.*

'Thank you,' I muttered in German, one of the few words I knew of that hated language, and slid past him, ignoring the rest of his company who politely stepped aside to let me leave the compartment first.

Most Danes avoided any kind of engagement with their occupiers wherever possible, but even as I loathed what they represented, I always experienced a small pang of guilt when cold-shouldering them. Especially when they were being friendly. It went against the grain with me to be rude, as it would with anyone who'd been brought up to be polite and kind, and in the end were they not just people like me?

I pushed open one of the three heavy wooden doors of the railway station and crossed the large square in front of it, then briefly I looked back at the station. Built in the style of a Renaissance castle with turrets and a crenellated centre gable, it was said to be the finest station building in Denmark, and it pleased me to see that despite its proximity to Helsingør shipyard, so far it had avoided being hit by the British Lancaster bombers.

After three years of German occupation and three years of what felt like endless bombing by the Royal Air Force, I still found it hard to see an end to the war. The British might be Denmark's friends and allies, but how could you appreciate this when you cowered in the basement, listening to the drone of aeroplanes, bombs whistling as they fell, the crash of impact deadened to a *thump* by the shelter walls? The not-knowing what might be gone the next day, your familiar landscape rearranged. People dead who had been alive yesterday. The bombers were careful not to target civilians, but they made mistakes. I shuddered at the thought.

Over the summer the mood had changed in

Copenhagen, and in other cities too. As people heard about the various German military defeats, which were reported by Danish newsreaders on the illegal radio station *Radio London*, they became bolder. Clashes broke out between young Danes and German soldiers, and the resistance movement upped their sabotage. The Germans demanded the death penalty for sabotage, the government refused, and on the 29th of August they had resigned. Martial law was imposed.

Denmark was fed up with being 'Germany's breadbasket', and responded with widespread strikes and civil unrest. The capital had been like a seething cauldron ever since.

So when I told my parents that I'd applied for a job as an assistant to a bookbinder in Helsingør, they were more than happy for me to leave the capital and stay with my father's brother, Uncle Poul, in the relatively quiet seaside town.

My uncle and his wife lived in a narrow cobbled street running perpendicular to St Olai Church Square. The cobbles were still slick with rain from earlier in the day, and to keep my balance in my heeled brogues I had to walk in the middle of the alley, stepping over the gratings covering the drains.

Still-flowering crimson hollyhocks framed the green-painted door of the small cottage, and as usual it was unlocked so I let myself in. My aunt, Marie, was in the kitchen, drying the dishes.

'There you are,' she said matter-of-factly, wiping her hands on her apron. 'I could've sent Jens to pick you up from the station, but I can see you made it just fine.'

I put down my suitcase and gave her a quick hug. 'It's not far and I enjoyed the walk.'

A young man appeared in the doorway to the parlour and sent me a lopsided grin. 'Hello, Inger.'

I stared at him for a moment, trying to place him. 'Jens? I don't believe it. You've grown so much!'

'I'm sixteen, actually.'

'Of course you are. Only, I didn't expect...'

He laughed. My cousin hadn't just grown. Broad-shouldered and square-jawed like the actor Cary Grant, he towered over his mother, and he'd become a man. Only his unruly thatch of fair hair remained of the boy I last saw five years ago.

'Jens is at the grammar school now,' said Aunt Marie, and even her usual no-nonsense demeanour couldn't quite disguise her pride.

'Here, let me take that.' With a cheeky grin, Jens picked up my suitcase and took the stairs at the back of the kitchen two steps at a time.

'Put it in Gudrun's room,' Aunt Marie called after him.

In our exchange of letters my aunt had suggested that I share with Gudrun, Jens's older sister, who was about the same age as me, instead of sleeping in the tiny unheated room behind the parlour which was mainly used for storage. I was grateful for that, but hoped it wasn't going to inconvenience Gudrun.

'Sure.'

Aunt Marie turned to me. 'I hope you're hungry. We're having fried pork with apples. I queued outside Kødbørsen, the butcher's, this morning and managed to buy eight slices of bacon. With potatoes and rye bread it should be enough for the five of us, even with Jens's appetite. We'll eat at six when your uncle is back. This evening he's helping to dig for peat, so it's a little later than usual. And Gudrun works at the brewery where they finish at five. In the meantime, I suggest you unpack your clothes and hang them in Gudrun's closet. She's made space for you.'

'Thank you, I'll do that. And I love *æbleflæsk*. I haven't had that in years.'

Aunt Marie made a sound which sounded like contempt for the kind of food 'city folk' might put on the table, and returned to her dishes.

The thought of dinner made my mouth water. It had been difficult for my parents to buy bacon as the Germans would confiscate most pigs, although farmers were allowed to keep some stock for rearing. It was fortunate that Aunt Marie had managed to get any, but Helsingør was surrounded by farmland, and I imagined it was easier to get in a town this size, as opposed to the capital.

I followed Jens up the stairs. Where my cousin had changed almost beyond recognition, Aunt Marie remained the same – a little intimidating, if I was to be honest.

Jens had left my suitcase on the bed to the left of the single window, and I looked out over the yard behind. It looked much the same; the old apple tree was still there, some of its branches now overhanging the neighbour's garden and there were some roses too. The only thing different from my last visit was a raised bed with potatoes where there used to be a bit of lawn and bushes at the end, separated from the narrow path by a row of boards. The boards were weathered with flaking yellow paint.

I squinted to see better, then turned to Jens in surprise. 'The outside loo has gone!'

Nodding, he went to stand next to me. 'We had a water closet put in two years ago. In the room next door. Now we have gooseberry bushes there and get lots of fruit. They're very good. Must be all that natural fertiliser.' Jens grinned.

I made a face. 'That was your bedroom, I remember. So where do you sleep now?'

'I'm in the attic.'

'Ugh. Doesn't that get cold?' I shivered in memory of the draughty space under the rafters and the rickety ladder leading to the loft, which Jens, aged eleven at the time, had mounted like a gazelle while his older sister had shouted for him not to wreck the bloody thing.

Jens shrugged. 'Dad managed to get some salvaged boards from a bombed-out building. They keep out the wind. But yes, I have some thick blankets.'

He left me to unpack, and I unpinned my hat and hung my clothes next to Gudrun's in the wardrobe. I hadn't brought much. Another suit beside the one I was wearing, a couple of plaid skirts and button-down blouses, a pair of slacks, a long-sleeved day dress, as well as a Fair Isle cardigan. Frivolously, I'd also packed a halter-neck evening gown in apple-green rayon, my peep-toe heels and the only pair of stockings I owned which had laddered and been repaired twice. The stockings and my smalls I put in the chest of drawers between the two beds.

Then, surprising myself at my own daring, I took a

quick peek at Gudrun's clothes. There wasn't a single dress amongst them, only shirts, trousers, and jackets in stiff cotton and wool, an oddly masculine, militant look. Or maybe not so odd; from what I could remember of my cousin, she'd never been one for dresses and pretty things. Apprehension crept into my previous excitement over seeing Gudrun again. How well did we actually know each other? And now we'd be sharing a room for several months until I'd earned enough in my new job to maybe get my own lodgings.

What if we didn't get on?

Pushing the thoughts aside, I closed the wardrobe and went back downstairs to see if I could help Aunt Marie in the kitchen.

'Could you set the table in the dining room?' she asked me. 'Normally we eat in the kitchen, but since it's your first day here, I thought you'd be more comfortable in there.'

'You don't need to go to any trouble for me.' I was touched by this and a little embarrassed that a fuss was being made. 'We usually eat in the kitchen as well.'

'Nonsense, of course I do.' Aunt Marie smiled for the first time. 'I'm glad you're here with us, Inger. We've missed you all, and Gudrun...' She didn't finish the sentence, instead turning away to stop the potatoes from boiling over, but I caught the lines of worry creasing her forehead. 'Well, Gudrun is Gudrun,' she added, and I wondered what she meant, but her closed expression warned me not to ask.

Not yet, anyway.

The parlour hadn't changed either since last time I was

here. In the corner by one of the windows, overlooking the garden, stood a bureau with a blotter and inkstand, beside it a low bookcase, a settee with antimacassars of hand-knotted lace, and a woollen blanket had been crammed against the opposite wall, with a sideboard by the door to the kitchen. The walls were hung with a small number of family photos as well as a painting, depicting Aunt Marie's family farm, now owned by her eldest brother. There was also a picture of Grundtvig, the nineteenth-century Danish pastor and philosopher.

'In my home we followed his teaching and would sing before dinner instead of saying grace,' she'd explained to me once, but to my disappointment she'd never demonstrated it. No one in my family was particularly religious, and Aunt Marie's background fascinated me.

But the pride and joy, a polished oak table with cabriole legs, dominated the tiny room. I moved the runner in the centre of the table and put it on the sideboard. The runner was embroidered with cross-stitch autumn leaves, and Aunt Marie had one runner for each of the seasons, just like my mother did. No decent home was complete without it, apparently.

I then laid the table with a crisp white table cloth and my aunt's blue fluted wedding china from Royal Copenhagen. There were eleven plates left, from a set of twelve, and only one had a chip in it, showing the care taken during my aunt and uncle's twenty-four years of marriage. We took care of our things at home too, but this single chip stood out to me as a reminder that even that which isn't perfect can be infinitely precious.

Jens came in, carrying a blue-painted chair from the kitchen. 'Mum says she'll have this one.'

'I don't mind what I sit on.'

'Oh no, God forbid hospitality should be lacking in this house. You know what she's like. Guests always come first.'

'But I'm not a guest,' I protested.

'Even so.' He shrugged.

I bit the inside of my cheek as a sense of uncertainty stole over me. I loved staying with my aunt and uncle and was grateful that I could take a job in another town and still be with family. I was grateful too, for the comfort it gave my parents to think me out of harm's way, but it embarrassed me to be singled out as a special guest, and I hoped it was only for this evening.

'How are your parents, then?' Uncle Poul asked when we sat down for dinner. Gudrun still hadn't returned, but had called the neighbour who had a telephone to say she would be delayed.

'They're both well.' Glad of the distraction, I draped my napkin over my lap. I'd sensed the tension in Aunt Marie, whose mouth had been like a thin line when the neighbour delivered this piece of news, although my uncle appeared unbothered by it. 'They send their regards.'

'I sure would like to see my brother soon, and your mother, but I don't suppose it's a time for gadding about at the moment.'

'The train was full of Germans,' I said.

'Mm. It'll be the Führer himself travelling on the Danish railways soon, with Comrade Stalin hot on his heels, if the news is anything to go by.' Uncle Poul chortled. 'Wonder if he'll be expecting us to salute and wave the swastika.'

'He'll be disappointed if he does,' snapped his wife as she began serving.

'Most of the soldiers were young. Some of them not much older than Jens.'

'They do regular changeovers at Kronborg Castle where some of them are billeted,' Uncle Poul explained. 'I'm told it's so they don't get too comfortable here before they're shipped off to the Eastern Front.'

His words hung in the air as he glanced at his son. The German losses at Stalingrad may have delighted the Allies, but even the enemy's mothers wept for their dead sons.

Aunt Marie changed the subject. 'When do you start at the bookbinder's?'

I put down my knife and fork, and used my napkin before answering. 'Tomorrow. I'm rather excited. I applied for a couple of places in Copenhagen, without any luck, but herr Kiær didn't seem at all surprised that a woman wanted to learn the trade.'

'Why should he be?' said Aunt Marie. 'One day women all over the country will be doing the same jobs as men, I'm sure of it.'

My uncle snorted, and Aunt Marie sent him a disparaging look.

The kitchen door banged open before this could escalate into an argument, and Gudrun came in, bringing with her cool, damp air from outside. She wrapped me in a massive hug, and my earlier misgivings that we wouldn't get on completely evaporated.

Of course we would; it was almost like the old days.

'It's wonderful that you're here.' She beamed, red spots of excitement on her cold cheeks. 'We're going to have such fun. There's this super dance on at—'

'Gudrun,' said her mother.

'Yes, yes.' Gudrun pulled out a chair and flung herself down on it, then tucked into her dinner. 'I'll tell you all about it later.'

She kept her promise. After we'd cleared up in the kitchen and gathered around the wireless for news on the war, Gudrun shared the plans she had for the both of us. That I hadn't had a say in these plans didn't seem to occur to her, but it hardly mattered. Getting ready for bed, I allowed the excitement to envelop me.

'…and you'll meet my friend Bodil. She's looking forward to getting some fashion advice from the big city. You've seen my clothes' – Gudrun rolled her eyes and laughed at herself – 'I'm really not the one to ask about things like that.'

I smiled. 'I'm not sure I'm the right person either, but I'd be happy to help.'

Gudrun slipped her nightgown over her head, then sat down on her bed and hugged her knees to her chest, a wistful, almost shy smile on her lips. 'And you'll meet Niels,' she added softly. 'My…well, we've been stepping out for a bit.'

How did she do it? I wondered. Not for the first time did I envy Gudrun's ebullience, her passion for life, coupled with enough self-confidence to show her softer side too.

'He's a fisherman, in the village of Gilleleje,' Gudrun went on in response to my next question. 'Dad says he'll have his hands full with me, and Mum tuts and tells him he should be grateful his fiancée has a brain. It's hilarious.'

I was reminded of my aunt's pinched expression earlier, and wondered if Gudrun's engagement had something to do with it. 'Does Aunt Marie like him?'

Gudrun blinked. 'Of course. Why shouldn't she?'

'Nothing. Just curious.'

So if Gudrun's young man wasn't the reason for Aunt Marie's vexation, had it simply been because she was late for dinner? Yet somehow that didn't tally with the concern I had sensed. Real concern.

In the darkness I tossed and turned as unfamiliar sounds kept me awake: the hoot of an owl, a dog barking, the stairs creaking, so quiet after the hubbub of the city. It was as if we were suddenly alone in the world. Gudrun's steady breathing and my tiredness from travelling eventually got the better of me, and I fell into a deep, dreamless slumber.

I was woken by a sound outside. Startled and disorientated, I took a moment to get my bearings, then I quietly pushed the blackout blind aside and peered down into the yard.

Jens had come in through the back gate, and the click from the latch as the gate fell shut behind him was like a pistol shot in the night air. Catching the movement in the first-floor window, Jens glanced up briefly, then let himself in through the back door. A moment later I heard his soft tread on the landing, the loft ladder groaning slightly under his weight.

What had my young cousin been up to after curfew? Maybe it wasn't Gudrun my aunt needed to worry about, but Jens.

Chapter Three

Helsingør

13th September 1943

K iær's bookbindery was on Stengade, a paved street with cobbles lining the narrow pavement on either side, and about ten minutes' walk from Uncle Poul and Aunt Marie's cottage on Kirkestræde. The sun was low in the sky, the streets shaded, and the air had that crispness which told you that summer was now a distant memory.

A German military car and a transport truck were parked outside the cigar maker's on Sct Anna Gade, which lay perpendicular to Stengade. I crossed to the other pavement to avoid having to squeeze past the three soldiers leaning against the truck, catching a cigarette break while they waited for their superior officer.

That didn't stop them trying to get my attention. '*Guten*

morgen, schöne fräulein,' said one, touching his cap cockily. *Morning, pretty young lady.*

When I didn't react and simply ignored them, the gallantry made way for crudeness. Or at least from their tone and body language it sounded crude because I had no idea what they were saying. Again, as I had many times since the occupation began, I regretted not having paid attention at school, but I'd never had an ear for languages.

Without warning, and so suddenly that I scarcely knew where it came from, fury welled up inside me. There was nothing, absolutely nothing I could do about their presence, and my own powerlessness in preventing it terrified me. This war, I just couldn't see an end to it. And when it did finally end and life went back to normal, so much would have changed forever. How could it not?

The reappearance of their superior officer and a sharp command put a stop to the heckling. The tension left my shoulders. German soldiers were not known for harming the general population in Denmark, but the fact that they were here was a constant reminder that they could, and would, if commanded to do so.

If only there was a way of fighting back, or at least to simply say 'enough'. The previous government had said it when collectively they resigned, and some people did too, risking their livelihoods and their lives. Throwing caution to the wind like that required bravery – or stupidity, depending on how you looked at it. For me, all I could do was bite back my anger.

Stengade number 68 was a tall, narrow three-storey building with a wide shop window and entrance. A

CLOSED sign hung on the door, and the shop lay in relative darkness despite catching the sun's rays this early in the morning. The side gate was closed as well. Briefly I wondered whether to knock on the glass or wait until it opened, but I was spared having to make a decision when I spotted movement behind the glass, and the door opened. A dark-haired man in his thirties with a brooding expression emerged from the shop, tipping his hat in greeting.

'Morning, miss. He's out the back,' he said, holding the door open for me.

'I beg your pardon?'

'My apologies. You must be the new assistant. In my line of business one often dispenses with the niceties.' His face transformed into a grin.

I recovered from my initial surprise. 'And what is your line of business, if I may ask?'

'I'm a journalist, at the local rag. Or more specifically, the Helsingør section of the regional newspaper, *Frederiksborg Amts Avis*. Børge Rønne.' He held out his hand for me to shake. 'Kiær binds all my books, and I have a lot of books, so I expect we'll be seeing quite a bit of each other.'

Tipping his hat again, this time in farewell, he sauntered down Sct Anna Gade, passing the Germans and whistling as he went as though summer wasn't just over, rationing didn't exist, and Denmark wasn't under occupation.

I stared after him. Something in his gait and the set of his shoulders had brought me up short, and the image of a young horse full of the joys of spring prancing past a tiger sleeping with one eye open entered my head.

Now where did that come from? I snorted at my own imagination.

A brass bell clanged as I entered the shop, and another man came out from the back room, wearing an apron over his shirt and slipover.

'Frøken Bredahl? I didn't expect you so early in the day.'

'I was anxious to get started, herr Kiær. To feel useful, I think. It's so easy to lose a sense of purpose in this war.' My own words surprised me, but I realised that this more than a need for change had spurred me on to take a job in another city, away from my parents and everything that was familiar. A place where perhaps I could discover more about myself. 'And the door was open. I hope I haven't overstepped any boundaries by walking straight in?'

Shaking my hand, he sent me a searching look. 'Indeed, indeed. And no, not at all. I'm very glad you're finally here. It's a busy time. At the moment I'm sourcing binding materials before the Christmas period. Books are popular gift items, for those who can afford the current costs.'

'I met one of your customers on his way out. Herr Rønne. I must admit I was a little taken aback since the sign on the door said the shop was closed.'

Kiær glanced over his shoulder, at the room behind, a distracted expression on his face. 'Yes, yes. Rønne likes to drop by before he starts at the paper. It's quieter in the mornings.'

'That makes sense.'

About my uncle's age, the bookbinder had light-brown hair, a slightly wide nose, and a cleft in his chin, and his kind smile, which reached a pair of gentle eyes, made me feel instantly welcome. I'd hoped I would get on with my new boss as I hadn't liked my previous employer much. Only now did it occur to me that this concern had dogged me from the moment I got on the train at Copenhagen Central Station. That, and the worry over travelling alone.

'Before we start,' he said, 'let me show you around.'

He gave me a quick tour of the shop, showed me some material samples and a small number of bound books on display, each in a different type of binding, to illustrate the various options to the customers. One particular book caught my eye – a collection of poems by Hans Christian Andersen, bound in decorative paper with a gold-printed leather spine. A string of twine had been wrapped around it, and a tag indicated it was paid for and ready for collection.

'It's for a lady,' Kiær explained.

I picked it up. 'This is why I wanted to become a bookbinder.'

'H. C. Andersen?'

'No, binding books. To me it's a work of art. On my confirmation my family gave me books, and not just the New Testament, and I usually get books for Christmas and birthdays too.'

One year my Christmas present from my parents had been the complete works of the Danish nineteenth-century romanticist Adam Oehlenschläger, and it had been bound in a similar fashion, which was why I'd noticed this book.

'What, no jewellery or gloves, or pretty dresses? You're a most unusual young lady. I should know; my wife and I have two daughters.' He couldn't quite disguise his amusement. Then he sent me a long look. 'I'm sure we'll find something very useful for you to do. This way.'

Kiær's workshop was much like Clausen's bookbindery in Copenhagen where I'd done my apprenticeship. A large square worktable in the centre with four wooden stools around it dominated the small back room. A piece of navy leather had been laid out, ready for clipping or cutting, a row of working tools hung above a workbench against the wall, and a stack of books lay on a windowsill, blocking out the daylight from one of the two windows facing the backyard. On the workbench a book was held in a press, the pages in the process of being stitched together with brown waxed thread. The combined smells of glue, leather, and the sweetness of old books – that unique and particular aroma I knew was produced by vanillin, toluene, and other chemicals – hung in the air. Drawing in a deep breath, I savoured the smell, and the prospect of my new job wasn't quite so daunting anymore.

The bookbinder went on to explain the job as his assistant, how my duties would consist mainly of manning the shop, receiving new orders, and delivering the finished products to those of their customers who were unable to collect.

'Before the occupation we sometimes delivered by car, depending on how far away the customers live, but now we cycle. I assume you ride?'

'Of course.' Having grown up on Frederiksberg, in the centre of Copenhagen, I was used to cycling everywhere, and it had made very little difference to me when my parents had been forced to put our car on bricks due to petrol rationing.

'The bike is out the back.' Kiær pointed to a black-painted bicycle under the cover of a lean-to, with a wicker basket on the handle bars. Next to the lean-to was a small brick outhouse similar to the one that used to be in Uncle Poul and Aunt Marie's back garden, and a far cry from the relatively luxurious indoor facilities at my old workplace in the capital.

It didn't quell my excitement, though.

'But not to worry,' he added, turning away from the window. 'You'll only be doing local deliveries as I need you in the shop. The son of a cousin on my wife's side will be doing those further afield. He works for the grocer's on Havnegade, near the brewery, and is keen to earn the extra coin.'

A couple of photos hung on the wall in the space between the windows. One depicted a soldier in the cavalry, the other the same young man on a mottled grey horse.

'Is this you, herr Kiær?'

The bookbinder nodded. 'I was a lieutenant in the cavalry, and after that I spent five years in Argentina where my brother worked as a cattle farmer. That particular breed of horse is a criollo. Very common in Argentina.'

I felt a stab of envy. Never in my wildest dreams could I imagine having the courage to travel to the other end of the world, or even get on a horse. 'Sounds like a very adventurous time.'

'Indeed it was. Although I'm not as daring as some.

Rønne, whom you met on the way in, once biked all the way to Gibraltar.'

'That's impressive.' I recalled the serious man in the doorway, and the way he had walked past the German soldiers, and thought how appearances could be deceptive.

———————————

For the next two hours we worked in companionable silence. Kiær had instructed me to prepare the cover for a lexicon in four volumes he was working on for the headmaster of the grammar school, and I began by scoring the cardboard using a folding tool made from bone. Then I cut out a piece of the dark-blue leather the customer had specified, and glued the two together.

Intent on my task, I lost track of time, and it wasn't until Kiær announced that we should break for lunch that I realised how hungry I was. Stretching, I massaged the small of my back which had become sore from sitting bent over the worktable, and followed him into a narrow kitchen to the side of the workshop.

'Would you like a cup of coffee, frøken Bredahl?' Kiær asked as I sat down at a small table and unwrapped my sandwiches.

Despite her protests, Aunt Marie had insisted on making them this morning – two slices of rye bread, one with dripping, the other with sliced cold potato and chives from the garden, and an apple.

'I make Gudrun and Jens's lunches, and your uncle's,

and one more won't make any difference,' Aunt Marie had replied. 'But it'll be nothing fancy, mind.'

Now, I hesitated at the offer of coffee. I'd never quite become used to drinking Rich's, the substitute brand my parents used. It was made from chicory, rye, and sugar beet mixed with real coffee, and the percentage of coffee beans became increasingly lower as the war dragged on. You could get other brands, similar in taste and texture, and each and every one of them made me shudder with distaste.

But the peat-burning stove in the workshop hadn't been that effective, and the prospects of wrapping my hands around the warm enamel mug my boss was holding out made me accept. I almost choked after the first mouthful and had to cough into my handkerchief, eyes watering.

Kiær smiled. 'My apologies, frøken Bredahl. Or, since we're to be working closely together, may I call you Inger? I should've warned you. It's real.'

'Yes,' I croaked in response to both, wiping away the tears brought on by my coughing fit, 'but how?'

Kiær tapped the side of his nose. 'It was a gift, from a friend. Probably best not to ask too many questions.'

'Yes, probably not.'

As I luxuriated in the rich, bitter taste, the image of Rønne returned. It wouldn't have surprised me to learn that he was the source. Journalists were bound to have all sorts of contacts, weren't they?

But, as Kiær had pointed out, it was best not to know too much. Trading on the black market was illegal and unpopular. Perpetrators could receive prison sentences and have their profits confiscated, and occasionally they risked getting beaten up by disgruntled members of the public. Even so, many established traders still sold their *bukkevarer* more or less openly, a nickname meaning *kneeling goods* because shopkeepers had to reach down under the counter for these illegal items.

———

Just before closing time, a woman entered the shop to pick up the bound poetry book. She wore a brown overcoat which had been repaired at the cuffs, sensible brown shoes and an unfashionable tweed hat, and looked nothing like the 'lady' I'd expected. My cheeks burned with shame at my own preconceived ideas, and I resolved to be extra kind. This was the provinces, not the capital, and some had been harder hit by the war than others.

'Is there anything else I can help you with?' I asked as I offered to wrap the book.

Unsmiling, the woman shook her head. 'Is the required paperwork inside?'

An odd choice of words. Why not just say 'the bill'? And why not just leave it on the top so the customer could check it before leaving the shop. Come to think of it, the book didn't have that newly bound smell I'd come to love; perhaps the woman had been prevented from picking it up before now.

I glanced at Kiær, who appeared in the workshop doorway.

'Yes, madam. Everything is as required,' he replied pleasantly.

Without another word, the woman picked up the book, put in it her grocery bag and left the shop in a hurry, the bell clanging loudly behind her.

'She can be a little terse, that one,' said the bookbinder.

'No need to explain, herr Kiær.' I'd met much ruder customers during my apprenticeship, and in some ways the woman had reminded me of Aunt Marie at her most formidable. Perhaps she had nieces too who were as fond of her as I was of my aunt.

'We also have German customers,' he added. 'Many of the officers are well-read, and we must treat them the way we treat all our customers, with the utmost courtesy and respect. I trust that won't be a problem?'

I thought of the jeering soldiers earlier, and the officer who had intervened. 'No, herr Kiær.'

Gudrun and I had arranged to meet after work. As I turned into Havnegade, Gudrun and another young woman pushing a bicycle were walking towards me.

'How was your first day at work?' my cousin asked, and before I had a chance to reply, she introduced the other woman as her friend Bodil, the one she'd mentioned to me last night.

'Welcome to Helsingør,' said Bodil. With short blonde hair and almost translucently pale skin, she had an asthmatic wheeze and the distinctive gait of someone who had had polio as a child. Her eyes, in contrast, bore witness that God wasn't entirely cruel; jade-green and fringed by long, curved lashes they saw right into me and made me do a double-take.

'Thank you.' We shook hands. 'Gudrun mentioned a friend. Pleased to meet you.'

Gudrun slung an arm around Bodil and gave her a loud smack on the cheek. 'Not just *a* friend, my *best* friend. And you're going to help her find an outfit for Saturday's dance.'

Bodil sent me a nervous smile. 'If it's no bother?'

Irritation crept over me that Gudrun had backed me into a corner. Not that I minded helping her friend, but I wished she'd asked me first before landing me in it. But I didn't say that. Instead I swallowed back my annoyance and did my best to reassure Bodil that I'd help in any way I could, but the wariness didn't leave her pretty eyes. Perhaps she was unused to kindness.

'If you're free Saturday morning, we could see what they have at the Høyer's. I've heard their prices are reasonable.'

'I'd like that,' Bodil replied.

'Let's go and sit on the harbour for a bit,' said Gudrun. 'I've got us something to drink.' She opened her satchel to reveal a couple of beers with the Wiibroe label. 'I pinched them off the production line.'

Bodil shook her head. 'You really shouldn't be doing that. It's theft, you know.'

'Oh, come on, they're not going to miss a couple of bottles. Besides, we have to celebrate that my cousin is here. You wouldn't say no to that, surely?' Gudrun winked at me, and although I was still annoyed with her, I found it hard not to laugh at this blatant manipulation.

'Sorry, but I have to go and help Father with the milking. See you tomorrow.' Bodil got on her bike and waved goodbye.

'Where does she live?' I asked my cousin.

'Between here and Snekkersten. It's about a mile. Her family have a homestead there. And her father's a bit of a tyrant, I believe.' Frowning, Gudrun watched her friend disappear into the distance, then she shrugged and slipped her arm through mine. 'Let's go.'

'Won't it be too cold?' After the sparsely heated workshop, I didn't relish the prospect of sitting on the concrete ramparts by the harbour for any length of time.

'We're only staying a short while. If I'm late for supper again today, there'll be hell to pay.'

As we headed towards the harbour with Gudrun's stolen beers, I wondered if my cousin was about to get me into trouble, and whether I truly minded. I'd never done anything as wild as cycling all the way to Gibraltar on the southern tip of Spain, or going horse riding in Argentina, but didn't they say that fortune favoured the bold? Perhaps it was time to live a little.

At any rate, what harm could befall two young women sharing a beer at the end of a hard working day, as long as we were well within the nine o'clock curfew?

Chapter Four

Copenhagen

October 2018

'Could it be the same person?' Cecilie had askcd her father, when after some deliberation she'd finally decided to show him what she'd found in the cellar.

'That's your mother's department,' he'd replied. 'I'm just the shoulder she cries on. Although perhaps now's not the time. It's like she's lost her sense of purpose.'

What purpose does any of us have now? Cecilie thought. *To God, if there is one, we're just grains of sand, insignificant in the big scheme of things.* She could still taste the bitterness in her throat, lodged there since her husband's betrayal.

Perhaps learning more about her grandmother would distract her from those feelings. It felt as though she was living her life in a haze of confusion at the moment, clarity both a thousand miles and a mere breath away.

She was nursing a rapidly cooling cappuccino on a wet October day in the centre of Copenhagen. Normally she'd be at home on a Saturday, marking essays on Shakespeare handed in by her English Lit class at Old Hellerup High School, but she had finally plucked up the courage to write to David Nathan. To her surprise, he'd explained that he was planning a visit to Denmark, and would be happy to meet at a café in Krystalgade, which suggested to her that he'd been to Copenhagen before.

Mr Nathan was late which added to her nervousness. Her rational self told her she had no reason to feel like this, but inexplicably, in her head, everything hinged on Cecilie doing the right thing and dealing with the consequences of her grandmother's theft.

If it was theft.

The centre of Copenhagen was strewn with cafés, and one could essentially 'café crawl' all the way down from Nørreport Station to the government buildings by Christiansborg Castle, and not be without a hot drink in hand. In the summer, tables would spill out onto the pedestrian streets, but in October the indoor season had already begun, and the only thing spilling out into the dusk were the warm, inviting lights from the shops and eateries.

The Danes loved their coffee and their cosy get-togethers, and nothing could keep them from it.

Cecilie had chosen a table in the centre, not too close to the window but close enough to the door so she could see whoever came in. The place was heaving, with people of all ages; young people tapping away at their laptops, middle-aged couples taking a break from shopping, friends catching up, tourists, and those borrowing books from Copenhagen Central library which housed the café. There were families too, it being a library, and one corner was given over to a soft play area with kid-sized designer chairs mimicking the ones the adults sat on and stacking blocks of green foam.

Christ, she groaned. You couldn't even go to a coffee shop these days without being surrounded by kids. She would *not* have chosen this place if it had been up to her.

Against her will, her eyes were drawn to a young family. The mother was keeping a squirming toddler entertained with a picture book, while the father was rocking a pram to settle a younger child. It seemed utterly normal and inconsequential, a natural tendency carried down generations of humans for tens of thousands of years, and would be continued for thousands more to come.

Swallowing hard, Cecilie looked away and began picking at her flaked almond pastry, hardly tasting it. She didn't really know why she'd ordered it; it wasn't as if she had much of an appetite these days, but it gave her something to do.

I suppose I ought to be thankful that they haven't put up Christmas decorations yet, she fumed silently.

She hated the sight of Christmas decorations in the shops in October – the end of November was fine – because it forced her to think about what was essentially a family celebration before she was even ready. And every year it got that little bit harder.

A glance at her phone reminded her that Mr Nathan was now almost half an hour late, and she wondered if he would turn up at all.

Oh, why hadn't she just mailed the jewellery to him, and been done with it? It would have been the most practical solution, and she wouldn't have had to come face to face with a person whom her grandmother had wronged perhaps.

The answer was simple: Cecilie was curious.

To take her mind off the impending Christmas doom, and Mr Nathan being late, for the umpteenth time she examined the contents of the cigar box. It had been made to resemble a jewellery box with homemade velvet lining glued inside, something a young girl might do.

Beneath the mustiness of being stored in the cellar for many years, the box smelled ever so faintly of the brand of cheroots her grandfather used to smoke before the doctors told him to stop, before the cancer took him. The smell invoked memories of fighting with one of her cousins, the one closest in age to herself, for the right to sit on Granddad's lap.

Their grandfather would always protest his lap was big enough for the both of them. 'I'm a large man,' he'd say and lean back in his chair so they could both cuddle up against him.

The memory made her smile, blasting away the clouds in her head. The content of the box continued to puzzle her though, and the note indicating ownership worried her. Perhaps it might have been better to let sleeping dogs lie.

She looked up as cold air blew in. A dark-haired man in

a navy-blue pea coat and grey snood held the door open for a man in an electric wheelchair. He appeared to be in his late twenties or early thirties, the other man a lot older, although how old it was hard to tell.

An instinct made Cecilie get up to remove her coat from the spare chair as the couple approached.

'Are you Cecilie Lund?' The younger man spoke in English with an American lilt, and added a pronounced *D* to her surname which was normally silent in Danish at the end of a word. 'Sorry we're late. My name is Rafi, and this is David.'

Cecilie shook hands with both of them. David Nathan grasped her hand and held it for a while. Despite being confined to a wheelchair and slightly hunched over, there was something urbane about him, with his closely cropped silver hair and dark, observant eyes, and in the self-possessed way he held her hand. Mesmerised, Cecilie found it easy to picture him being very attractive as a young man.

'Miss Lund, I am so pleased to meet you at last.'

She absorbed the words, and it took a moment or two for her to realise that he had addressed her in perfect Danish.

'You speak Danish?' she replied in her own language. Surprise and nervousness made the question come out like a squeak. She cleared her throat. 'Have you travelled in Denmark a lot?'

'I have,' he replied, 'and I was born here. Rafi, would you?'

'Certainly.'

The young man helped David Nathan take off his coat,

then he hung it over the back of the wheelchair, took off his own, and went to the counter to order.

'Rafi is my carer,' David Nathan explained. 'And he knows how I take my coffee.'

'Eh, right.'

'You may wonder at my choice of meeting place. I love libraries, adore the smell of books, and I like the view.'

'The view?' Cecilie looked out the window at the row of bicycles parked outside and the yellow-brick building opposite. Then the penny dropped; the Tel Aviv address, the surname, one of the jewellery pieces in the cigar box, a golden Star of David.

'The synagogue,' she said. 'Of course. You're Jewish.'

David Nathan sent her a mischievous wink. 'Took you long enough.'

'I don't…really think about these things. Whether people belong to this religion or that. Maybe I should.'

'It's rather moving for me to see it standing there, freely and undestroyed,' he went on as a solemn look flashed briefly across his face. 'It reminds me that they didn't get rid of us.'

'Yes, I can see that it would.' Cecilie felt suddenly foolish for not thinking about his culture and history. She wasn't sure she'd ever met a Jewish person before, certainly not someone who was likely to have been around during the Second World War, but maybe she had and had never even been aware of it.

'As for having a constant awareness of other people's religions,' he said, partly echoing her thoughts, 'there's a risk we might end up overthinking it. To my mind it's always best to take people as you find them. Cecilie – may I call you Cecilie?'– she nodded – 'and please call me David. I believe you have something for me.'

She pushed the box across the table to him, suddenly reluctant to let go of this link to her grandmother's past and a side to her she could never have imagined and still didn't understand.

David placed his hands on it slowly, as if he was just as reluctant to open it as Cecilie had been to give it up. She noticed they were shaking, and she had to stop herself from reaching out and placing her hand over his to still them. He seemed distant, lost in time, and might not have welcomed it.

Rafi returned with a tray of coffee and pastries still warm from the café's oven. He placed a cup in front of Cecilie.

'I noticed yours had gone cold. Cappuccino, was it?'

Gratefully, she nodded. 'Thank you.'

He flashed her a smile which lit up his golden-brown eyes, then he set about the task of stirring two sugars into David's coffee and cutting up the pastry into bite-sized portions. He had large hands, Cecilie noticed, tanned and strong, yet his movements when quartering the delicate pastry were gentle.

Briefly Cecilie wondered what those hands would feel like against her skin, but immediately looked away when his gaze caught hers so he couldn't see the flush that crept across her cheeks.

Don't even go there.

The old man, his hands still cradling the cigar box,

didn't notice. The air around him was like glass ready to shatter at the wrong word, and cruelly wrench him from the place his mind had sought.

But Cecilie had to know. 'I have no idea how your jewellery came to be in my grandmother's possession, but if she…if it was in any way unlawful, I'm truly sorry.' She couldn't quite bring herself to use the word *stolen*.

Mr Nathan appeared to shake himself out of his trance-like state as a number of different emotions dashed across his face: confusion, anger, sadness.

'No, no, I don't think she stole it. I believe there must be more to it than that. And the jewellery doesn't belong to me; it belonged to my mother. She died many years ago.'

'Could she have known my grandmother?'

'We both did. Briefly.'

Silence fell between them. Cecilie's mind was racing with unvoiced questions. Had Inger met them on her many travels, or here in Denmark? Was it before she'd met her husband? Had they perhaps had an affair? It wasn't that great a leap since the youngest of her uncles was quite dark, like Mr Nathan would have been in his youth.

Perhaps more significantly, she remembered a conversation she'd had with her grandmother when things had begun to sour between herself and her own husband.

'Maybe I didn't always love your grandfather as I do now,' her grandmother had said as Cecilie was wiping her eyes. 'Love is a living thing; it waxes and wanes, and sometimes it sickens and needs a little help. And sometimes it dies. But when it does, there is always another place for it to grow.'

At the time she'd been rather appalled by the thought that her grandparents hadn't always been in love, but now she allowed herself to be intrigued by it; there was so much she didn't know about Inger Jensen.

And she definitely preferred the idea of infidelity as opposed to theft.

The carer was the first to speak. 'May I see it?'

'Of course, Rafi. Of course.' Carefully the old man passed him the box, then produced a handkerchief from his trouser pocket and dried his eyes. 'I met your grandmother in 1943, in Helsingør. Or Elsinore, as Rafi here would call it. The circumstances were…difficult.'

He picked up a piece of pastry and took a small bite.

What, Cecilie wanted to say, *what happened?*

But she waited while he finished chewing. She could tell he wasn't really tasting it, rather it seemed for the carer's benefit as Rafi had patiently tried to coax him into eating something.

Eventually he said, 'For many years I simply focused on living my life, to live in the present and look forward, not back. Then about five years ago I had a stroke, and while I was recovering I received a letter from your grandmother who'd managed to track me down after all these years.' Folding his handkerchief, he put it back in his pocket.

'I didn't reply straight away,' he continued, and looked at Rafi examining the contents of the box. 'I think it might have been at least a year. My wife had passed away, but I had my children and grandchildren as well as great-grandchildren around me, and that was enough. I didn't want to get dragged back into the past.' A shadow crossed his face. 'But illness changes your perspective. In the end we began an irregular correspondence. At no point did she mention the jewellery and I've absolutely no idea why it was in her cellar and why she didn't tell me when she had the chance.'

'Maybe she meant to,' said Cecilie, suppressing the urge to take his hand in hers. He was another link to her grandmother whom she'd adored, but perhaps never really known. It was becoming clear to her that Inger had kept secrets from her, from everyone in the family. But she must have had her reasons.

'This might tell us,' said Rafi.

The carer had worked loose the velvet lining on the base of the box, and pulled out a thin leather-bound notebook.

Cecilie could have kicked herself. Why hadn't she noticed? In her preoccupation with the notion of theft, and the need to keep her suspicions from her mother, she hadn't thought to look further than the jewellery. Why would she? Rafi holding up a notebook, possibly a diary which had been hidden for years, cast further doubt in her mind, and it made her feel terrible.

Despite her intense curiosity, she told Rafi to give it to David Nathan. After all, he was more entitled to an explanation than she was, if that was what the notebook offered. But the old man shook his head.

'Would you do me the honour and read it for me?'

Her fingers itching with barely suppressed excitement, Cecilie replied, 'But wouldn't you rather do this yourself, in private? Since it was found in the box, it may have been intended for you.'

David Nathan gave her a sad little smile. 'Alas, I can speak Danish, but due to an old head injury I haven't been able to read or write it for many years. It sometimes happens with head injuries, I'm told.'

'If you're sure.'

'I'm sure.'

'Don't keep us in suspense,' said Rafi. 'Please.'

Cecilie met the carer's eyes. His gaze was direct, and his lips curved in a soft smile which sent shafts of electricity down her spine. What was it about this man that had her nerve-endings tingling? She had no idea, and now was not the time to think about that. Looking down, she opened the notebook carefully to avoid tearing the fine paper on which were tightly written lines in fading ink, and took a first step into her grandmother's past.

Chapter Five

Helsingør

14th September 1943

G udrun and I stayed at the harbour for about an hour watching the fishing boats coming in – mostly small motorised boats with a mast and a wheelhouse aft, big enough for two people standing up. Soon the harbour was busy with fishermen bellowing and swearing as they unloaded their catch, stacking crates of cod, herring and plaice, most of which had already been gutted on the return journey. Seagulls circled overhead, on the lookout for fish guts, their eerie cries travelling inland. The stench of fish, saltwater, and spilled fuel hung in the air.

A father and his young son watched them working, the little boy pointing with excitement. The fishermen took no notice of their spectators, and they didn't look at us either.

Gudrun lit a cigarette and offered one to me.

I shook my head. 'You smoke too? Do your parents know?'

'Are you going to tell?'

'Of course not!' I pulled my coat tighter around me, a little shocked that she could think me so fickle. 'I'm just not sure it's what a young woman should be doing.'

Laughing, Gudrun removed a piece of stray tobacco from her lip. 'You've got a lot to learn about what girls can and can't do.'

I shrugged. 'Probably.' Gudrun was still shy of the legal drinking age and since I was the older of the two of us by almost a year, some might say it was my responsibility to stop my cousin from doing something stupid. Also, I didn't want to get in trouble with my father's family. They had very little and shared what they did have, but they'd been good to me and hadn't complained about having me to stay. I'd given Aunt Marie my ration stampsbecause she would need these to feed an extra person in the household, and I intended to pay some kind of rent once I had my first pay packet.

'Anyway, Niels doesn't mind. He says I'm spirited.'

'Oh, if he likes it, everything is all right then.' I couldn't stop my tart reply.

Gudrun rolled her eyes and stubbed out her cigarette. 'It's getting cold. Let's go.'

There was a little bit of cold tea left in Gudrun's flask, and we rinsed our mouths with it. Grimacing, I longed for a peppermint drop, but sugar rationing had put that tiny luxury firmly in the past. We were given chocolate stamps, but I had handed those to my mother before I left.

Aunt Marie didn't suspect a thing, or if she did, she chose to ignore it. She only raised an eyebrow when Gudrun claimed we'd been for a walk.

I was starving when we sat down to eat. 'All that sea air,' my mother would probably say.

Dinner consisted of *vandgrød*, porridge made from water and rolled barley, and Aunt Marie's homemade apple sauce which made it marginally palatable. Uncle Poul had swapped some apples from the tree for a bag of plums, which we had for dessert. It was ages since I'd eaten a plum, and I chewed slowly, savouring the soft, sweet flesh, and licking the juice which had run down my hand.

Like at home, we had the leftover porridge the next day for breakfast with warm milk. That I had to force myself to eat; had I been at home, I'd have preferred to go hungry, but I didn't want to appear rude and ungrateful to my aunt and uncle.

Even so, my stomach rumbled on the way to work, and already I was looking forward to my two slices of rye bread with dripping in my lunch, plus a few extra plums. So far we hadn't starved under the German occupation, but food had become a little uninteresting, and for a while I'd forgotten the joy of eating.

Kiær was already in the workshop when I arrived, as well as a young man I hadn't seen before, sitting on one of the stools and talking to Kiær as he worked. Smiling, he rose and introduced himself as I shrugged off my coat.

Still bent over the page press, Kiær said, 'Herr Jensen is related to me on my wife's side. He does some of our deliveries, which I believe I mentioned yesterday.'

Grimacing, he shook my hand. 'Hans-Peter, although some people call me HP.' He pronounced it 'Ho-pea' in a slight country burr I couldn't quite place.

Tall and slim – well over six feet – he had large hands, short blond hair and an easy manner. Despite his size and the way he towered over me, he was soft-spoken and had trouble hiding the mischief in his blue eyes. An image of him as a young boy going scrumping in a neighbour's garden or climbing down the drainpipe in the night for an adventure with his friends popped into my head and tugged at the corners of my mouth. Then the heat rose in my face as he held onto my hand for longer than necessary. When he finally let go, I felt oddly bereft.

'Inger Bredahl,' I replied, and searched my brain for something clever to add, but nothing came to me. To explain that I was the new assistant seemed trivial; he already knew that.

I was saved by a sharp bark coming from the backyard. Hans-Peter opened the back door, and with a clatter of claws a small dog appeared. Black and tan with short legs, it tilted its head sideways and regarded me with intelligent obsidian eyes.

'You have a dachshund!' Completely forgetting my embarrassment, I knelt down and beckoned the dog closer, then scratched it behind the ear. 'Aww, look at you! Aren't you a good boy?'

'It's my mother's dog.' Hans-Peter explained. 'She's away visiting my auntie in Odense. She asked me to look after him, but I'm not allowed to have him in the grocery shop with me, and my father can't take him to work at the shipyard.'

'What's he called?'

'Franklin.'

'Franklin?' Cradling the dog on my lap, I sent him a curious look from my position on the floor.

'As in Roosevelt. You know, the American president.'

'Oh, right.' I'd seen a picture of the president in the newspaper. 'Well, he doesn't look like him at all. With a monocle maybe.'

'It could be worse,' Hans-Peter grinned. 'My mother wanted to call him Adolf, as a joke, but my father vetoed that. "It's me or the dog," he said, and for once he had his way.'

I grimaced at the name. 'That would've been cruel. A dachshund's legs are far too short for goose-stepping.'

We both laughed, and the little dog joined in with a muffled bark. I kept stroking him. 'I've always wanted a dog, or a cat even, but we live in a flat on the third floor, and my parents aren't keen.'

'You can borrow him,' said Hans-Peter. 'As long as I get him back eventually.'

'Oh, I can't promise that.'

Kiær looked from me to Hans-Peter with a bemused expression on his face. 'We can keep him here during the day. He's so small he won't get in the way.' Then he turned pensive. 'Perhaps Inger could even take the dog with her on some of her deliveries.'

'Of course,' I said. 'He'll fit in the bicycle basket. If that's all right with you?'

Hans-Peter smiled. 'He likes riding on my bike, but I can only do that when there's space on the carrier.'

'Talking of which...' Kiær fetched a stack of books – an encyclopaedia in six volumes, which belonged to a local shipowner. The books had recently been given a new binding and were tied together with twine in the usual manner of the workshop. 'Since you're going to Hornbæk, could you please deliver these for me?'

'Certainly.' Hans-Peter took the stack of books and cradled it under his arm as if it weighed nothing. 'It was nice meeting you, frøken Bredahl...'

'Please, call me Inger.'

'Inger,' he repeated, and for the first time his easy confidence seemed to falter. 'Well, uhm, there's a dance on this Saturday at the inn in Snekkersten. I, er...'

'My cousin mentioned it.'

'Good, great.' His smile returned. 'Then perhaps I'll see you there?'

'Perhaps.'

Frowning, I watched him through the shop window as he secured the books on the rectangular carrier on the front of his delivery bicycle and set off.

I was suddenly sad to see him go. He'd lit up the workshop and although I usually held back a little when meeting new people, I'd liked him instinctively. I didn't take him for a smooth operator, but the sudden change in him from confidence to self-consciousness puzzled me. Was he truly that shy? Or did he like what he saw when he looked at me? I certainly liked the look of him.

I thought that perhaps I should mention it to Gudrun, then dismissed the idea; it would only lead to teasing. And I wanted to keep his easy smile to myself for a bit longer. Sharing a private moment with others too soon carried a risk of devaluing it.

It also puzzled me why he was doing deliveries in Hornbæk, besides the books for Kiær. I'd been to the village with my parents last time we visited Helsingør, and as far as I could remember it had its own grocery store, but perhaps it wasn't there anymore. Or perhaps the delivery was for a picky customer not content with what the local shop could offer.

Turning away, I went to the kitchen to fetch a bowl of water for the dog, then sat down at the worktable and began my tasks for the day. Franklin lapped up the water noisily, then curled up by my feet. An unaccustomed calm settled over me, and I sighed with contentment.

———————

In the afternoon I had a couple of deliveries, none of them as far afield as the one Hans-Peter had done, and I was thankful for that. The sky had greyed over and an easterly wind blew in from the sea, and I had to wrap a kerchief around my hair to keep it in place.

My first stop was a doctor's practice, belonging to a Dr

Winther. In the waiting room sat a small number of patients, including a heavily pregnant woman with a little boy on her lap, a uniformed railway worker with a makeshift bandage on his hand, and an elderly couple, the woman patting her husband's hand when he was beset by a coughing fit.

The door to the doctor's consultation room was closed, and as there was no receptionist, I could do nothing but wait. Fortunately, I didn't have to wait long. The door opened, and a patient came out, thanking the doctor.

The doctor was female, and wore a white coat with a stethoscope around her neck. Her salt and pepper hair had been gathered in a bun at the back of her head, but even without her dowdy tweed hat, I recognised her as the taciturn woman who had picked up a book of poetry from the workshop the day before.

'Ah, the bookbinder,' said the doctor. 'I must settle your bill. Please come in. Fru Svendsen, I'll be with you in just a moment.' She nodded to the pregnant woman and ushered me into the consultation room.

The doctor sat down behind her desk. As I waited for her to write a cheque for yet another beautifully bound collection of poems, I took the opportunity to look around the room. Mahogany bookshelves lined the walls behind the doctor's desk on one side of the room, and the other side of the room was taken up by an examination table, a tall glass-fronted medicine cabinet, weighing scales and various other instruments. On the wall beside the large window overlooking the surgery front garden hung a Snellen eye chart for testing a person's vision.

Dr Winther handed me a cheque and another book to

take back to Kiær. It was wrapped in newspaper and tied with string. 'Some of the pages are coming loose, so I thought it safer that way,' she explained.

'I'll see that he gets it.' I turned to leave.

'How are you settling in?' the doctor asked.

'Er, well, I think. Thank you.' Dr Winther's kind question made me warm to her.

'I know your aunt and uncle,' the doctor said, smiling briefly. 'Your aunt told me a few weeks ago that you were coming to stay. I hope it all goes according to plan.' She looked as if she meant to add something else, then thought better of it. 'Well, I bid you good day. I'm sure we'll meet again.'

I got back on my bike. It had started drizzling, and I was glad I'd left the dog fast asleep at the workshop, but fortunately the wind had almost died down, and cycling wasn't as unpleasant as it might have been.

The next delivery gave me pause, as it had when I first saw the name and address. An officer residing at Sveahus, the German headquarters in Helsingør.

Kiær had told me that the German soldiers used to occupy the villa of Wisborg on the southern coastal road Søndre Strandvej, which had been a youth hostel before the war. In late summer the Gestapo had moved in, and the military had also taken over the larger villa across the road.

There were stories about what went on at Villa Wisborg, about the prison and the interrogation room in the basement, and my heart began to race almost to the point of causing a pain in my chest the closer I came to both buildings.

Even so, I couldn't stop stealing a glance across the road. Surrounded by tall deciduous trees, Wisborg had been painted in camouflage colours, the windows dark and empty to the casual observer, although probably not empty at all. Through the amber-coloured leaves I spied the sea. The Sound, as this particular stretch of water was called, lay like a grey slab, silent and brooding as though waiting to unleash its powers.

Shuddering, I turned away. With nothing to hide I had no need to worry, and as much as I hated the Germans, and especially the Gestapo, I wasn't planning on causing any trouble.

If you discount drinking a stolen beer by the harbour, that is.

Still, I couldn't shake off the feeling of being watched as I handed over my papers and the wrapped parcel to one of the two young soldiers on guard duty.

'*Was wollen Sie hier, fräulein?*' he asked gruffly, which was strangely at odds with his young boy's face. *What do you want here?*

'*Ich habe*, er, a delivery,' I tried in my halting German. '*Für*, er...' I showed him the tag on the string-tied book, and with hand movements managed to convey that it was to be paid for.

The soldier handed back my papers and the book. '*Bitte, warten Sie.*' *Wait, please.*

While I waited, the other soldier, his rifle slung over his

shoulder, searched my pockets and my handbag, then removed the string from the book and flicked through the pages. The bookbinder's bill fell out, and he returned it, then shoved the book back at me with a casual movement.

The first soldier returned and swung open the barbed-wire barrier, indicating that I could enter.

My stomach began to quiver with unease as I followed him, pushing my bike. A number of vehicles were parked in the yard in front of the house: a tank, several khaki military trucks, and a couple of anthracite staff cars. The tank was covered by a camouflage net.

At the soldier's direction, I left the bike against a tree in front of the house and went inside as the soldier returned to his post. A junior officer behind a desk demanded to see my papers again, then showed me into an empty office facing the yard.

Now what? Should I remain standing, or sit down? No one had said anything. But I found I couldn't move and remained standing.

I started as the door opened, and an officer came in. Tall, with an upright bearing and greying hair, I judged him be somewhere in his mid to late forties.

'Fräulein Bredahl?' he queried.

I wondered how he knew my name, then realised the junior officer who had inspected my papers the second time around must have told him, and the tension in my stomach loosened.

'Ja.'

His eyebrows rose. '*Sprechen Sie Deutsch?*' *Do you speak German?*

'No.'

'English?' he asked in English.

'Not much.' If only I did.

'We shall speak in Danish, then. You must forgive me; it is the language of my mother, and I have not spoken it in many years. She came from Schleswig-Holstein in Northern Germany, and taught me as a child.'

'That would be fine,' I replied in a neutral tone. Kiær had stressed the importance of being polite, even to the occupying forces, and my sense of self-preservation dictated the same. But I didn't have to like him.

He put his hand out. 'My book, please.'

I handed him the book and pointed to the bill.

'*Natürlich.*' Of course.

He settled the bill, and I put the money in an envelope I kept in my handbag. I wanted to leave, but he hadn't exactly given me permission to do that so I hesitated.

'Do you know the story of *King Lear*, fräulein?'

'Shakespeare? I'm afraid I've never read that particular play.'

'I bought this when I was studying in Oxford in 1920. In fact, I bought all of Shakespeare's plays when I was there, but this one is my favourite.'

'Why?' I blurted out, regretting it immediately.

He laughed softly, and a shiver ran down my back. Did he just want to discuss literature – a favourite subject of mine, but he didn't know that, surely – or was he angling for something else? It suddenly struck me that perhaps he was simply lonely, in another country away from family and friends, and generally loathed. Then I steeled myself; he was enemy.

'Because of its probing observations on kinship, and the nature of human suffering,' he said. 'And because it is my son's favourite.'

'I see.'

'He is on the Eastern Front. I have not heard from him in a while. Do you know what that means?'

I shook my head although I had a fairly good idea what it meant. The German losses at Stalingrad had amounted to half a million, according to Radio London. The officer's son was likely to be either dead or maybe captured by the Russians.

'Sometimes it is not easy to tell friend from foe, fräulein,' he said as if he'd read my thoughts, then added cryptically, as he held the door open for me, 'Not all Germans are your enemy, and not all enemies are German. Please convey my thanks to herr Kiær. This is very beautifully bound.'

'I will.'

'*Auf wiedersehen.*' *So long.*

Cycling back, I went over our rather one-sided conversation in my head. It had disturbed me slightly. The officer wasn't unlikeable, and on an intellectual level I understood what he meant when he'd said that an enemy could not be defined in terms of black and white. He was a husband and father, like my own father and Uncle Poul. A son and a brother too, perhaps. A friend and neighbour, a workmate.

At the same time, it *felt* very black and white. Denmark was under occupation, the Germans could do what they wanted, and the only way to interrupt their activities was to fight back even if you did nothing more than ignore them. One enlightened and philosophical person could never invalidate the acts perpetrated by all the other ruthless individuals, and even thinking that would make me an enemy of my own country.

I wondered why Kiær had asked me to do this particular delivery. Perhaps it was because I'd told him of my love of literature, and he knew the German officer liked to discuss the subject. Or perhaps he wanted to emphasise the need to be polite to all our customers, and had deliberately thrown me in at the deep end.

I didn't know. Maybe there was no reason at all, other than business as usual. But it had made me feel uncomfortable.

Chapter Six

Helsingør

16th September 1943

The rain clouds had dissipated the next day, and the sun was shining as I walked to work. The golden trees in the churchyard around St Olai Church stood slender and proud like sentinels protecting the faithful, and the cobbles in the lane where Uncle Poul and Aunt Marie lived were almost completely dry, which made walking easier.

Despite my defiantly cheerful surroundings, a strange tightness held my chest in a vice, a feeling that something bad was about to happen. It had started yesterday, after my meeting with the intelligent German officer which, as much as I tried to deny it, had rattled me. A peculiar sense that I was sitting on the fence and had to make a decision one way or the other had beset me in the night and resulted in a series of fragmented dreams.

This morning, while getting ready, I'd told myself over and over that there *was* no other side to choose, if that was what the dreams actually meant. There was only you, your family and getting through this horrible war the best you could.

I hadn't mentioned my discomfort to Kiær when I returned to the workshop, and he hadn't asked. Nor had I mentioned it to Gudrun, knowing exactly what she would say: 'You think too much.' Which was probably true, but in my opinion Gudrun didn't think enough.

It was still early when I arrived, and the front of the workshop appeared dark and empty so I let myself in through the side gate using a key Kiær had given me on my first day.

My employer arrived with today's copy of the local paper, as well as Hans-Peter and Franklin in tow, just as I was cutting a sheet of coloured paper with a fleur-de-lys design to size. Hans Peter smiled broadly when he saw me, and my stomach fluttered a little from pleasure.

'Morning, Inger,' said Kiær, putting the paper down. 'Ah, I see you're working on the Holberg plays for the provost's wife. Excellent, excellent.'

'Hello, again.' Hans-Peter unclipped the dog's lead. 'I was hoping you wouldn't mind looking after Franklin again today. My mother has decided to stay in Odense for another few weeks.'

'Of course not. He's no trouble. In fact, I might take him

with me on the bike this afternoon if that's all right with you.'

'Absolutely. It'll do him good.' Hans-Peter had come up to the worktable and picked up the coverless book lying next to me. Turning the pages, he said, 'So, the provost's wife is reading Ludvig Holberg. That's very enlightened of her. I thought she was a dried-up old prune.'

'Evidently not.' His cheekiness made me smile.

'*Jeppe on the Hill* is my favourite comedy,' he said.

I nodded in agreement. The ribald play was about a drunken and abusive farmer getting his come-uppance when the local baron played a joke on him by letting him think he'd suddenly become a rich man. 'Mine too.'

Hans-Peter flipped a page. 'I particularly love this quote from Jeppe himself, "Everybody says that Jeppe drinks, but nobody asks why Jeppe drinks." He is, of course, trying to rationalise his alcohol abuse as a sensible reaction to his miserable life.'

So, Kiær's relative was bookish. The thought pleased me. Yet, at the same time, this unexpected desire to discuss literature with me reminded me of my encounter with the German officer yesterday, and my skin prickled from the memory.

'What do you think, Inger? Can Jeppe use his poverty as an excuse for his bad behaviour?'

I assessed him briefly. Somehow I didn't think he was referring to the play, and was instead testing me for reasons of his own, and I tailored my answer carefully.

'I like to think that good people can do bad things for

the right reason, and that sometimes bad people can do something good.'

Hans-Peter grinned. 'That's a very diplomatic answer. And the Nazis? Are they good people doing bad things for the right reasons?'

I stared at him, incredulous. 'What a question! I don't think that at all.'

'Are they all bad, then?'

'Probably not, but there must be…' I searched for the right word. Responsibility? No, that wasn't it.

I was still trying to figure it out when Franklin suddenly jumped up and ran to the front of the shop where he started barking. We all followed him.

Led by a standard-bearer, a platoon of German soldiers was marching down Stengade, singing a patriotic song in German and swinging their arms in tune with their high-stepping. Arms crossed, people watched in silence from behind shop windows, others in shop doorways, as the soldiers paraded past, their boots stomping brutally on the old cobbles and pounding them like fragile sea shells beneath their feet.

Finally, the platoon turned the corner, and the sound echoed and died. Without a word, the spectators turned away and went about their tasks as if this was nothing but an unwelcome interruption or a nuisance.

Although I didn't understand the language, I understood the message. It was a show of force, and a keeping up of morale amongst the troops, and although we'd been spared the usual 'Heil Hitler!', it worked.

My heart sank. Forgotten by the rest of the world and

left to struggle on our own, what chance did tiny Denmark have against such might? I sensed Hans-Peter beside me, felt the feather-light touch on my shoulder, and swallowed back the tears.

On my other side, Kiær was laughing quietly as if to himself. As my surprise sank in that he could be laughing, actually *laughing*, at a time like this, I noticed the harshness in his laughter and the curl of his lip. Perhaps he had the right idea. These strong-arm tactics deserved our contempt, not our sadness or feelings of helplessness.

Contempt, and a determination to overcome this. I tightened my fists and returned to my work station.

As Hans-Peter left, he mentioned the dance again, and I assured him I'd be there. It was only after he'd gone that the word I'd been searching for earlier came to me. *Accountability*. The German officer had suggested that he wasn't my enemy, but he was part of Hitler's army. Somehow I doubted he could have an opposing opinion and live to tell the tale. Perhaps by being seen as a moderate by those he'd helped occupy, he thought he could save his own skin when the war ended.

And surely it must end. The defeat at Stalingrad had demonstrated that.

When was another matter. Almost three and a half years of curfews, restrictions, and shortages of even the essentials seemed like an eternity to me. How much longer would we have to endure it?

There was only one delivery in the afternoon, another parcel for Dr Winther, and Kiær suggested that I gave Franklin a run around in the local park afterwards, or maybe let him walk beside me for some of the way. I put the parcel in the basket and pushed the bike as I held onto the dog lead. Although I didn't know much about dogs, Hans-Peter had told me he was quite young, and I reckoned he would be able to keep up with me for a few blocks. Then I would put him in the basket.

As I turned into the road where the doctor's surgery was, a cat emerged from a hedge and slunk across the street. Franklin reacted immediately, and before I had time to think, he'd pulled the lead out of my hand and taken off in pursuit of the age-old enemy, the dog lead trailing after him like a brown leather snake.

'Franklin! Dammit!'

Steadying the bike, I leaned it against the hedge and ran after the dog. By the time I caught up with him a few houses further down the road and in the opposite direction to the surgery, the cat was up a tree in a private garden, eyeing the barking dog with disdain.

'You naughty boy!' I picked up the lead and tried pulling the furious dog away without harming him, when the front door to the house opened and a middle-aged woman with her hair in curlers came out and stood at the top of the steps.

'Clear off!' she shouted in a tremulous voice. 'This is private property. You have no business here!'

'Sorry, I was just—'

'We've done nothing wrong!' Her lips trembling, the

woman shook a defiant fist at me and went back inside, slamming the door.

I stared at her, mouth wide open. Then I noticed the paint, and the word in crude white lettering.

Værnemager.

Collaborator.

The owner had made an attempt at washing off the paint, but not very successfully, and the accusation was still legible for anyone walking past on the pavement outside.

Backing away, I pulled the reluctant dog with me. You heard it all the time; talk of people collaborating with the Germans, those actively seeking to do business with them, but I'd never met anyone in person who'd been accused of it. This woman didn't look like she was collaborating with anyone; she'd seemed scared more than anything.

In my haste to chase after Franklin, I hadn't secured the bicycle properly, and it lay sprawled on the pavement. I righted it and returned the old towel to the basket which was meant for the dog to sit on, and picked up Dr Winther's parcel as well. The brown wrapping paper had ripped from the fall, and the doctor's paperwork was sticking out from between the pages.

On impulse I brought the book to my nose, and as with the last book I'd delivered to the doctor it didn't have that smell of new leather and fresh glue; not something most people would necessarily notice.

I examined it more closely. The paper cover and leather spine were both in good condition but, to the trained eye like mine, at least ten years old judging by the slight scuff along the bottom edges from average shelf wear.

Odd, I thought. I doubted very much that Kiær could be cutting corners to save money; that didn't tally with the man I was slowly getting to know.

Checking that I was alone in the quiet residential road, I carefully eased the paperwork out from between the pages. It wasn't a bill as I'd expected, but somebody's identity papers. Or false identity papers, more like, given the furtive nature of the delivery.

It wasn't someone I'd heard of, and why would I have? I hadn't even been in Helsingør for a week yet.

The enormity of what I was holding in my hand slowly began to sink in. Who would need false papers, unless they wanted to hide their real identity? And what sort of people would that be? I could take a guess: anyone having fallen foul of the Nazis, political opponents, saboteurs.

Resistance fighters. Spies.

Could it be that Kiær and the doctor were helping smuggling people in and out of the country, out of reach of the Germans?

And who else might be involved? Hans-Peter? Rønne, the newspaper man? And now myself, just by knowing about it.

That's what you wanted, wasn't it? A chance to fight back.

I pushed the little voice to the back of my mind. Getting involved required courage.

I'm not brave.

I froze as a car turned the corner and chugged past me, the smell of smoke escaping from the wood-burning gas generator at the rear, but the driver paid no attention to me and disappeared down the road.

Heart thumping, I stuffed the papers back inside the book and arranged the wrapping paper as best I could beneath the twine, then continued to push the bike the rest of the way to the doctor's house, keeping a firm grip on the dog lead. I needn't have worried. Exhausted from his exertions, the little dog trotted softly beside me and allowed me to tie the lead to a tree in the front garden without protest. I left the bike against another tree in case Franklin was dumb enough to get himself tangled up in the frame.

Like yesterday, I was ushered into the doctor's treatment room straight away and handed over the parcel, apologising for the state of it. 'I had a little accident on my bike and dropped it, I'm afraid.'

Dr Winther arched an eyebrow. 'Not used to cycling?'

'It's been a while,' I lied. I wasn't sure how the doctor felt about bringing a disobedient dog with me on deliveries.

'You must be more careful, frøken Bredahl.' I felt the doctor's suspicious eyes on me as she settled the bill. 'You never know where your errands might take you.'

'I will.'

Once outside, a shaky little laugh escaped me as the tension left my shoulders. You could read Dr Winther's ambiguous message about safety in two ways; perhaps she suspected me of peeping. Which I had, of course.

The question now was whether I should confess to Kiær what I knew, or stay out of it. The discovery weighed on my mind, but at the same time I felt rejuvenated by it, because it had woken me to the possibility of doing something worthwhile, something *important*, instead of endlessly accepting the rule of the Wehrmacht.

Franklin woke up when I returned to the bike, and I took him to a small park with a lake and let him run around for a while. After that he was clearly tired, and I put him back in the basket.

'Poor Franklin. I forgot you've only got tiny little legs.'

His response was a soft, warm tongue on my chin.

Turning into Stengade, I ran into a German patrol on the pavement, and I stepped out into the street to walk around them.

'*Schau dir den kleinen Hund an!*' one of them laughed to the other, and I didn't need a translator to know what he meant. *Look at the little dog.*

Buoyed up by my discovery earlier, I was in a good mood and felt I had one over them so I nodded curtly.

I parked the bike in the backyard. The sun was setting, and the house opposite cast a dark shadow over the yard. Through the window of the dimly lit workshop I saw that Kiær had company – Rønne and two other men I hadn't met before. Bent over the large worktable, they were looking at what appeared to be a map, and didn't notice me until I came in through the back door.

Kiær jumped up immediately and stopped me with a smile. 'Inger, I've got some guests with me today. Would you mind getting us some soda waters from the grocer's? And get yourself one too. We'd be honoured if you would join us.'

'Er, of course.' I took the money he handed me and

headed back out, after leaving Franklin in his basket by the door.

When I returned, whatever the four men had been studying so intently had been cleared away, and they were now engaged in a discussion about petrol shortages.

Kiær introduced the taller of the two men to me as police officer Thormod Larsen, who looked to be of a similar age to himself. Larsen had light-brown hair, regular features, and the remnants of a summer tan.

He smiled warmly as he shook my hand up and down. 'Ah, the famous frøken Bredahl. Kiær has told us all about you, and of course we had to come and see for ourselves.'

'He has?'

'Hard-working, intelligent, and not easily intimidated.'

Herr Larsen winked at me, and a flush spread across the back of my neck. That didn't sound like me at all.

The other man, almost as tall as the first and at least a decade younger, with short, wavy fair hair, shook my hand gruffly. 'Ove Bruhn, police clerk. A pleasure to meet you.'

The men stayed for another hour, talking mainly about the war, and the new government which had replaced the recently resigned government. Martial law, which the German occupiers had declared immediately after, was very much on the everyone's mind. Only Bruhn was quiet, merely putting in a word here and there, as though the conversation bored him.

'How are you finding Hamlet's city of Helsingør?' he asked me.

I explained that I was lodging with my aunt and uncle and had visited before, which led to a conversation about the city itself and its history. Initially reserved, the subject seemed to brighten up herr Bruhn; even so, once or twice I got the impression his mind was elsewhere.

My own mind kept going round in circles and returning to the same question. Whatever Kiær and Dr Winther were involved in, and possibly Rønne too, did this include a police officer and a police clerk?

I felt a tightening in my chest when it occurred to me that perhaps this was bigger than I'd first imagined. The comment about me not being easily intimidated puzzled me. Was I slowly being drawn into whatever they were engaged in, just by sitting here and enjoying the company of these very different men?

And that perhaps I had, unwittingly, taken the first step from the moment I set foot in Kiær's workshop.

The thought both excited and scared me.

Chapter Seven

Helsingør

17th September 1943

As we'd agreed, I met Bodil after work on the corner of Havnegade. Gudrun was there too and had taken her bike to work this morning.

Seeing the two of them coming towards me, each with their own bicycle, I felt a sudden yearning for the bike I'd left behind in Copenhagen, because I hadn't wanted to take it on the train with me. I'd asked Kiær if I could borrow the one at the workshop to go to the dance on Saturday, and was grateful for his reply that I could take it whenever I needed it.

Gudrun waved when she spotted me. 'I'll leave the two of you to your clothes shopping,' she said.

This morning she'd told me she was having dinner with

her fiancé Niels's family for the first time since they became engaged. I knew they lived in the fishing village of Gilleleje, northwest of Helsingør, but only now did I realise she intended to cycle there.

'How long will that take you? It's quite far.'

Gudrun shrugged. 'About an hour along the coast road.'

'Are you completely mad? Why not get the train?' City girl that I was, I gawped at her, and out of the corner of my eye I noticed Bodil shaking her head slightly.

'I like cycling.'

'You're not going to make it back in time for curfew. And what if you have a puncture?' Procuring rubber was practically impossible these days, and the tyres on my own bicycle back at my parents' had been patched and repatched several times.

'I will if I leave by eight o'clock.' There was a stubborn set to Gudrun's jaw.

I just stopped short of rolling my eyes at her. 'Well, you'd better get going. And, Gudrun—'

'Yes?' Gudrun turned to look back at me.

'Be careful.'

As I watched my younger cousin setting off, the gentle on-shore wind lifting her short, wavy blonde hair at the back of her neck, I experienced a sudden chill that something terrible would happen to Gudrun and it would be all my fault for not stopping her.

Which was, of course, utterly silly. Gudrun must have cycled the twenty-five kilometres to Gilleleje many times before, and because she always wore trousers, today she'd have no problem either.

I had to stop worrying so much.

Bodil more or less echoed my thoughts. 'That's how they met. On the coast road. She had a flat tyre, and Niels stopped to help her. That was back in May. Sometimes on Sundays they meet halfway and go for a walk on Hornbæk Beach.'

'I didn't know that,' I said.

'That's Gudrun. Sometimes you can't get a word in edgewise, other times she doesn't tell you things because *she* doesn't think it's important. Never mind what anyone else thinks.'

Bodil sounded amused rather than dismissive, and, I realised, this was the most my shy new friend had ever said to me, and I liked the sound of her slightly wheezy voice with its hint of film star quality to it. Looking forward to our time together, I suggested we get ourselves to the store before it became too busy.

Høyer Trikotage was a newly renovated three-storey building on Strandgade. Two large windows facing the street had been dressed with skirts, dresses, and knitted tops using fishing wire and pins to display them, and a wooden display case inside the porch showed gloves and handkerchiefs as well as a range of haberdashery items.

Bodil leaned her bike against the wall and we spent a few minutes looking at the window display. Last night I'd asked Aunt Marie where would be a good place to find a skirt or dress for a dance, and she'd suggested Høyer's.

'Let's go inside,' I said, then noticed Bodil hesitating. 'What's the matter?'

'I think it might be expensive,' Bodil replied in an almost-whisper.

'It can't be; my aunt shops here. Where do you normally buy your clothes?'

'I, er, don't buy much. Usually I take in the hand-me-downs from my older sister. They're always too big, but she got married and moved away, so...' Forcing a smile, she trailed off.

For a moment wrong-footed, I hesitated as well. I'd just assumed that Bodil must have had at least a little bit of money to spend, but now I realised that it was Gudrun who had set this up and had, in her usual fashion, failed to give me all the pertinent facts.

I held out my hand to Bodil. 'Well, let's just see what they have, and then we can think of what to do next.'

A sylph-like shop assistant with crimped hair greeted us expectantly, but when Bodil shook her head at everything the woman showed her, after checking the price tag, she directed us to the bargain rail on the first floor.

'It'll mainly be past season if that isn't a problem for the ladies,' she said, casting an expert eye over my city clothes.

'Yes, I should like that,' Bodil replied, and her shoulders dropped with relief.

Upstairs, after a quick browse, almost as if it were a sin to take her time over it, Bodil decided on a grey-green wool skirt, and the first-floor assistant showed her to a small changing room in the corner.

I made a face. It wasn't what I'd have chosen; the colour was too much like the German uniforms, and therefore hateful. To counteract this whimsy of mine, I picked out the brightest item I could find on the bargain rails, a rose-red A-line skirt with fabric-covered buttons, white button holes and white piping down the front, and finished with white piping on the lower edge of the waistband.

It was so striking, I'd have been tempted to buy it for myself except it was too small. I went to find Bodil in the changing room.

'What do you think of this?'

Bodil peeped out from behind the curtain. 'Ooh, but that's...' her eyes lit up, then immediately a shadow crossed her face, '...too lovely.'

'I think it'll suit you. Why don't you try it on?'

'That is a beautiful skirt, madam,' the shop assistant remarked. 'It's a copy of a Parisian model.'

'But I don't think...'

'Go on,' I insisted. 'At least try it.'

Bodil went back inside the changing room and appeared again a few minutes later. The red skirt clung to her body, but instead of making her look slimmer, which would have been the reason for me to buy a skirt like this, it accentuated what curves she had. She'd pushed her wispy fair hair back and removed her work shirt, but kept her grey slipover on, and the soft lighting on the shop floor made her pale skin glow and her green eyes stand out.

'You look amazing,' I said, for a moment convinced I must be looking at some other-worldly creature. I heard the catch in my own voice, a mixture of envy and pride; perhaps this was how it felt to be an older sister, something I'd always wanted to be.

When I get married, I'm going to have lots of children, not just the one.

'I do?'

'Truly.' I nodded. 'Although you should probably wear a white blouse with it. Have you got one?'

'There'll be one in my mother's closet.'

'Good.' I took Bodil by the shoulders to turn her around so I could see the fit of the skirt at the back, and noticed a set of dark bruises at the nape of her neck.

'Did you hurt yourself?'

Bodil ran her hand over the bruises. 'Oh, that. Not really. One of the cows pushed me against the pen yesterday when I was milking her. She's got a bit of a temper.'

'Right,' I said. The bruises looked like fingermarks to me, but what did I know?

———

Outside, as Bodil hung her parcel wrapped with paper and string over the handle bar, I suggested we took tea at Hotel Øresund in Stengade which was a couple of hundred metres from Kiær's workshop. I often walked past it and had made the decision I'd have tea and cake there the first opportunity I got. Asking Bodil to join me seemed only natural.

'It's my treat,' I said in response to her look of apprehension.

'If you're sure. I don't want to take any more of your time.'

'You're not.' I gave her a reassuring smile. 'I'm still

trying to get to know the town, and I'd like your company. Unless you have to get back.'

A moment's pause. 'I don't have to be home early on Fridays. Father usually goes to the inn for a drink or two, and my younger brother is happy to do the milking.'

'Doesn't he need your help?'

Bodil shook her head. 'We don't have that many cows. Sometimes I suspect my father doesn't need my help at all, he just likes me to be there. But I'll have to be back in time to cook dinner so there's something for him to eat when he returns. He's hungry when he's been drinking. He works hard,' she added and looked away. 'It's only reasonable.'

Despite her excuses, the bruises on her neck suggested to me that Bodil's father was free with his fists, and anger rose in me that anyone could hurt this gentle, unassuming woman. The brute sounded like Jeppe from the play, except this was real life, not eighteenth-century satire. I was glad I'd been able to help Bodil, if only in a small way, and I didn't tell her that I'd swapped the price tag on the skirt for another, cheaper one. The shop assistant hadn't noticed, but I had an inkling Bodil would have refused to buy the skirt if she'd known about it.

I'm as bad as Gudrun and her stolen beers.

Chapter Eight

Gilleleje

The same evening

Having said goodbye to the others, Gudrun soon found herself on the edge of town and away from the shelter of the houses. On the coastal road the wind picked up, and she stopped for minute to tidy her hair away in her hat to stop it blowing in her face.

She'd only just finished crocheting the beret from some leftover yarn she'd found in her mother's sewing box, and because there hadn't been enough wool for a hat of just one colour, she'd chosen blue, white, and red like the Royal Air Force roundels. With just enough yarn for that, she was proud of her hat. Prouder still because the Germans didn't like it, and she felt like she was doing something to show them they weren't welcome here, something for the war in her own way.

She hadn't admitted to Inger that cycling twenty-five kilometres after a long day at work was a hard slog. Her cousin was so uptight, and so...so fancy, and Gudrun couldn't compete with her city ways.

Yet, sometimes you'd think Inger had grown up in the back of beyond, always on about what you couldn't do, and shouldn't do, instead of just *doing*, but maybe that's what having overprotective city parents did for you.

The sudden stab of jealousy that her own parents had never regarded her as someone needing special protection made her pedal faster, and she nearly toppled over when she had to swerve to avoid a pothole in the road.

When this war is over, I'm going to learn to drive, she cursed.

Fortunately she had the wind behind her and made good progress, and it wasn't long before she could see the tall masts from the boats used for sailing freight between Copenhagen and the Danish mainland, the so-called 'wind drivers', on their stopover in Gilleleje Harbour.

Niels's fishing boat had just come in – his father's boat, really – and Niels was sorting out ropes while his father was unloading today's catch. Gudrun stopped her bike and leaned against the handle bars as she watched them.

The sun had almost set, and the two chimneys of the fish smokehouse, cones ending in a rectangle, cast a curious shadow over the pier like an upside-down chicken. Seagulls dipped and mewed in the sky or padded alongside the mooring boats on their webbed feet. One regarded Gudrun with beady, amber eyes, then pecked aggressively at the ground with its yellow beak.

Niels and his father didn't notice her. Securing the ropes with jerky, angry movements, her fiancé was frowning, and the two of them seemed to be engaged in an argument, in low hissing tones to avoid being overheard. She was too far away herself to hear what they were saying, and although curious, she stayed back until Niels spotted her.

His face transformed, and he was by her side in a few strides. 'There you are,' he said, and pulled her behind a wooden shed. 'Where's that kiss?'

Gudrun laughed as he pulled her into his arms. 'Right here,' she said and breathed in his familiar scent – a mixture of engine oil, sea air, and fish. The embrace didn't last as long as she'd hoped.

'Is something wrong?' she asked when he pulled away.

He shook his head, but his earlier frown had returned. 'It's nothing. Just missed you, I suppose.'

She cupped his face in her hands. 'If we marry, we can be together every day.'

'I know.' He sighed. 'But war is not a good time to get married. And we can't afford it either.'

Gudrun dropped her hands, disappointed and irritated that the war kept getting in the way of everything. And did he truly love her? You heard stories of women being led astray and giving themselves to a man before marriage. And babies being born out of wedlock. Jesus, that would shock her parents.

Niels forestalled her outburst. He took her hands in his

and kissed both of them in turn. 'But you must believe me when I say I'm sincere.'

'Must I?' She sniffed derisively.

'Yes. Do you believe me when I say that the day we met was the best day of my life? That I'd go to the ends of the earth for you? Do you?'

Gudrun examined his face and read no guile in his clear blue eyes, only affection. And concern that maybe *she* didn't love *him*. What had made her doubt him? Her feelings of inadequacy in relation to Inger? Those feelings came from herself, not her cousin. And certainly not from Niels.

And he was right; now was not a good time to get married.

'I do,' she replied.

Niels's mother had prepared fried breaded plaice with potatoes and carrots from the joint garden behind the row of tiny fisherman's cottages a few minutes' walk from the harbour, where Niels, his parents, and his two younger brothers were crammed into two small rooms. Niels's parents had the small back room, and the younger boys slept in the attic under the rafters while Niels had the settle in the kitchen-cum-living room, which doubled as a bench during the day.

Fru Andersen, a rotund, smiling woman with big, capable hands, tried to make conversation during dinner by asking Gudrun lots of questions about herself although they had met on several occasions before, but her jolly attempts at making conversation fell flat in the sulky atmosphere between Niels and his father.

'What in God's name is eating you two?' she snapped eventually, after the younger brothers had been allowed to leave the table.

'I'm thinking of bringing some goods back from Sweden,' her husband replied slowly.

'Smuggling,' Niels sneered.

'Call it what you will, son, but there's a tidy sum to be made.'

'All of Denmark is in the same boat here, doing our best to make ends meet,' Niels replied. 'There's no shame in solidarity.'

'Why suffer in sympathy?' his father argued. 'Makes no damned sense to me when there's money to be had. People will pay for anything if they're desperate enough.'

Niels crossed his arms. 'Whatever they pay won't be enough if we risk our boat and our livelihood. And for what? Coffee? Whisky? It isn't worth it.'

'Pah!' His father waved a dismissive hand. 'The coastguards don't care, as long as they get first pickings. They'll look the other way. I'm right, aren't I?' Niels's father asked Gudrun. 'That's what your father does, isn't it?'

'Actually, my father works for the coastal police as a clerk.'

'Ach, same difference,' he scoffed, but Gudrun had the pleasure of seeing the colour rise in his face.

As much as she loved Niels and respected his mother, she'd never quite found it in her heart to extend this to his father. Fishermen lived a hard life, and she could see why many of them came across as grim and forbidding until you got to know them, but there was something uncommonly harsh about this man, a deep resentment that he'd been short-changed in life and would do whatever necessary to get what he was owed. And pity the person who got in the way of this.

Gudrun shuddered at the thought and turned to Niels's mother, who was more than happy to talk about the wedding and dresses and the many grandchildren she was hoping to have, although she also insisted they must be patient and wait until happier times.

Niels sent Gudrun a grateful smile. His father was leaning back in his chair, giving monosyllabic answers whenever his wife directed a question at him, making clear his contempt for what he thought of as 'women's talk', but at least for now the conversation had been steered away from dangerous territory.

'I'll ride with you,' Niels said when Gudrun announced she had to get back.

'But that means you'll be out after curfew,' she protested. 'I'll be all right.'

He pulled her close in a brief, passionate embrace. 'When you're my wife, I won't have you gallivanting around after hours like this.'

'Is that so?' Gudrun cocked her head to one side and sent him her best coquettish smile. 'It sounds like you want to own me.'

'Would that be so bad? You'd own me too, you know. And by the way, if I see a patrol, I'll throw myself in a ditch.'

Gudrun laughed. He would; she could just picture it. 'Well, in that case, sir may escort me.'

At the outskirts of Helsingør they kissed goodbye, whispering soft words and the promise that they would have every dance together tomorrow night.

'You'll meet my cousin,' she sighed against his jacket. 'I hope you'll like her. But don't you dare like her too much.'

Niels kissed her forehead. 'Never.'

When she returned home, her parents, Inger, and Jens were listening to Radio London in the parlour. She poured herself a cup of coffee from the blue enamel pot on the stove in the kitchen, and joined her family, squeezing onto the settee next to her brother.

Huddled around the radio, they listened to the news that the Russian army had recaptured a port city on the Black Sea from the Germans, and that the recently overthrown Italian dictator, Mussolini, had been restored to power.

Gudrun's mind wasn't really on the news. Instead she focused on the coffee substitute she was drinking. She'd almost, but not quite, got used to the taste of it – not like Inger who hated it – but knew Niels's father had been right when he'd insisted people would pay for anything if they wanted it enough, and had the money.

At my wedding lunch we're going to have proper coffee, she thought. Another reason for her and Niels to wait.

The calm, quiet mood in her parents' parlour was interrupted by a sudden rap on the window at the front of the house. Jens quickly switched off the radio, and her mother draped an embroidered tablecloth over it. Listening to the radio wasn't forbidden, but the Germans took a dim view of broadcasts from the BBC, and it was better to be safe than sorry in case they confiscated it.

Her father turned off the lights and opened the door, with Gudrun and his wife almost right behind him.

'Yes?'

'*Ihre Verdunkelungsvorhänge!*' came the sharp command. *Your blackout blinds.*

The soldier had used the butt of his rifle to knock on the glass which fortunately hadn't shattered, and was explaining that a tiny sliver of light was escaping, and that they must cover up properly.

Gudrun's father apologised and promised to sort it out.

'*Und lass es nicht noch einmal passieren!*' the soldier barked as the two-man patrol continued down the street. *Don't let it happen again.*

'*Jawohl, mein Herr*,' her father muttered sarcastically, and adjusted the blinds to make sure no light could be seen from outside.

'Oh Lord, are we now to be murdered in our beds?' his wife said and pulled her cardigan tighter around her against the draft. 'I thought my heart was about to leap out of my chest!'

Gudrun laughed. 'I don't think it'll come to that, Mum.'

Returning to the parlour, she sent up a silent prayer in the hope that Niels had made it safely back to Gilleleje without being stopped. And without having to hide in a muddy ditch.

Still grinning at her father's irreverence, she glanced at her cousin, expecting her to join in with the mirth. To her surprise, Inger was clutching her arms and had gone as white as a sheet.

Chapter Nine

Helsingør

18th September 1943

'What a pretty skirt!'

Bodil had joined Gudrun and me in our shared bedroom, where the three of us were getting ready for the dance together, and Gudrun was admiring the red skirt Bodil had bought yesterday

'Inger found it,' said Bodil. 'We went to Høyer's, in the upstairs room, where they have a bargain rail. I've never been to Høyer's,' she added with a shy smile.

'Honestly, how long have you lived in this town?' Gudrun rolled her eyes.

I sent Gudrun a severe look, and had the satisfaction of seeing her flush with embarrassment over her thoughtless comment.

Taking the hint, she said, 'Well, I'm really glad you managed to find something nice. I told you Inger would be the person to ask, didn't I?'

'You flatter me,' I replied mildly.

'Perhaps you could find a skirt or a dress there sometime,' Bodil suggested with a gentle smile.

'A skirt? Me? I'm telling you this, me and skirts are not the best of friends! Anyway,' Gudrun threw out her arms, 'this dance is going to be such fun, so let's do our lips.'

'Do you have any lipstick?' I asked.

'No, I thought I'd use yours.'

Laughter bubbled up in me. Gudrun was impossible. 'Oh, you did, did you? Why don't we do our hair first?'

Which meant that Bodil and I pinned each other's hair up in a roll at the back of the head as Gudrun refused to do anything with her just-above-the-shoulder hairstyle other than brushing it.

A knock on the door, and Jens popped his head around the door.

'What's going on in here? Sounds like a gaggle of geese.'

'Oh, go away!' Gudrun threw her hairbrush at him, and her brother ducked out of the door just in time, laughing.

As I did Bodil's hair, I noticed a faint smell of the cow shed on her, and so suggested we all had a dab of the perfume my father had brought back from Paris five years ago for my mother, and she'd subsequently passed on to me. It was far too heady a scent for my mother who preferred subtle florals, but perfect for a younger woman, and normally I hoarded the expensive drops ridiculously.

Bodil's eyes nearly popped out of her head. 'Perfume? Oh Lord!'

A warm feeling spread in my chest at Bodil's uncomplicated delight. Standing behind her, I looked at us both in the mirror; me in apple green and Bodil in red and white like the Danish flag. Both of us glowing with...well, what exactly? I searched for the word and settled on happiness. Surrounded by laughter and excitement and the two almost-sisters I'd gained within the span of a week – what else could it be? Even so, I experienced a twinge of guilt that I could be content when there was so much misery and death all over the world, but I didn't allow the feeling to ruin the mood.

If only I could frame the precious feeling I had right now and come back to look at it again and again, drinking it in like a restoring tonic, when life was tough.

But we were young and lived for the moment.

Uncle Poul had borrowed a car from his place of work and offered to drive us to Snekkersten Inn.

'Can't have you girls cycling in your finery, now, can I? And there's room for this young lady's bicycle on the roof too.'

Bodil shook her head. 'It's very kind of you, herr Bredahl, but we're going for a bike ride tomorrow, and I've arranged a lift with our neighbour to pick it up then.'

We clambered into the car, Gudrun in the front seat next to her father, with me and Bodil at the back. There was a bag of firewood on the backseat, smelling strongly of resin, and I moved closer to Bodil to avoid snagging my coat on the rough bark.

'That's for the gas generator,' Uncle Poul explained as we set off. 'Clever things they are, if a nuisance. Don't know if you girls know how they work, but—'

'Dad, we're not interested,' Gudrun interrupted.

'I am,' I said.

My parents had put their own car on blocks when the war led to petrol shortages as, strictly speaking, we didn't need to use it, but others had chosen to install a gas generator on the back, so they could still drive their trucks, vans, and taxis, and some private cars had one too. I was getting used to the sight of horse-drawn cars or vans as well, since only doctors and midwives could get petrol rations.

Uncle Poul went on to explain how burning wood generated a gas which could be used to power the car, and that sometimes a whole load of firewood was needed if you were going on a longer journey. Gudrun groaned, and I couldn't help giggling at her exasperation with her father. He chuckled as well.

'I'll pick you up later,' he said. 'About eight-thirty so we can get back in time before curfew. And girls' – we all turned, fearing that he was suddenly going to place conditions on our fun – 'don't do anything I wouldn't do.'

'That's a good one, Dad.' Gudrun laughed. 'I happen to have it from the highest authority that you were something of a daredevil back in the day.'

'Is that so? I'd better have words with Mother. Fancy

spilling all my secrets like that.' He waved goodbye and drove off back towards Helsingør.

Snekkersten Inn was a wide, two-story pavilion on Strandvejen overlooking the sea. There was a central gable at the front with a vine-clad balcony, and we entered through the main entrance to the left of the gable.

We left our coats with the cloakroom assistant, who gave us each a token. I slipped mine in my evening bag, a black bead-embroidered velvet one with a metal clasp, which my mother had lent me before I left for Helsingør.

'My dancing days are over,' she'd said, which was utter nonsense. My mother was still light on her feet and able to turn a head or two.

The dance hall was decorated with colourful streamers and was already heaving, with over fifty people, most of them a little older than the three of us, in their mid-twenties to early thirties. There seemed to be all sorts of people, from ship-builders and factory workers to shopgirls and bank clerks, but in common they'd all made an effort and were looking their best. If it hadn't been for a cluster of German soldiers huddled together in one corner like a blob of Wehrmacht grey, you could easily picture everything being back to normal.

Aunt Marie had warned me that the place was well-visited by the Germans, but in my naiveté I hadn't actually expected to see any this evening. I was relieved I'd persuaded Bodil to buy the red skirt and not the grey.

We ignored the soldiers, and I allowed an excited Gudrun to drag me across the floor and introduce me to her fiancé and a couple of his friends.

'This is Niels.' Gudrun beamed and clutched his arm possessively, barely reaching to his shoulder.

'Hello, nice to meet you.' As we shook hands, my fine-boned hand was dwarfed by his giant, gentle paw.

I could see why my cousin found Niels attractive. Tall with thick blond hair, piercing blue eyes, and a bronzed face, he reminded me of a saltwater version of Hans-Peter.

Come to think of it, where was Hans-Peter? He'd told me he'd be here, but, after scanning the room, I couldn't see him. Perhaps he intended to turn up later.

One of Niels's friends asked me to dance, and I accepted gladly. It was a lively jitterbug, and afterwards I excused myself and went to the powder room to freshen up. I wet my handkerchief and dabbed it against my hot cheeks, luxuriating in the coolness, then reapplied my lipstick.

On my way back from the powder room I spotted Kiær and the other three men sitting together around a table in the taproom. While I dithered whether to go and say hello, there was a tap on my shoulder.

'Hans-Peter! You came!'

He smiled, and I experienced a pleasant little flutter in my chest. 'I said I would. Now, how about that dance you promised me?'

I pursed my lips in mock seriousness. 'I don't think I did, but…all right.'

I slipped my arm through his and we went back into the dance hall. This time it was a slow jazzy tune, and we were able to talk while I relaxed into his arms. He danced well, leading firmly without treading on my toes like so many other young men did.

'I wonder why Kiær is here tonight,' I said. 'Don't they all have families at home?'

'Having a beer, I should think. It is allowed if you're of age.'

I laughed. 'Yes, of course it is. I just wondered. Anyway, did you come alone, or with friends?'

'Alone,' he replied. 'And you?'

'I'm here with my cousin and a friend. That's my cousin over there.'

Hans-Peter looked in the direction of my nod. 'The woman in slacks, dancing with that tall man?'

'That's Gudrun and her fiancé.'

'Fiancé, eh? Well, he looks like a decent sort. Do you think they're right for each other?'

'Eh yes, I think so.'

The question threw me. From my first meeting with him, Niels had given me the impression that he might be the right sort of man to keep my impetuous cousin in check, but on second thought, from the way he looked at Gudrun, he may well have met his match. I could imagine them sparring like my aunt and uncle.

Changing the subject, I said, 'I'm going on a bike ride tomorrow with Gudrun and her friend. We're off to Julebæk for a walk on the beach. I wondered if Franklin would like to come.'

'Yes, please. Take him away.'

'Why? What's he done?'

'He chewed one of my shoes this morning. The little beast.'

'How can you say that?' I tutted. 'He's adorable. He

might not win any wars like we're hoping his namesake will, but he's definitely won my heart.'

'I'll have to ask him what his secret is.'

I blushed furiously at that and lowered my head to hide my flaming cheeks. But there was something else I'd been meaning to speak to Hans-Peter about, but I didn't quite know how to approach the subject.

'What's the matter? Did I say something wrong? I apologise if I embarrassed you.'

You did, I thought, *but that isn't it.*

'No, no, but say you…' I began. 'What if you knew someone was doing something which was strictly illegal, but right at the same time?'

'That's a little too cryptic for me,' he replied. 'Can you be more specific?'

I met his eyes, but read only curiosity. Could I trust him with my discovery? He and Kiær were related, on Kiær's wife's side, and familial loyalty must count for something, but I'd noticed in him a genuine willingness to help. He seemed to have understood my despondency when we'd watched the German soldiers march past the shop window.

Hesitantly, I confided in him, my mouth close to his ear, although with the music in the background we were unlikely to be overheard.

'Inger,' he said, and I felt his arm tightening around my back. 'Whatever you saw, it's best you forget it.'

'So you know about it?'

His mouth a thin line, Hans-Peter didn't answer. Then he let out a long sigh. 'The less you know, the safer for you. Kiær would agree with me.'

'But—'

'I like you,' he went on. 'I wouldn't want anything to happen to you. Sure, I understand how frustrated you are. We all are. But if I could ask for one thing not to be tainted by this war, it would be you.'

An odd tingling flooded my body as he pulled me closer. No one had ever held me like this before – no one had ever wanted to – and I allowed myself to be swept up in the dance, in the moment.

At the same time, I couldn't deny the warring emotions in my chest. A deep satisfaction that this handsome man liked me and wanted to protect me, coupled with a slight resentment that I was being patronised.

I'm not a child, I wanted to say. *And you're not my parent.*

On the one hand I had to do something before this pent-up anger I carried deep in my stomach got the better of me. On the other hand, I knew it was likely to be dangerous, and I couldn't exactly walk up to Kiær and demand to get involved. We were only acquainted, and he had no real reason to think I could be trusted.

Why did it have to be so complicated? And why couldn't I just let it rest?

Chapter Ten

Snekkersten

The same evening

From her seat along the wall, Bodil watched Inger dance with Niels's friend, then later with the handsome shop assistant from the grocer's on Havnegade. Gudrun was deep in the arms of her fiancé, and no one seemed to have noticed Bodil.

She was used to it, but couldn't avoid the shrinking feeling of disappointment inside her. She'd hoped that with her new skirt and Inger's lipstick, she might have caught the eye of a young man, but she should have known by now that wasn't going to happen.

Making a brave attempt at just enjoying the music, she smiled in encouragement when a man she recognised from the brewery came towards her, but he stopped a few chairs away from Bodil and invited the girl who sat there to dance.

She resigned herself to not dancing this evening, which was probably just as well as she'd never learned it properly. The only time she'd danced was when her father was out and her mother would put on the wind-up gramophone so Bodil and her older sister could practise in the parlour. But that was long ago now.

Smoothing down the white blouse she'd borrowed from her mother's closet, she wondered where her mother was now. After she'd left, she'd never returned for the rest of her clothes, nor her two youngest children. It should make Bodil angry, but in some strange way she understood that she and her brother had fared better where they were. Her mother had no income and relied on her relatives for help, and wouldn't have been able to support them.

Still, if only things could have been different.

Lost in thought, she didn't notice the man standing in front of her at first. Looking up, she took in the grey trousers and grey jacket with a black collar, his black belt and the silver eagle emblem on his field cap.

German.

He bowed gallantly. 'Fräulein, may I have this dance?'

Bodil hesitated, searching for her friends, but they were too busy dancing to notice, nor did anyone else in the room. Why would they? No one had any interest in the lame girl.

Rebellion stirred inside her like a waking lion, and she rose, accepting his outstretched hand.

'Yes, I'd be happy to,' she said in German.

'You speak good German,' he said as he guided her to the dance floor.

'*Ich habe es in der Schule gelernt.*' *I learned it at school.*

He smiled, showing off a set of even teeth. 'That's fortunate because I don't speak Danish. *Ich heisse Oskar.*' *My name is Oskar.* 'And you, fräulein, if that isn't too forward?'

'I'm Bodil, and no, it's not too forward. We're not our parents.'

'Indeed.' He laughed.

She gave herself over to the pleasure of dancing; it had been so long, and at one point she stumbled slightly.

'I'm terribly sorry,' she said, heat rising in her face as she thought he'd probably escort her back to her seat now and be done with her. 'I'm not a very good dancer, I'm afraid.'

'Because of your foot?' he asked. 'Polio?'

Nodding, Bodil reddened even further.

'Two of my sisters had polio so I know what it does,' he said. 'One we lost, but the other lives and is still beautiful. Like you, fräulein. You have beautiful eyes. *Schöne Augen.*'

'Thank you,' she whispered. 'And I'm very sorry to hear that you lost a sister. Do you have other family?'

As they danced, Oskar told her about his family. Five siblings all together; himself, one brother still at school, three sisters in between the two boys.

'I have a brother, too,' said Bodil. 'He finished school last year and wants to continue his studies one day, but my father needs him at the homestead, which is just outside town. And my older sister has married and moved away.' She didn't mention her mother.

'I also come from a farm. In Bavaria.'

Bodil listened intently as he described the place in the mountains, her lips parting with longing and envy. She'd never felt any love for her home, never felt much love *at* home. From the age of five she'd been chased out of bed before dawn, tasked with carrying heavy buckets almost as big as herself across the muddy field with feed for the cows, and in winter having to knock the ice off the water pump so there would be water for everyone to wash. The harsh words, the brooding atmosphere, the clip over the ear if she dropped or forgot something. The bleak realisation that the next day it would be the same all over again.

In contrast, Oskar's home sounded enchanting, but perhaps this was how he chose to remember it. Reality might be different.

A shadow crossed his face. 'I just realised that I haven't seen my family in over four years.'

'I wish for you that you soon may.'

'Thank you.' The dance ended, and he bowed. '*Auf Wiedersehen, fräulein Schöne Augen.* May we meet again.'

'I hope so,' she replied without thinking.

Gudrun and Inger had finished dancing as Bodil returned to her seat.

'I saw you dancing with a German,' said Gudrun. 'Be careful you don't get too close to them. People talk and say horrible things about girls like that. You don't want anyone calling you *tyskertøs*, do you?'

German-loving hussy.

Bodil felt a shadow cross her face. 'Yes, I know what they say. It was only a dance.'

Later, Gudrun's father dropped Bodil off by the lane leading to the homestead. 'Thank you, herr Bredahl. It's very kind of you, but I could've walked.'

'Nonsense. I said I'd bring you girls home, and that's what I'm doing.'

Having waved goodbye, Bodil headed down the lane and let herself into the dark house. To her surprise her father was in the small parlour, which was lit only by a paraffin lamp.

'Where have you been?' he demanded.

'At the dance at the inn,' she replied. 'I told you about that three days ago.'

'Hm, you may well have done. But surely there was no need to paint your face like that. No one's going to look at you anyway.'

'It's just a bit of lipstick, Father.'

He frowned as if only really noticing her for the first time since she came in. 'And *what* is that you're wearing?'

Bodil stuck out her chin. 'A skirt I bought. With my own money.'

'Not that whore's get-up. The blouse that's your mother's. How many times have I told you not to touch her things? That's why she left, because of her useless children, and you, the worst of them all with your gimpy leg! Useless girl!'

His words stung a little. She'd heard them many times before and believed what he said, feeling small and pointless. But this time it was as if his words held no power over her and she could simply peel them off like a bit of dry skin.

Emboldened by her evening out and the German soldier's compliments, she answered back. 'No! She left because of you. Because you're a miserable old bastard!'

The ensuing slap made her ears ring, but through the darkness which threatened to overwhelm her came a perceived image of the Bavarian landscape: the mountains, the green pastures, the wild flowers in the grass. Instead of her father's tirade she heard the echoes of a clanging cow bell, the call of mountain birds, the eagles, the choughs, the grouse.

For once she had somewhere for her mind to seek sanctuary, and her father couldn't ruin it for her.

As the blows rained down on her, her thoughts were of Oskar and the hope that she might see him again, and bugger the consequences. There was nothing to keep her here. Her brother would leave soon, just like her mother and sister already had.

And if she never saw the handsome soldier again, after the war she would visit Bavaria and lie on the grass amongst the mountain flowers.

Chapter Eleven

Helsingør

19th September 1943

O n Sunday morning after the dance, Aunt Marie got
us all out of bed in time for morning service at St
Olai Church.

We'd returned home last night just before the nine
o'clock curfew, but after that Gudrun had spent the next
three hours dissecting everything that had happened at the
dance; who had said what, what people had worn, how
many times she'd danced with Niels (all evening), and
wasn't his friend nice, and what about Bodil and that
German soldier. It wasn't until I could barely keep my eyes
open that her endless stream of words finally came to
an end.

Stretching, I felt as though I could sleep for another hour

at least, but Aunt Marie had insisted, in a sternly gentle way, that I join them for the usual service even though my parents and I weren't regular churchgoers. God's displeasure I could live with, but not my aunt's.

Aunt Marie huffed quietly to herself during the short walk that St Olai wasn't like her own denomination, but that it would have to do.

I slipped a tired arm through Uncle Poul's, and he sent me a sympathetic grin. 'Could have done with a bit more kip myself but, unfortunately, I don't have a bloody say in the matter. On Sundays Mother rules.'

His comment earned him a Gorgon's stare from his wife because he was swearing, and on a Sunday too. Most likely, Mother ruled every day.

Bodil met us at the house afterwards, and we packed the picnic Aunt Marie had insisted on putting together for us despite our protests that we could do it ourselves.

Aunt Marie handed Bodil a little parcel wrapped in greaseproof paper, as she ran a critical eye over Bodil's figure. 'I noticed yesterday how thin you are. Think we need to put a bit more meat on those bones.'

Bodil beamed in thanks, but also blushed from embarrassment.

On our way out of town I picked up Franklin as agreed with Hans-Peter. My heart skipped a beat at his beaming smile, but I was still a little annoyed by his patronising comments last night, and didn't linger.

Besides, we had to get going if we were to get the most out of the day. The dog immediately began sniffing around when I put him in the basket, and I asked Gudrun to put my packed lunch in her panniers before he sank his teeth into it.

Julebæk Beach was about five kilometres out of town on the northern coast road, a little less than halfway to Hornbæk Harbour, where Gudrun and Niels would sometimes meet, according to Bodil. Typical of September, the sun was noticeably lower in the sky day by day, but there were no clouds, and only a gentle breeze buffeted us along.

We left our bikes amongst the tufts of prickly lyme grass, then spread out our blanket on the sand and ate our lunch, while Franklin whined for titbits. In the end we all sprinkled the last few crumbs from the paper-wrapped lunch into the palm of my hand, and I let him lick. The greaseproof paper we folded carefully so it could be used again after a wipe-down.

'Don't they ever feed him?' Gudrun asked.

'Of course they do. Hans-Peter said he just had breakfast before we picked him up.'

After lunch we kicked off our shoes and ran down to the surf, an excited Franklin hot on our heels.

'Here, boy!'

Gudrun had found a sun-bleached stick and tossed it for the dog to retrieve, and Bodil joined in with the game. The little dog ended up running between the two of them, confused as to whom he should hand the stick over to, then dropping it at the feet of the one who begged the loudest.

Their laughter carried out over the sea, insubstantial and lightweight like a bird.

I dug my toes into the cold grey sand and watched them play. I'd noticed the discolouration on Bodil's cheekbone when we met up earlier – and although I wanted to ask her what had happened this time, I refrained from doing so – but Bodil seemed to have livened up since then. For the second time it occurred to me just how enchanting she was, and was again perplexed that anyone could wish to harm her. It was akin to squeezing Thumbelina in your hand or gutting the Little Mermaid… Just wrong.

In my view, if anyone deserved a little bit of happiness, it was Bodil.

Eventually Franklin was tired out and he trotted back to me, covered in wet sand and shivering from the cold. I picked him up and dried him with the towel I used for lining the bicycle basket, then let him curl up on the blanket and go to sleep.

Red-cheeked and giggling, Gudrun and Bodil dropped down beside me, and Gudrun poured us all a mug of tea from her flask.

I'd hoped she'd finished talking about last night, but no. As soon as we were settled with our tea, she was onto the subject of men. I suppressed a smile, and when I caught Bodil's eyes over Gudrun's head, I noticed Bodil doing the same.

Even so, when Gudrun mentioned Hans-Peter, his

comment about winning my heart came back to me, and I blushed just at the wrong moment. Then there was no escaping the teasing.

'Bodil had an admirer too,' I said and wished I hadn't.

It was Bodil's turn to blush. 'His name is Oskar. He was nice.'

Gudrun rounded on her. 'I don't care what his name is. He's the enemy.'

'Is it really that simple? Because he's the enemy, he can't be a nice person?'

Picking at her fingernails, Gudrun shrugged.

'And what about the British who drop their bombs on us?' Bodil went on. 'You try explaining to a young child that they're our friends, and that the pleasant young man who smiles at you in the street is the monster. They don't understand. And neither do I sometimes.'

From the set of Gudrun's shoulders I could tell that she was getting Bodil's point but was refusing to back down. 'Well, you should be more careful,' she said. 'You don't want to get a reputation, do you?'

'And you should be careful about that stupid hat you're wearing,' Bodil snapped back. 'It'll get you into trouble.'

I sighed. Gudrun and Bodil had retreated to their opposite corners like two fist fighters waiting for the sound of the gong. The mood was ruined, and I got up, drinking in the last sunshine of the day, rose-gold and purple brushstrokes tinting the sky in the west above slow-moving, puffy blue-grey clouds. The wind was coming from the west now, which was fortunate, but it was time to head home.

Silently we got our things together, and I put Franklin back in the bicycle basket. He gave a little growl of complaint, but fell asleep again.

After a couple of kilometres we came upon a German motorcycle patrol. The two-man team had parked the motorbike with a sidecar right across the road, blocking the traffic, and one of them was smoking a cigarette. When they spotted us, the smoker flicked the cigarette to the ground, while the other held up a hand for us to stop.

'*Papiere, bitte,*' he demanded. *Papers, please.*

'What? It's hours until curfew,' Gudrun protested. 'You can't do this!'

I handed over my identity papers, and Bodil did too.

'I'm not doing it. They have no right!'

'Gudrun, please,' I said.

Shaking her head, Gudrun crossed her arms and sent the soldier a defiant look. The soldier took her by the arm, and she pushed him away. They faced off, glaring at each other, neither willing to back down. I felt my lungs constrict and suddenly couldn't breathe properly. What on earth was the matter with Gudrun? She was going to get into serious trouble.

'*Verdammt noch mal! Verrückte Frau!*' *Crazy woman.*

Angered, the soldier ripped the RAF hat off her head, and Gudrun shrieked as some of her hair was pulled out along with it. Stamping on it, he tossed it across the field. Franklin woke and started barking and snarling, which seemed to startle the German at first.

Then he laughed. '*Das ist kein Hund. Es ist eine Ratte!*' *That's no dog. That's a rat.*

The other man joined in, and suddenly the tense atmosphere was diffused. Climbing onto their motorbike, they drove off, both laughing.

Gudrun started crying. I desperately wanted to put my arm around her, but I was balancing the bicycle with the terrified Franklin in the basket, and she would probably shrug me off anyway. Besides, she had no one to blame except herself, and she knew it. Instead I gave her my handkerchief to hold against her scalp, which was bleeding slightly.

Bodil put her bike down on the ground and went to retrieve the hat. The field had been ploughed, ready for winter, and she had to step over the deep furrows, which obviously made it slow going.

'Here.' She handed it to Gudrun when she came back. 'You can wash it. It'll be as good as new.' I read the *I told you so* in her eyes, but at least she had the decency not to say it out loud.

Wiping the tears from her face, Gudrun merely sniffled and nodded, then got back on her bike, and we followed her, none of us speaking the rest of the way.

When I dropped off Franklin, Hans-Peter wasn't there and instead his father took in the dog. herr Jensen looked so much like an older version of Hans-Peter that I chewed my lip with disappointment. Some instinct told me that although Hans-Peter could be patronising, he'd have understood the complicated emotions inside me, and I wanted to talk to him about it.

Both Gudrun and Bodil had been right. Bodil may have met a genuinely nice soldier – they existed of course; he was a person like everyone else – but in this I had to side with Gudrun. It was quite simply a case of *us* and *them*.

I'd seen the fury in the soldier's eyes earlier, and felt the fear deep in my stomach. Had it not been for his amusement over Franklin, who knew what he might have done? And this Oskar person, when it came to following orders I had no doubt he could be as brutal as the rest of them.

———

When I got back, Uncle Poul was in the parlour reading the Sunday papers.

'There's a letter for you,' he said, pointing to an envelope on the gleaming oak table. 'I believe it's from your parents.'

I looked at him in surprise. 'On a Sunday?'

'It was misdelivered to one of the neighbours a few doors down. He only just brought it round this afternoon.'

I joined him in the parlour. I recognised my mother's sloping handwriting and felt a touch of guilt that I hadn't written to my parents other than to say I'd arrived safely and had started work. Hungry for news from home, I ripped the envelope open.

The letter started with a few trivial things about the weather and how long she'd had to queue for butter, as if she merely was warming up to what she really wanted to say. Then it came.

...with a heavy heart that I tell you that young herr Nørregaard from next door has been killed. The Gestapo came in the night, with their black cars and trampling boots, and I have to tell you, I've never experienced such fright before in my life. Young herr Nørregaard managed to evade them by taking the back stairs, but they caught up with him in the street and gunned him down like an animal.

Now fru Nørregaard sits in our kitchen with the light gone out of her, while old herr Nørregaard is trying to get to the bottom of why this happened. Not that it will bring their boy back, but I suspect it offers him some kind of peace knowing that he's doing something at least, to get an explanation.

I felt myself crumple inside at my mother's words, like a tin can being crushed. The realisation gripped me that I wouldn't see his teasing smile again or hear his sing-song voice as he spoke my name in friendly mockery, and selfishly I wished I'd had the courage to smile back at him, just the one time. Now I never would.

...wonder if perhaps it was a case of mistaken identity, and the Gestapo were after someone else, and we praise ourselves lucky that you are safe in Helsingør. We had thought of coming up to see you for the day next Sunday, and the rest of the family, but I'm afraid we're needed here now.

The letter went on to reassure me of their love, but my mind was incapable of taking in the rest of it. Stunned, I stared ahead of me, the single sheet of paper clutched in my hand.

'Bad news?' Uncle Poul took his glasses off and put the newspaper down.

My throat had suddenly constricted, and, gasping for air, I dashed out through the kitchen past my startled aunt who had just come down the stairs.

I grabbed the workshop bike and began to pedal – going where I had no idea, I just kept riding, my legs pounding, my heart a lump of ice in my chest, my rage building until I thought I would explode. Eventually I had to stop. Turning another street corner, I threw the bike on the ground and leaned with my back against the wall of a house, my body shaking from fear and anger, my jaw tight from clenching my teeth.

A woman carrying a shopping bag sent me a wary look and crossed to the pavement opposite.

Pounding my fists against the rendered wall until they hurt, I forced myself to breathe. At some point the anger began to subside, leaving me spent, and slowly I peeled myself away from the wall and picked up the bike.

My subconscious had made the decision while I fought to get my feelings under control. The Germans had hurt my cousin, almost tearing her hair out, and now they had murdered a young man I admired who'd had his whole life ahead of him. Like Old herr Nørregaard I had to do something, get involved, take a stand, even if it turned out to be futile.

I knew I was about to cross a threshold from which there could be no return, but I couldn't stand idly by when I had an opportunity to do something, however small my involvement.

And working for Kiær had provided me with that opportunity.

After lunch the next day I approached Kiær at his workbench where he sat bent over a volume.

'Herr Kiær?'

'Yes, Inger. Is there a problem?'

'When I delivered that parcel to Dr Winther the other day, I...' Hesitating, I bit my lip.

'Yes?' He looked up, a slight frown creasing his forehead.

'Well, I dropped it, and some papers fell out. I didn't mean to drop the book, but I wanted to ask you if the identity papers were false.'

'Perhaps it's best you forget that,' he said mildly and returned to his work.

'I can't. Whatever is going on, I want to help. I want to get involved. Anything, other than this'–I pressed my hand to my chest – 'this pain in here because I just have to put up with everything. And I have my reasons.'

Sighing, he put his tools down and turned to face me fully. 'You're awfully young, Inger. Not much older than my own daughters. If I got you involved, I'd feel responsible for you. And if anything were to happen...well, I'm not sure I could forgive myself.'

'I may not be very old, but the occupation affects me too.' I mentioned Gudrun's run-in with the German soldier yesterday, and told him about the letter from my mother.

Kiær's eyes went wide. 'That was very brave of your cousin. And stupid. As for the events in Copenhagen...' His face darkened.

'I agree, but it made me realise that I need to do my part. Maybe being young is an advantage, and people, even some of the Germans, seem to find it either enchanting or amusing that I cycle around with a small dog in a basket. I suppose it looks innocent and homely. Why not use that to our advantage?'

Kiær regarded me with a thoughtful expression, as if he were seeing me for the first time. He didn't question why the content of the letter had affected me so much; it would affect anyone who cared about others, even those we didn't know well. But he was wrestling with his own mind.

'It's not without danger, as you now know. If you're caught, it's Horserød prison camp at best. At worst, Gestapo. Like your neighbours' son.'

The double mention of the harsh-sounding word was like a snarl in the air between us. The image of Villa Wisborg came back to me, the camouflage-painted exterior and those empty windows behind which a malevolent darkness waited to devour those unfortunate enough to end up there.

I drew myself up. 'I know, but how else can I prove who I am and what I believe in?'

Kiær assessed me again, his shrewd intelligence battling with his conscience as a person responsible for me, but practicalities won out. 'Very well,' he said. 'Rønne and Bruhn have worked on an illegal newspaper for a while, and Thormod has been contributing for a couple of years now. Rønne even has a press at home in the laundry room of his apartment.' Kiær put down the volume he was working on.

'But these newspapers need to be distributed, and that's where Hans-Peter comes in. As a delivery boy for the grocer's, he has an excuse to be cycling back and forth, and no reason for the Germans to search him. Perhaps your idea isn't so bad, that cycling around with the dog in your basket will have the same effect.'

'I hope so.' In my own head I was both eager to get started, but also breathless with a mixture of fear and excitement.

'Are you absolutely sure about this, Inger?'

I swallowed hard. 'This may sound strange, herr Kiær, but I've never been more sure of anything in my entire life.'

'It will just be the newspapers. The less you know about anything else, the better.'

'I understand.' And I did – he would need me to prove myself trustworthy before I could be given any more serious tasks. That was to be expected, but at least I was doing something and it was a start.

'Well, no need to wait for Hans-Peter today, then,' he said resolutely.

He opened a box of book-binding paper, and lifted up the decorative sheets. Underneath was a thin stack of one-page newspapers with a single centrefold as large as an oversized pamphlet, which he handed to me.

'Rønne dropped off the latest edition early this morning, but just one stop for you today. The rest can wait until tomorrow.'

He gave me a name and address, then a parcel for the provost's wife with the bound Holberg play, which was now ready for delivery.

As before, I put Franklin in the basket with his towel and the parcel beside him, but this time the towel was covering the illegal newspaper. To my horror, Franklin began to scratch at the towel.

'No!' He stopped at my sharp command, tilting his head and regarding me with his chocolate-brown eyes. Then he decided it wasn't worth defying me, and settled down as if he couldn't wait to begin today's adventure.

Still thinking about the horrors my neighbours must be reliving, and despite knowing this was no child's play, I stroked the dog's tiny head. 'That makes two of us.'

The drop was a small public house in Havnegade, a street full of pubs and restaurants. The pubs, I knew, were frequented mainly by brewery workers, fishermen, and those working in the shipyard, and not a place I'd choose to venture on my own late in the day.

I entered through the gateway to the cobbled yard behind the pub. A middle-aged man with sideburns who was dressed in a long white apron with the brewery logo on the front met me. Without a word he took the newspapers and handed me two soda bottles from a beer crate in return, then put the papers in the beer crate and carried it back into the pub.

The whole exchange had lasted less than a minute. I'd

been about to say that I wasn't thirsty when I understood his meaning. I put the sodas in the basket, covering the sharp bottle tops with a bit of the towel so Franklin didn't cut himself.

Then I set off for the provost's residence, on my legal errand.

When I returned an hour later, pushing the bike through the side gate, I heard raised voices coming from the workshop. I entered to find Kiær and Hans-Peter in a heated argument.

'You shouldn't have let her!' said Hans-Peter.

I knew they were talking about me. The other night Hans-Peter had told me to forget about it, and now I'd done the exact opposite. Again that slight resentment curled inside me; it wasn't his decision. And he didn't know about the letter, and why I felt so strongly that I had to play my part.

Kiær replied to that effect. 'We all have a duty to defend our country, in whichever way we can. That goes for pretty, young girls too.'

The two men stopped talking when I closed the back door behind me. 'Carry on,' I said dryly.

'I think we've said what we need to say on the subject,' said Kiær. 'Hans-Peter here has come to walk you home. Perhaps you should let him.'

It wasn't a suggestion. Nodding, I put the two sodas on the worktable to indicate a successful delivery, then got my things together, and put the lead on Franklin.

Hans-Peter laid into me the moment we were out of the door. 'I wish you'd listened to me.'

'I'm aware of that but I couldn't stand by any longer without doing something.' I told him about Nørregaard and also what had happened on the way back from the beach yesterday.

'Christ,' he muttered, his shock palpable.

'Anyway, it's only a newspaper.'

'An illegal newspaper,' he said. 'I want you to be careful.'

I glared at him. 'Why is everyone saying that? Why not say thank you? I'm not a child, and I feel this anger inside me, this…extreme hatred. If I don't do something to harness it, I think I might explode!'

How could he not understand? I was no different to him, or anyone else wanting to fight in whatever way they could.

Perhaps he realised he had no right to lecture me. 'I beg your pardon. You're right; it's important to make a stand.'

But the concerned glance he sent me made a shiver of unease slither down my back. What if he was right and I should have left well alone? Except now I'd taken that first step, and I couldn't back down. It was too late for that.

Chapter Twelve

Copenhagen

October 2018

'Thank you, Cecilie.'

Hands trembling slightly, David Nathan slumped back in the wheelchair. 'I think that's enough for now. I'm rather tired and should like to go back to the hotel now. Rafi, would you…?'

The carer rose and coaxed the old man's arms into the coat sleeves – gently, like you would with a child – and Cecilie noticed how thin David was despite his tanned complexion. Now that she looked more closely, she could see an odd bluish tinge to his lips, as if he wasn't getting enough oxygen, and the thought filled her with anguish that this was one more person who would soon disappear from her life. The feeling surprised her; she had only just met the man.

The old man took her hand. 'I'm grateful to you for bringing back my mother's jewellery. I expect you'd like to keep the diary since it was written by your grandmother.'

'Thank you, yes,' she replied in a thick voice.

'It would please me greatly if you could read some more of it to me. Perhaps in a day or so if you're not too busy.'

'I'd like that,' she replied.

Rafi held the door open for them both, and David steered the electric wheelchair outside, then smiled at Cecilie as she passed him.

'Walk with us for a bit?' asked Rafi.

'S-sure,' she stammered and looked away from those amber eyes, which seemed to see right inside her.

Outside they turned right and walked past the synagogue. A police car was parked at either end of the long yellow-brick building, and a battle-dressed crew guarded the entrance.

'Some things never change,' muttered David, and Rafi touched his shoulder briefly.

The pavement was narrow, and David rode ahead of Cecilie and Rafi who had to walk very close together to let other people pass.

'Have you had a chance to see much of Copenhagen yet?' she asked, to make conversation.

He shook his head. 'There were a couple of places David wanted to visit, but we haven't done the tourist trail yet. Not sure he's up to it, and since it's my job to look after him, that'll have to be my priority.'

'Well,' she said, and pointed to a spire just ahead of them, 'one of our famous landmarks is coming up in a moment.'

'The church?'

She grinned. 'No, it's what is attached to the church that is more interesting.'

'You've got me there.' Rafi smiled, and she smiled back, holding his amber gaze for just a fraction longer than necessary.

Chuckling, David turned his head. 'Heh, I know what she's talking about. Rundetårn.'

'Er, what?'

'The Round Tower,' said Cecilie. 'Or at least I think that's what it's called in English.'

The road opened out into a partly pedestrianised crossroads with a long red-brick building on the right and a small square with a cylindrical tower in masonry of alternating yellow and red bricks.

'There's your Rundetårn,' she said.

Rafi looked up at the eight-storey building with four sets of arched windows on each floor and a balustraded lookout platform at the top. 'Is that a prison?' he asked. 'Attached to the church?'

Cecilie burst out laughing, and the last of her tension since she'd found that cigar box melted away. 'It's a seventeenth-century observatory. Obviously isn't not used as an observatory anymore because of the pollution, but there's a wonderful view of the city. On a clear day you can see as far as the Øresund Bridge and Sweden.'

'Wow,' said Rafi. 'And the church is part of it?'

'It was part of a complex for scholars back in the day, but now it's sometimes used for concerts.'

'And what about that one? Is that part of it too?' Rafi pointed to the red-brick building across from the tower.

'That's a dormitory. For university students.'

Rafi's eyebrows rose in astonishment. 'Students live there? Lucky them – what a fantastic place this is!'

A young man wearing cargo pants and a thick sweater grinned as he walked past pushing his bike, before disappearing through a gate to the dormitory.

'It can be,' said David, his voice tinged with sadness.

Cecilie had never really thought of Copenhagen like that; she just lived and had studied here, but seeing it through Rafi's eyes she felt a sense of pride in her hometown. It *was* a fantastic place, at least these days. She could understand why David might view it differently though – there had been a dark shadow over the place when he knew it during the war.

'Well, it's far cry from my digs when I was a student,' Rafi commented.

'Mine too,' Cecilie agreed. She hadn't been fortunate enough to live in the centre of town during her student days, but instead in a modern apartment-type building a little further out.

They carried on down the pedestrian route and turned left into Copenhagen's main shopping street which housed all the expensive brands and luxury items.

Even on a Sunday the place was teeming with people – cyclists pushing their bikes, families, shoppers, tourists, all dressed in coats or colourful windbreakers to protect against the fresh easterly breeze. David stopped the wheelchair for a moment and raised his face towards the wind, a wistful smile creasing his features.

Cecilie wondered where he was staying, but since there were plenty of hotels all over central Copenhagen, in varying price brackets, it could be anywhere.

To her surprise it turned out to be Hotel D'Angleterre, considered to be the best and most exclusive hotel in town.

Reading her mind, he said, 'I'm not a rich man, but all my life I've wanted to stay here, just the once. It always rather amused me that the fanciest hotel in Denmark essentially means "Hotel England" but in French.' He chuckled. 'Danish people are such polyglots,' he continued, 'like the Israelis, but for different reasons. Israel is a melting pot, and you receive a good language education here.'

'With a minority language you have to if you want to connect with the wider world,' Cecilie replied. 'I'm an English teacher, so I suppose I'm always looking outward.'

'You don't have to be a teacher for that.'

'No, you're right.' She expected him to elaborate, but he didn't.

Instead he told Rafi that he would go straight to bed. 'I'll order room service and sit by the window. It's a wonderful view,' he added to Cecilie, 'overlooking the square and the Royal Danish Theatre. I saw *The Nutcracker* performed there once.'

'I did too, when I was a child.'

'You have that to look forward to one day, Rafi,' he said. 'Wherever in the world you choose. Ballet needs no words. Nor does love.'

An awkward silence ensued at this unexpected turn in the conversation and Cecilie and Rafi exchanged a slightly flustered glance. 'Well, I'd better get going.' Cecilie tightened her scarf and prepared to say goodbye.

'Not so fast,' said David. 'Rafi here hasn't seen much of the city. Perhaps you could show him a few places? I mean, if you're not otherwise engaged, of course.'

This was such an obvious attempt at matchmaking, and normally Cecilie would have deflected it with a laugh, but she'd become tongue-tied all of a sudden and was only able to make a small, non-committal sound.

Rafi shrugged slightly and sent her an embarrassed smile. 'Only if you have the time.'

She thought of what she had waiting for her – nothing but an afternoon on her own in her flat. It was cosy enough, with its sanded floorboards, the upcycled furniture, and the framed 1930s and 40s Hollywood film posters her husband had hated because they weren't 'posh enough': *Casablanca*, *Gone with the Wind*, and her favourite, *It's a Wonderful Life*, for the sheer joy it conveyed. The three rooms were her sanctuary, the place where she could express herself. But her self-expression aside, the flat felt particularly empty these days with no one to come home to, not even a cat.

'Yes, I've got plenty of time.' To David, she said, 'Perhaps we could meet on Tuesday. I only have one lesson in the morning, and another at two o'clock.'

'Perfect. Come for lunch at my hotel.'

'That's not neces—'

'I insist.' David cut off her protest. 'Now, I must deprive you of Rafi's company for about ten minutes or so while he helps me upstairs. I look forward to seeing you again on Tuesday.'

While Rafi helped the old man into the lift, Cecilie sat down to wait in the foyer. She'd never been inside the hotel before, and could see why it was celebrated for its luxury and style. It was the perfect balance between nineteenth-century architecture of the historic building and the graceful simplicity of Danish design. The foyer was light and airy with gleaming floors and luxurious velvet furniture.

When Rafi returned, she suggested they go to Nyhavn which was just across the large square from the hotel.

'Nyhavn means "new harbour",' she said, 'but paradoxically it's actually the old harbour, and it had a pretty bad reputation in the past. Now it's reserved for veteran ships and is considered very exclusive. There's also a boat theatre.'

Rafi seemed fascinated with this potted history and asked her lots of questions. Cecilie answered them as best she could, realising with embarrassment that she didn't know that much about the city's history.

'What's that at the end?' he asked her when he'd admired the narrow canal-front townhouses, each painted a different, vibrant colour – red, blue, yellow, green, white.

'It's a footbridge, although you can cycle across it as well.'

'And where does it lead?'

'To an island. We call it Papirøen, which means "Paper Island". It's a nickname really because it was used mainly for paper storage.' *That* she did know. 'It's been developed, and now there are quite a few restaurants, including Noma, which is, as far as I know, ranked the best or the second-best restaurant in the world.'

'I've heard of Noma,' said Rafi. 'It's a shame I can't take you there, but it's a bit above a carer's budget.'

Cecilie smiled. 'You'd have to book months in advance anyway. But...' Doing up the top button of her coat, she looked away.

'But?'

Surprising herself, she looked up at him. 'There are plenty of eateries here in Nyhavn, as you've probably noticed. In case you still wanted to, you know, have dinner together...'

She felt her ears go hot despite the brisk wind coming in from the harbour. What had made her say that? She'd had no interest in men at all since her divorce, and the few times she'd been asked out, she'd found an excuse to say no. But for some reason she found herself reluctant to end their time together.

She couldn't deny Rafi was attractive. With his Mediterranean colouring and those golden eyes, what was not to like? But it was more than that. There was something about his gentleness and patience with the older man, a compassion which reminded her of her grandfather. Her husband may have been fun, but the laughter they'd shared once couldn't quite disguise the core of steel inside him, the drive to succeed and to create the kind of life for himself he felt he deserved.

And Cecilie had fallen by the wayside.

'I'd love to have dinner with you,' Rafi replied, with a

direct gaze that should have made her cringe with embarrassment but instead gave her confidence.

'Great,' she said and touched his arm briefly. 'Let's see if we can get a table.'

They found a table at one of the restaurants on the pedestrianised side of Nyhavn. It was outside, overlooking the old harbour, but there were patio heaters and fleecy blankets available to help customers stay warm. Rafi immediately covered his chair with a blanket and wrapped it around his legs.

'I'm not quite used to the temperature here yet.' He smiled.

'Trust me, neither am I. I hate being cold.'

He laughed. 'Not much of a Viking, then.'

'Nope. Having said that, I'm not sure what it means to be a Viking, though.'

'That's a Viking,' said Rafi and pointed to two teenage girls sitting on the concrete pier, tapping away on their mobile phones, with no blankets, hats, gloves, or scarves in sight.

'I don't know – the stupidity of youth seems more like it.' They grinned at each other.

Having placed their order, they started talking about the differences between their countries, and their impression of each other's homeland. Inevitably, the talk turned to politics, but Rafi had a remarkably balanced view on the issue of Palestine, and he rose in her estimation. The thought of how the jewellery ended up in her grandmother's possession came back to her, as well as David Nathan's words that there had to be more to it.

Nothing was ever black and white, except perhaps to the very young, like the two girls on the pier.

And even they weren't that much younger than her grandmother had been when she'd taken a dangerous step into the unknown.

But that was for another day. Right now, Cecilie found herself in the moment, enjoying the hubbub of voices around her, the smell of oil and brine from the harbour, and the little bubble of light and warmth under the parasols that kept the encroaching darkness at bay.

'Have you always wanted to be a teacher?' Rafi asked her.

'Well, not really,' she replied. 'I did English at university and sort of fell into teaching afterwards. It was only later I realised how important it is to me, to be able to share what I know and pass on my knowledge. Even on days when the kids aren't as receptive as I'd like them to be.' She made a face.

He smiled. 'I can imagine.'

'And you?' She took a sip of her red wine. 'Did you always want to be a carer?'

She hadn't intended for the question to sound so flippant, but the wine had suppressed some of her inhibitions.

Fortunately he took it in good humour. 'I only knew that I wanted to do something that involves helping other people. Nursing seemed the obvious choice. To me, life is precious in all its chaos, young as well as old. Teaching is another way to give to others.'

How different he is from my ex-husband, Cecilie thought.

When they were married, Cecilie had always had to defend what she loved, and live with his scorn that if you weren't making a lot of money – which teachers have never done – you were essentially a failure.

The fact that Rafi was so comfortable in his own skin, so sure that what he was doing was right for him, and without seemingly having the need for validation in the form of clawing his way up a career ladder to get rich, was incredibly appealing. Cecilie had never realised before quite how much her husband's ambition and greed had repelled and irritated her. She felt a definite stirring of attraction for the strong man sitting opposite her, so undeniably male despite his caring profession.

'The carer part I did sort of fall into,' Rafi was saying. 'The thing is, David is actually my great-grandfather. He's quite frail, and when he had his stroke and needed almost full-time help, it made sense for me to move in with him so he could stay in his own home rather than go into a nursing home. Great-grandpa would really hate that.'

He spoke in a soft tone expressing both love and respect, and Cecilie's breath hitched in her throat as she realised once again that her own grandmother was gone for ever.

'But I'm not entirely altruistic,' Rafi continued with a smile. 'I'd recently split up with my long-term girlfriend and was looking for a place to stay. It benefits us both.'

'That makes two of us,' she sighed. 'The splitting up, I mean, not needing a place to stay.'

'So, there's no Mr Lund.' Was she imagining things or was there a glint of interest in Rafi's eyes?

Cecilie shook her head. 'I'm divorced. He's now married

again, and they have a child. His new wife was pregnant almost immediately, so I'm thinking they knew each other before we broke up.'

'A child that should've been yours?' he guessed. 'That must hurt.'

'It would never have been mine anyway – I can't have children.' Honesty compelled her to tell him, just in case he *was* attracted to her and was counting on having a large family one day.

She looked away to hide the sudden tears in her eyes, not from the loss of what might have been, but from the unexpected sympathy. When he took her hand across the table, she let the tears run freely down her face without wiping them away and telling herself to be strong. Instead she allowed herself the feeling until the pressure in her chest had disappeared. It was cleansing, healing somehow.

He took her hand again as they headed back across the square to the hotel, then gave her a quick kiss on the cheek as they said goodbye.

'If I had a special and gentle person such as you in my life, I'd never have been unfaithful.'

Blushing, she said, 'Thank you. That's really kind.'

'Not kind. True.'

Walking back through the now quieter shopping streets to Nørreport Station where she'd come from, her steps lighter than they had been in a long time, Cecilie thought about Rafi. Touched by his kindness towards her – a complete stranger – and also flattered by his attention, she knew it could never be. Rafi lived in Tel Aviv, and she'd built up a life here in Copenhagen.

But a voice inside told her that maybe it was time to look at it all from a different perspective, to get out of this rut and stop feeling like a victim. There had to be more to life than having a husband and children. Perhaps she had been become too single-minded, and instead needed to just live and see what happened.

Perhaps, like Inger, she was about to take a step into the unknown, but unlike her grandmother, who had decided to take a stand despite the dangers involved, the issue for Cecilie was whether she dared to embrace life as a whole and live it to the full.

Chapter Thirteen

Helsingør

22nd September 1943

On Monday, Bodil tried to catch Gudrun's eyes across the brewery factory floor, but she was frosty and withdrawn and averted her eyes, and Bodil didn't press her.

The encounter with the German patrol had clearly shocked her friend – shocked both of them – although it shouldn't have, but Bodil knew Gudrun well enough to know that her pride was wounded more than anything else.

So, she was pleased when the next day Gudrun caught up with her outside the brewery gates.

'I want to thank you for your help on Sunday,' she muttered, looking at her shoes. 'You didn't have to, and after what I said to you, you could've just left it. I would have.'

'It's fine,' Bodil replied.

Gudrun shrugged inside her jacket and looked suddenly very young. 'I don't know what's the matter with me at the moment.'

'Like I said, it's fine.' Knowing that this was the nearest she'd ever get to an apology, she squeezed Gudrun's shoulder to show her she'd been forgiven.

After having mulled it over, Bodil was inclined to think Gudrun might be right about the business with Oskar despite her clumsy way of saying it, but she wasn't going to give her the satisfaction of admitting it. For once in her life someone – a man – had made her feel genuinely attractive, and she wanted to hold onto that feeling for as long as she could. To treasure it and relive that one perfect dance in her head, alone in her bedroom at night.

As she cycled past Snekkersten Inn on her way home, she wondered if she would ever see him again. Helsingør wasn't that big a town, and it wasn't exactly overrun by Germans either, so there was a good chance that they might meet again, and she'd have to figure out how she was going to react if they did.

With regret, she knew it was probably for the best if she rebuffed him, except she also knew she'd find that difficult. His guileless attention towards her had awakened something inside her, a sense of self-worth she'd never felt before. The fact that it was a German man who'd caused this stirring was neither here nor there.

A group of soldiers stood outside the inn, and she was about to turn around and take a detour to avoid them, when someone called her name.

Her heart gave a little jolt when she realised it was Oskar who had called out. She couldn't very well ignore him now; that was just plain rude. She stopped and got off her bike.

'Hello again,' he said, and bowed like the first time they'd met. 'What a pleasure it is to see you again.'

One of the other soldiers made a rude gesture, and Oskar rounded on him, firing off a string of words in German too fast for Bodil to follow but she got the gist of it. The other soldier turned red from embarrassment and, clicking his heels together in a formal salute, nodded to Bodil.

'*Entshuldigung, fräulein*,' he said. *Apologies.*

The other soldiers went inside the inn, leaving only Oskar outside.

I must look a mess, Bodil thought.

She straightened her hair which had been blown about from cycling. There was nothing she could do about her work clothes though, and a part of her wished she'd at least worn a nicer skirt.

Oskar noticed her discomfiture and as if he'd read her thoughts, he commented, 'You needn't worry, fräulein Bodil. *Sie sind noch immer hübsch.*' *You're still pretty.*

'Thank you.' She blushed.

'Would you like to take a walk with me?' he asked. 'We could go to the beach opposite. I can see other people so we wouldn't be alone if you're worried about my intentions.'

Bodil felt torn. She actually did want to go with him, but what if someone saw her? Gudrun's words still echoed in her mind and she swallowed down her disappointment.

'Sadly I'm not able to. I have to get home and help with the milking.'

'Is it far?'

'No, it's not far.'

'In that case, may I walk with you? I'm off-duty this evening.'

Bodil nodded and let him push her bike for her. Suddenly conscious of her limp, she tried as hard as she could to disguise it by walking on the tip of her foot, but he seemed not to have noticed. Instead he talked about the weather, the landscape, as well as the farming methods on his family's farm, and she soon relaxed.

At the top of the lane they stopped. 'Might you be free tomorrow evening?' he asked.

Bodil chewed her lip, again torn between wanting to and being afraid to say yes. 'I'm not sure. I still have to help with the cows.'

'Well, if you change your mind, fräulein Bodil, you will find me on the beach tomorrow, waiting.'

'We'll see,' she replied, and thanked him for taking her home, then headed down the lane.

She could ask her brother Aksel if he would do the milking in her stead. Their father never paid him anything for working on the farm, and Bodil sometimes slipped him a bit of her own earnings when she'd handed over the lion's share of it to her father.

Aksel always protested that she should keep whatever she had for herself, but to her it wasn't right that a young man had no money of his own.

The argument with Gudrun had complicated matters,

even though they had made up now. After the dance, Bodil's head had been full of life's possibilities, but the reminder that Oskar was the enemy was still niggling. If she began stepping out with him, there would be no return.

Her father was already in the stables, and she quickly changed into the overalls and gum boots she wore around the farm.

'What time do you call this?' he grumbled.

'I'm sorry, Father. Gudrun wanted a quick word with me when I left.'

'Hmph. Young girls – nothing but nonsense and fripperies on their minds.'

If only you knew, she thought to herself. At least he hadn't seen her with Oskar.

'Sorry,' she said again and tried to sound contrite, but she couldn't quite hide the surge of energy inside her and the feeling that the world looked suddenly brighter and more beautiful.

The dirty-white rendered stable walls, the soggy straw, the uncooperative cows, everything had taken on a rosier tinge, and Bodil moved as if in a slow dance. In the end her father exploded.

'What's got into you, you useless girl?' Her clipped her over the ear and sent her indoors to prepare dinner.

Walking across the muddy yard, her hand pressed against her burning ear, she made her decision. Happiness wasn't going to come all by itself; she had to grab any opportunity that came her way.

'What do I tell him?' her brother asked before she left for work the next day.

'Tell him…tell him that I have an errand in town. To do with women's problems.'

He grimaced. 'Ugh yes, that'll do the trick.'

Bodil had hoped for decent weather, and she was in luck. A grey and overcast morning had given way to watery sunshine and a tranquil sea, perfect for an autumn stroll.

Oskar was exactly where he'd said he'd be. She left her bike against the fence beside the inn and walked down the slight slope to the water. She'd chosen a nicer skirt today, with a wide hem so she could cycle, but she hadn't reckoned on the scratchy dead wildflower stems and brambles and had to pick her way carefully.

Smiling, Oskar extended a hand. 'Here, let me help.'

To call their meeting place a beach was being generous. Instead of the fine grey sand on the northern coast, the shoreline by Snekkersten was strewn with boulders, pebbles, and dried seaweed, but she supposed that to a person from landlocked Bavaria, to all intents and purposes it was a beach.

Bodil smiled and took his hand, then let go of it again, flustered, when she reached him.

They took a stroll along the water, with Oskar adjusting his masculine stride to accommodate Bodil's smaller steps and reaching out to steady her where the ground was particularly uneven. His attentiveness warmed her; it wasn't intrusive, but it was there, for support, whenever she faltered.

They talked about this and that, polite small-talk to begin with.

'I've received a letter from my sister,' he said. 'Things seem to be difficult at home, but at least they're still all together, and my brother hasn't been called up yet.'

'Is he likely to? Isn't he just fourteen?'

'Yes.' Seemingly deep in thought, Oskar stopped to look out over the sea. Bodil went to stand beside him. Behind them, the sun was setting, and their bodies cast two long shadows across the gently rippling water, like an artist's impression of poplar trees.

Could it be true? she wondered. That a fourteen-year-old boy could be called up? Perhaps this was a sign that Germany were losing the war.

The thought brought mixed feelings with it: happiness that the occupation might soon come to an end; sadness that it meant Oskar would leave. Concern for the brother whom she hadn't met.

His thoughts echoed her own, in part. 'When the war is over, would you like to see my home? I would dearly love to show it to you.'

'Yes, I'd like that very much.'

'Then I promise to take you there one day,' he added, then heaved a sigh. 'If I survive.'

'Why wouldn't you? Denmark is peaceful, despite the occupation. Yes, there are a few saboteurs but there haven't been any German casualties.'

She was deliberately understating this, out of respect for him, but in November last year resistance fighters had derailed a train near the town of Espergærde, south of

Helsingør, and this year in August a bomb had shattered the shipyard. The same night, a group of locals had started a fight with three German soldiers, who opened fire and killed two of the locals.

The shock had reverberated through the whole community, but she didn't think Oskar would understand how that felt.

'No, I'm not worried about saboteurs. They'll be rooted out and punished.'

Bodil opened her mouth to protest that two Danes had died, then thought better of it.

Clearing his throat, he said, 'It's the fighting in the east that worries me. Several men I know have already been transferred. Denmark is only a temporary placement for many of us. They don't want us to get too comfortable here.'

She took his hand, hoping to reassure him and smooth away his pained gaze. 'I'm sure it won't come to that.'

But what do I know, she thought?

They remained standing like this for a while, just holding hands and watching their own elongated shadows until they disappeared from sight. It was time to get back; even though her brother was doing the milking for her, Bodil still had to prepare dinner.

Something hit her on the back of the head. Crying out, she turned around and was hit again, this time on the forehead.

'Ouch!'

Some local boys stood at the top of the slope and were hurling pebbles at her.

'Take that, you filthy whore!'

'Hey!' Oskar ran up the slope, and the boys scattered in different directions, laughing and chanting 'Feltmadras! Feltmadras!'.

One of them, more intrepid than the others, stood his ground for a moment longer. 'My father catches you, he'll cut off your hair and chase you naked through the streets so everyone can see how ugly you are!'

Then he scarpered, narrowly escaping Oskar's grip, and Oskar was left holding the boy's jacket. Furiously he tossed it on the ground and returned to Bodil.

'If I get my hands on them...'

Bodil held her palm against her forehead. It still stung, but the pain was already subsiding.

'It doesn't matter. They're just kids.'

'Let me see that,' said Oskar. 'Ooh, that looks painful. Think you'll get a bump on the head. What can I do? I don't have a handkerchief but I can dip my uniform sleeve—'

Bodil shook her head. 'I'll be fine. Believe me, I've had a worse. My f— The cows can be temperamental sometimes.'

Oskar studied her for a moment, but if he'd heard what she almost said, he obviously decided to let it go for now.

'What were they shouting?' he asked.

'Like I said, it's not important.' She couldn't bring herself to repeat it.

'Bodil, I want to know.'

Closing her eyes to banish their angry, contorted faces, and to hold onto the last remnants of her dignity, Bodil told him. 'They called me *feltmadras*. It means a camp bed that soldiers lie on when they're away from barracks.'

It was the most natural thing in the world that he took her in his arms. 'I'm so sorry…'

She let him hold her, just for a moment, allowing him to comfort her and realising just then that all she'd ever wanted in life was to feel cherished.

Chapter Fourteen

Helsingør

The same day

Over the next few days, I did several deliveries – legitimate ones as well as the illegal newspaper. As I'd hoped, people got used to seeing Franklin in my basket on the handlebars, as he looked straight ahead like a captain steering a ship.

Old ladies would smile, small children pointed and begged their mothers to lift them up so they could pat the little dog's head, and, best of all, German patrols began recognising me and the dog as a regular feature in the streets of Helsingør and greeted us with a nod.

Franklin was a German breed, after all.

When that happened, I forced myself to smile back so they had no reason to suspect anything.

Occasionally, when I was pushing the bike down a crowded street, some people would offer him titbits if they'd managed to pick up something from the butcher's shop. In the end, much to his disgust, I had to put a stop to it.

'You'll be a proper sausage dog if I don't,' I said in response to his disappointed yap.

It was going so well that at first I didn't notice when a patrol flagged me down and therefore almost cycled past them.

'Halt!'

The sharp command was followed by a yank as a strong hand caught the carrier at the back of my bike, and to prevent myself from toppling over I put my foot down on the ground hard. The sudden movement sent shooting pains up my leg.

'What on earth are you doing?' I shouted as shock and anger gave way to caution. I put a hand on Franklin's head to calm him down. The little dog was quivering uncontrollably.

'*Stoppen Sie das Fahrrad!*' came the command again. *Stop your bicycle.*

Although I didn't understand what the soldier was saying, I couldn't mistake the word *stop*. There were two of them, dressed in their habitual grey-green uniform, black boots and helmets, and armed with a rifle each and a cosh tucked into their cartridge belts. Fear rose in my throat at the thought of the neighbours' son lying bleeding in the street, and the memory of what had happened on Sunday on the way back from the beach.

My mouth suddenly dry, I fought to get my voice under control.

'*Entshuldigung.*' *Sorry.* 'I didn't see you.'

'*Was sagen Sie?*' snarled one contemptuously, with a grimace that was at odds with a pimply face which had never needed a razor.

The other soldier, who obviously spoke some Danish, translated for him. 'She says she didn't see us.'

'*Ihre Papiere!*' snapped the first man, and I handed him my identity papers. 'And your bag!'

With my lips in a thin line to stop myself from crying out in alarm I slipped off my leather satchel and handed it to him, wincing as he went through my personal belonging with rough, uncaring hands.

If only there had been a handkerchief in there with a big gob of snot on it.

But I wasn't concerned about my personal belongings. When I'd handed over the last batch of newspapers, I'd kept a copy for myself, to take home to Uncle Poul who would enjoy reading it. That newspaper was now folded up inside the towel Franklin sat on.

The soldier pushed my handbag back at me. 'Your basket,' he said.

Think, Inger. Think.

'*Bitte. Mein Hund,*' I said, swallowing hard. *Please, my dog.*

The soldier moved closer to lift Franklin out, and a scented, pungent odour hit me – a mixture of wool and boot polish, and something chemical...mothballs perhaps. Franklin, whose sense of smell was infinitely better than mine, bared his teeth in terror, and the soldier took a step back.

'You do it,' said the other man.

Gently so as not to frighten him, I put my hand under Franklin as well as the towel, and lifted him out under the pretence of swaddling him. The soldier searched the basket but found only a paper-wrapped parcel for a customer.

He ripped the paper off and flicked through the pages, then broke the spine of the newly bound book in his search. I flinched at the sound. It was a beautiful first translated edition of *Wuthering Heights*, and it belonged to a young bank clerk who had inherited it from her mother. Finding nothing, the soldier tossed the mistreated book back in the basket, and the other soldier, the one who knew some Danish, told me I could go about my business.

Feeling his eyes on me as though he was trying to penetrate my mind, I kept my face averted, and instead spoke soothingly to Franklin as I returned him to the basket.

I got back on the bike and continued in the direction I'd been heading. Over and over in my head I kept saying to myself that this was merely an unpleasant interlude, but my head wasn't listening. When I rounded a corner, I had to stop. I shivered all over, and the muscles in my legs had almost seized up. Until I found the strength to cycle again, I had to walk.

If the soldiers had found the illegal newspaper, the one who spoke Danish would have known what it meant and would have demanded to know where I'd got it from. Of course, I could have said I'd simply found it, but they might not have believed me, especially as I'd hidden it away. And if they started applying pressure – what kind of pressure, I didn't even want to contemplate – I wasn't sure I could have withstood it.

I'd been so excited about playing my own small part in the fight against the Germans that I hadn't thought much further than that; only now did I fully comprehend that this was deadly serious.

Perhaps Hans-Peter and Kiær had been right, that I was far too young to willingly get involved. Perhaps they'd seen that I was more vulnerable than I thought I was. And yet, I believed myself to be stronger than that.

I swallowed hard. Was I afraid? Yes. But perhaps with that fear came caution and maturity. Could I get used to encounters like these and train myself not to react so strongly? I had yet to find out, but I needed to grow a backbone, and fast.

Because the book was almost ruined, I couldn't get around not telling Kiær about it, but for as long as possible I would avoid telling Hans-Peter. If I shouldered the burden of his worry on top of my own justified fears, I might not have the courage to carry on.

Chapter Fifteen

Later the same day

When I returned to the workshop, after having done a little detour to avoid running into the patrol again, I showed Kiær the ruined book.

Touching it gingerly, he asked, 'What happened?'

'German patrol.'

My two-word reply was sufficient. He examined the book, opening up the cover board and checking the coloured threads which held the pages together. 'It's just the hinge, you know, this section here between the cover board and the spine. The leather is fine, only the paper on the inside of the cover needs redoing, but we can save it. You needn't worry about it, Inger.'

He put the book down. 'More to the point, how are you?'

I noticed his hand trembling before he managed to still it, but whether it was fear or anger he was trying to keep in check, I couldn't tell. I considered his question, then answered as truthfully as I could.

'Conflicted but determined,' I said, clearing my throat.

He nodded. 'I wouldn't expect you to feel anything else. It'd be surprising if you weren't a little shaken by such an encounter. Just as well this is it for now. When the next edition is ready, we can see how you feel then.'

'It won't change anything.' Pressing my lips together, I hugged my arms.

He nodded again, but more to himself this time. We returned to the tasks we'd been working on before I'd gone out on my errand. Slowly I felt the tension leaving my body as I allowed my hands to take over and guide the rest of me. There was comfort in the familiarity of my work.

Though I'd never admit it, I was relieved this was the end of my involvement for now. I'd sensed Kiær's conflict too as he veered between wanting to protect me and giving me the opportunity to do what I saw as my duty.

I wondered what other activities he was involved in, apart from the illegal newspaper and people needing false documentation, but now was not the time to ask. The less I knew, the less risk to him and his family.

On Friday I met the girls by the harbour after work. This time I'd brought tea in a flask – and made sure to tell Gudrun about it in the morning – to stop Gudrun stealing beers. Although I experienced a certain thrill at the thought of doing something illegal, Gudrun liked her job, and it would be a shame if she lost it. I particularly didn't want to be the cause of it in case she was doing it to show off a little in front of her city cousin, which I suspected was the reason last time.

They were already there when I arrived, and I listened to their easy chatter as I approached. Pealing with laughter, Gudrun seemed to be in high spirits, and although Bodil as always was more subdued, her usually throaty wheeze had a new quality to it, like meltwater trickling out from underneath a sheet of ice. It pleased me that they seemed to have buried the hatchet after Sunday's argument.

Just as well, I thought, as I sat down next to them.

Bodil was the first to acknowledge me. 'Hello. How was your day?'

'I had a good day, thank you,' I replied, which was true. An uneventful day until Hans-Peter dropped by and asked if he could walk me home. I explained that I'd arranged to meet my friends, and we'd agreed on a stroll along the pier later after dinner instead.

'Would seven o'clock suit you?' he'd asked.

I didn't tell Gudrun or Bodil any of this though, nor did I mention what had happened on Thursday.

I was getting adept at hiding my feelings, but still couldn't decide whether this was a good or a bad thing.

Pouring us all some tea, I joined in with the chat, but in the end took a backseat and let them do the talking. I'd noticed a bump on Bodil's forehead, but respected her privacy and didn't ask.

Gudrun was more direct. 'What actually happened? Your father again?'

Shrugging, Bodil blew on her tea.

'That old bastard!'

'It wasn't him.'

'Well, who was it then?' Gudrun scowled.

Bodil hesitated. 'Swear you won't have a go at me?'

'I swear. We both swear, don't we, Inger?'

I nodded. 'Of course we won't.'

'I went for a walk on the beach with Oskar. You know, the German soldier. And, well, some local boys threw stones at me and, um, called me names…'

I bit my lip, not sure how to react to this. I'd never had to deal with such a situation before. In theory, I ought to have been horrified that Bodil wanted to fraternise with the enemy, but on the other hand I thought I knew her well enough now to realise it wasn't as simple as that. Gudrun was different though. To her, everything was black and white, and she looked set to explode.

'You promised.' Bodil held up a hand in warning. 'I know what you think, but he's not like the rest of them, just looking for, well, you know…' She flushed. 'And I really like him. As a person.'

'A German person.' Gudrun frowned.

'I know.'

Gudrun, to my surprise, showed more maturity than usual. Sighing deeply, she said, 'I suppose we don't get to choose who we love. Just promise me you'll be discreet.'

'It's a little reckless,' I remarked, far more diplomatically than I felt.

Bodil wasn't stupid; surely she knew that with people being unable to vent their frustrations on the Germans without going to prison, they would find an easier target like herself, and there would be nothing her beau could do about it. Matters like that were for the Danish police to deal with, and they would probably take a dim view anyway and tell her it was her own fault.

Which would be completely unfair, but this wasn't about fairness, it was about loyalty. Why couldn't Bodil see that?

The conflicting feelings churned in my head. One minute, I wanted to shake Bodil and tell her to wake up, but at the same time I wanted her to be happy. And if she really was with this man, who was I to tell her what to do?

'I promise we'll be discreet.'

We fell silent after that, the relaxed atmosphere gone. I thought of the patrols I'd encountered here in Helsingør, and once back in Copenhagen when I'd been out shopping with my mother, and knew that I could never feel the way about a German soldier the way Bodil clearly did, no matter how nice he was. It was the casual brutality I'd witnessed, and the way they had gunned down a young man in the street for whatever reason, which I was glad I *hadn't* witnessed. The very air around them became charged and noxious. Besides, I was too angry and still grieving over the senseless loss to regard them as people, and I hated it when my thoughts took me in that direction. It made everything all too complicated.

We stayed silent as we watched the ferry *Svea* from Helsingborg in Sweden mooring by the pier at the far end. It felt good, just sitting here letting the breeze caress my cheeks and threaten to whip off my red hat which I'd secured with a pin. The wind these days was a constant, whether a light breeze like today or stronger, and the reliability of it was something for me hold onto. So too were the sounds and smells of the harbour. I realised I should have come here on Thursday, straight after my run-in with the patrol, instead of going home and pretending everything was normal.

Uncle Poul had sent me a mischievous grin when I handed him the newspaper and hadn't asked me where I'd picked it up – which, frankly, was easy enough if you knew who or where to enquire. Nor had he noticed how my hands were shaking, and when Aunt Marie asked him about the paper, he'd simply replied with a shrug.

Perhaps covert activities weren't as rare here as I'd thought; the town was small enough to know what others got up to, at least to an extent, and turning a blind eye and pretending not to know was in itself an act of subversion.

Finally, Bodil rose and handed back my enamel mug. 'I need to go now. Father is waiting.'

There was an eagerness to her, combined with a rosy tinge to her cheeks, and I suspected she wasn't rushing home to help out on the farm. But the less said about that the better. Gudrun hadn't noticed, just got up quietly and suggested we walk back too.

Her preoccupation continued while I was redoing my hair later, her teasing about my meeting with Hans-Peter half-hearted as she lay on top of her bed twirling her hair brush in her hand. I'd never seen her quite so subdued, and I wondered whether she was worried about Bodil. Or maybe it was something to do with Niels?

Selfishly I chose to ignore it otherwise my evening stroll with Hans-Peter would be spoiled.

———————

Hans-Peter was waiting in the square in front of the railway station, a lone tweed-clad figure amongst a sea of grey-green uniforms.

'What do you think is going on?' I asked him, as German soldiers carrying knapsacks or suitcases continued to spill out of the tall triple doors of the station building – more troops than any of us had seen in Helsingør before. 'Looks like they're preparing for an invasion.'

His hands deep in the pockets of his jacket, Hans-Peter shook his head. 'I don't know, but whatever it is, it can't be good.'

I had to agree with him on that, and seeing his knotted brow I was relieved that he didn't know about my second run-in with a patrol.

'Could they be worried about a Russian invasion?'

'I strongly suspect Stalin is too busy elsewhere, although I wouldn't rule out that it's crossed his mind,' he replied acidly.

I shuddered. As much as I hated being under German occupation, something told me it wouldn't be any better under the Soviet leader.

'I wonder where they're going to put them all.'

'Some at Kronborg Castle no doubt, and in various other places around town, mainly the infantry. A lot are in Hornbæk further north. I think there are about 5,000

German troops there, which is more than the entire population of the town.'

Hornbæk was where Gudrun and her fisherman often met, and to me that was a little too close for comfort. 'Well, I hope Hamlet's ghost shows up. Then we'll see how brave those officers are.' According to legend – and Shakespeare which I'd read many years ago – Kronborg Castle was supposed to have been the home of the mad prince.

Hans-Peter laughed. 'It was Hamlet who saw the ghost of his father, not Hamlet who was a ghost.'

I punched his arm lightly. 'Now you're just being pedantic. Let's go. I'm tired of this view.'

Narrowing his eyes as if he were doing an inventory, Hans-Peter continued to stare at the many German soldiers swarming the area. It suddenly struck me that perhaps he was involved in something more than the illegal deliveries, and a similar fear to the one I felt for Bodil crept over me.

'Hans-Peter…' I began.

He turned, smiling, and the memory of the way he'd held me close during the dance – daringly so – came back to me. Without realising it, I'd allowed Hans-Peter to sneak under my defences, and the thought of anything happening to him, of the light in those honest blue eyes going out, was almost unthinkable. But the thought refused to go away.

'Yes?'

'Are you…it's just newspaper deliveries that you do, isn't it?'

He gave a brief nod, then held out his arm. 'You're right, let's get out of here.' Away from the station, with the sound of hundreds of boots on the cobbles still echoing behind us, and looking out over the Sound, he said, 'I do feel I could do more, though. Ought to do more.'

As well as worrying for his safety, I couldn't help admiring him for his courage which I feared I might lack myself. At the same time, I was dealing with the aftermath of the fright I'd had and not wanting him to know about it.

How was it possible to feel so conflicted?

———————

The next day, Gudrun's fiancé came to dinner. Niels had brought some freshly caught cod with him, earning him a loving pat on the cheek from Aunt Marie.

My aunt had simply boiled it in saltwater and served it with potatoes and a white parsley sauce she'd made from her last knob of butter. As usual there was plenty of rye bread to fill up on and Ramona spread. It was a poor substitute for butter or even margarine, but in contrast to the coffee substitute, which still made me gag a little, I didn't find the combined taste of carrot and rosehip too unpleasant.

For dessert we had red-berry fruit compote with milk in place of cream. As a child I'd loved mixing the red fruit and the cream together until it had the colour of American bubble gum, but this didn't quite work with milk.

Uncle Poul and Niels were discussing the current political situation in the world, and also what had occurred closer to home. Gudrun and Aunt Marie would occasionally remark on what they were saying, with Jens listening intently.

I was content to just watch Gudrun and Niels and the occasional look which passed between them, and I noticed an unusual softness to Gudrun. The same expression had been on Bodil's face yesterday, now I came to think of it.

Is this what my face looks like when I think of Hans-Peter, I wondered? And was that really what I wanted?

To me, Bodil was putting herself in a vulnerable position by going with an enemy soldier, but Gudrun looked vulnerable too. It seemed the more people you loved and respected, the more exposed you became. I thought of the neighbour's son and his teasing smile. Was I ready to put myself in that position? But perhaps I was getting ahead of myself. It wasn't as though Hans-Peter had declared his undying love for me, or anything that melodramatic. We'd stepped out together twice, that was all, and were only just beginning to get to know each other. Time enough to worry about the consequences of falling in love as and when I was sure it had happened.

'Hold on a minute.' Uncle Poul rose from the table to rummage in a drawer, then returned with the illegal paper. 'In case you haven't already got a copy.'

'No, I haven't. Thank you, herr Bredahl.'

'Mind you, you'd better stuff it down your trousers on your way home.'

Niels grinned. He didn't ask where it had come from, and Uncle Poul didn't volunteer the information but winked at me.

As the women began clearing away the plates, I felt Gudrun's eyes on me, causing a prickling sensation on the back of my neck. I pretended not to notice and busied myself with the washing-up while Aunt Marie made coffee.

'I heard a little bird singing at work about some fishermen taking it upon themselves to smuggle goods in from Sweden. Have you ever been tempted?' Uncle Poul asked Niels.

'Dad! You can't ask questions like that. Of course he hasn't!' Gudrun looked outraged and almost dropped the stack of plates she'd piled into her arms.

'I'm sure Niels here can speak for himself. And take a joke.'

Shaking his head, Niels spoke mildly, like the gentle giant he was. 'No, herr Bredahl, I haven't. I'll not be risking my livelihood for luxury items. If someone was in dire need of my help, that'd be a different matter.'

'Well said, young man. Sounds like you're the kind of chap who can keep my daughter in check.'

'That I doubt I'll ever manage,' said Niels, and we all laughed, even Gudrun – although her frown told me that Uncle Poul had yet to be forgiven.

This was the second time I'd met Gudrun's fiancé, and he struck me as a man of simple principles, what with being against smuggling. At the same time, I'd rather enjoyed that cup of real coffee Kiær had given me on my first day at work. Which, of course, made me a terrible hypocrite.

Aunt Marie hovered by the door while the young couple said goodbye outside in the lane.

'Come away, Mother. Let the young ones have some privacy.'

Jens sniggered suggestively.

'Just so she knows to be careful,' Aunt Marie protested.

'She will be,' Uncle Poul replied, frowning slightly as he twiddled to knob on the radio.

Having witnessed how foolhardy Gudrun could be, I suspected my aunt and uncle were talking at cross purposes.

In the bedroom later, Gudrun asked me about the illegal newspaper.

'Did you have anything to do with that?'

'Of course not. Why would you even ask that?' A flush spread at the back of my neck, and I averted my eyes from Gudrun's in the mirror, as I continued plaiting my hair for bed.

'Well, Dad looked at you when he gave it to Niels.'

My hair done, I climbed under the covers. 'It was one Kiær had lying around, and he gave it to me. So I passed it on.'

'Uh-huh. And does he print them?'

'Not to my knowledge. Can we have lights out, please?'

To stop Gudrun asking further questions, I pretended to fall asleep immediately. Except I couldn't sleep. Troubling thoughts beset me. Gudrun was suspicious of me, and though I was pretty certain Gudrun would praise me for my efforts, as little as it was, I worried she might inadvertently say something to the wrong person.

Suddenly, everything and everyone was a threat and it was an uncomfortable thought.

The more you knew, the more you exposed the ones you loved, and the more you loved, the more you stood to lose. But someone had to make a stand, whatever the cost. I owed that to my country and all those suffering at the hands of the Germans.

Chapter Sixteen

Copenhagen

October 2018

A s arranged, Cecilie returned to David's hotel. She came straight from the high school where she taught, jumping on the train from Hellerup Station, where she had no trouble finding a seat since it was outside rush hour.

The train swayed softly, an almost silent journey. Having been both to London and Paris a few times, and seen the state of the underground trains there, she was grateful for the cleanliness of Copenhagen's easily navigated S-tog system. Or *Stadsbanen* as it had originally been dubbed, and which she could best translate as 'city train' to her English friends and colleagues.

There were no loud-mouthed lounging teenagers this time of day, just a few pensioners, young mums, and dads pushing prams, and the odd cyclist in the designated area for people with bikes.

At the hotel reception she asked after a David Nathan, explaining that she was having lunch with him here, and was shown into the restaurant. It turned out to be an almost overwhelmingly opulent room with champagne-coloured drapes, purple unholstered chairs and crisp white tablecloths. Their progress through the tables was muffled by the silver-grey deep-pile carpet, and Cecilie felt as though she ought to whisper so as not to disturb the diners they passed. David and Rafi were already there, sitting at a square table designed to seat four, one on each side, but Rafi rose when she entered and gave her quick kiss on the cheek.

'Here, let me take your coat.'

Her face grew hot as she was suddenly conscious of his nearness, her old duffel coat, which had seen better days – why, oh why, had she not paid attention this morning instead of just whipping it off the clothes rack? – and her scuffed leather rucksack that she kept her school papers in. They all made her feel very out of place in these posh surroundings.

'Thank you.'

Rafi handed the coat to a member of staff who took it away. 'My pleasure.'

Putting her rucksack on the floor, Cecilie sank into a chair. A waiter handed her a menu, and she chose an autumn salad made with Jerusalem artichokes, pumpkin, and cabbage sprouts. Not because she was a vegetarian but because it was the cheapest dish on the lunch menu, and David had said he wasn't a rich man. Also, she wanted to avoid anything with pork in it out of respect for David and Rafi whom she was pretty sure wouldn't be eating that and she didn't want to offend.

Then she stopped herself. *They* had picked the restaurant, not her, so why would they be offended by her choice at all? She was, as David had put it on the day they met, guilty of overthinking the situation.

Just relax and be yourself, she thought.

While they ate, they talked about an anniversary event David was planning to attend at a church in Gilleleje to mark the seventy-fifth commemoration of the events in Denmark which had eventually brought him to Israel. Then the talk turned to David's wife – Rafi's great-grandmother – who had passed away only three years previously.

'We had a good life together,' the old man said with the wistful smile of a person who knew he'd been blessed. 'We met on a boat out of Italy in 1948. I was planning to finish my studies to become a lawyer, and she was a teacher, like yourself, and when we arrived in Jaffa – which is called Tel Aviv now – I started working for a firm of solicitors. Later I set up my own practice, specialising in litigation. Two of my sons took over the firm, and it's since passed to one of my grandsons, Rafi's father.' David patted Rafi's hand with an indulgent smile.

'Trust me, my father wasn't too happy when I announced my intention to do nursing instead of going into the family firm.' Rafi grinned. 'He called it a woman's job, and more besides. Questioned whether I was a proper man.'

Not a proper man? A flush spreading on the back of her

neck, Cecilie regarded Rafi out of the corner of her eye. How could anyone be in doubt about that?

'Fraud, defective products, and unpaid bills just isn't for me,' he added.

David waved a hand dismissively. 'Ach, my grandson's a fool. He'll come round. I expect one of your cousins will be interested, and if not' – he shrugged – 'young people have to go their own way.'

'And what about your parents?' Rafi asked, putting down his cutlery. 'Are they happy with your choices?'

'Yes, they are. I can't fault them; they're always there when I need support.' Most recently, in connection with her divorce, but she steered away from that as the subject had a tendency to make her feel sorry for herself. Right now she wanted to think positively.

'I'm an only child,' she went on, 'although I've always been close to my cousins. They're almost like brothers and sisters to me. I guess you could say we're a close family, and I hope we'll stay that way now my grandmother is gone. She was like the glue that held us together.'

'Ah yes, your grandmother.' David sighed. 'Would you be so good as to read some more of her diary for us? When we've finished eating?'

'Of course.'

Over coffee, Cecilie got the diary out of her rucksack and opened it on the page when they had last left Inger. She'd been itching to finish the rest of the diary by herself, but it was quite emotional for her and it didn't feel right to read it without David somehow. Besides, his – as well as Rafi's – presence somehow made it more bearable.

David had known her grandmother, in a different capacity to herself of course, but last time they'd met, she could tell that he had at least liked Inger, and Cecilie wanted them to share her grandmother's story together.

David and Rafi listened intently, David slumped in his wheelchair bowing his head, and Rafi with his arm resting casually over the back of Cecilie's chair.

When had he moved his chair closer? Or had Cecilie moved hers?

...The more you knew, the more you exposed the ones you loved, and the more you loved, the more you stood to lose...

'Saturday the twenty-fifth of September,' said David with a distant look on his face. 'That was four days before it all happened. On the twenty-ninth. Terrible moment. I was there.'

'Yes, I can imagine,' said Cecilie.

Although how could anyone imagine what it felt like to be persecuted this way? No one could, really, unless they had experienced it for themselves. In reality, it was beyond most people's comprehension.

Rafi echoed her thoughts. 'Part of the culture in Israel is defined by the Holocaust, the Hebrew language, and the need to band together against conflict with hostile neighbours. Some Jewish people outside Israel don't always identify with that. Although sometimes we can be the hostiles too.'

'Let's not have that discussion again, Son.' David's face was drawn, and suddenly he looked every bit his age.

'You're right, Grandpa. Let's not.' Rafi turned to Cecilie. 'I like the way your grandmother writes. I can literally feel her conflict and fear.'

'Yes.' David's eyes had welled up, and his hands shook. 'I like hearing her voice too, and her story of the past,'

Clearly moved by whatever distant memories Inger's words had invoked in him, he was staring straight ahead as though watching an old film being replayed before him.

Revealing another hidden part of her grandmother, the diary had touched Cecilie too. This brave young woman Inger had been…did it tally with the person Cecilie knew? She realised it had never even occurred to her.

Her grandmother had, like a benevolent matriarch, gathered her children around her as often as she could and found every excuse to spoil her grandchildren. Even during the inevitable disagreements in such a large, close-knit family, she had, in a firm but tender way, coaxed the combatants into seeing each other's perspective.

Yet, she had also been fierce in her love. Once, when Cecilie's mother had had a persistent cough, she'd practically frogmarched her daughter to the doctor to get antibiotics for what turned out to be a mild case of bronchitis.

Always with the power of her convictions, she'd been a force to be reckoned with. Perhaps that was the ingredient which made a person brave.

As these thoughts flew through Cecilie's head in the few seconds it took for her to formulate them, Rafi, ever the carer, put his hand over the old man's.

'Grandpa? Would you like to rest up for a bit?'

'Rest?' David seemed to have withdrawn into himself. 'Yes, yes, I will rest now. Truth be told, I am rather tired.' He turned to Cecilie. 'But if you're not bored with an old man yet, may I suggest we all have dinner in Tivoli this evening?'

'That's sound lovely.'

'What's Tivoli?' Rafi asked.

David gave a low chuckle. 'You'll see. Something for you to look forward to. But no reading tonight, just enjoyment.'

'Agreed,' Cecilie replied.

She returned to the high school just in time for her afternoon lesson at two, then back to her flat for a quick cup of tea and to change for the evening. She needed to prepare for her lessons tomorrow but would get up early and do it then.

Despondently, she looked at the contents of her wardrobe. Downsizing from the home she'd shared with her husband had given her the perfect opportunity to declutter, and she had done just that. Except for her wardrobe, which was still in a bit of a mess; she had too many clothes she hardly ever wore.

It had also been ages since she'd been for a night out which didn't involve family in one way or another, but this was an-almost-but-not-quite-date, and she wanted to look good for both Rafi and David. The question was what to wear for a night out in Tivoli Gardens in October, which would be mainly outdoors.

Once, she'd read a book about the different ways of dressing amongst women in several parts of Europe, as well as North America. According to the author, Scandinavian women were 'a colourful lot', but in winter you 'hardly ever saw their legs'.

'Because it's too damned cold, dear author,' she muttered and selected a knee-length black velvet skirt and a pistachio-green oversized jumper with slits on the hem like an upside-down crenellated tower.

She finished it with a matching woollen scarf, black gloves, and a pair of stupidly expensive silver brogues she'd bought on a whim. The aim was to appear both hip and feminine – *showing my legs (in tights), hah!* – and be warm as well.

'Oh, God,' she groaned as she took one final look in the mirror, but it was too late to change again.

She met them again that evening outside the main entrance to the famous amusement gardens near Copenhagen city hall.

'You look nice,' said Rafi. 'A proper Viking.'

She laughed at his reference to their conversation in Nyhavn, and lowered her eyes so he couldn't see just how much the compliment meant to her.

David noticed her reaction and smiled as if to himself.

Once inside the amusement park, Cecilie persuaded David and Rafi to try the famous soft ice. Rafi helped David wrap a couple of napkins around the cone like you would with a young child to stop them getting ice cream all over themselves, and David sent Cecilie a mischievous wink. Rafi was fussing, but she could tell David enjoyed the attention.

The gardens were crowded, with both tourists and locals, families, but also many young people in groups of varying sizes, including a stag party. For some reason these groups felt it necessary to walk several people abreast, so David rode in front of Cecilie and Rafi like an icebreaker boat ploughing through the masses, which he seemed to find amusing. She and Rafi would occasionally bump into each other, and each time she was intensely aware of him, her body tingling with anticipation.

She could tell he felt the same by the way he kept throwing her heated glances, his eyes smouldering in the light from the old-fashioned lamps.

They had dinner at the restaurant in The Chinese Tower, overlooking the roller coaster and a small artificial lake. This time she dared to order a proper meal as she had gathered neither man would be bothered whatever she chose. She persuaded them to end the meal with Danish *æblekage* and custard, her favourite dessert and something most people enjoyed. This proved to be the case here as well.

Afterwards David fell asleep in his wheelchair, and Rafi

pulled the blanket he'd brought with him further up to cover the old man's chest.

'He could be pretending,' he said, but with fondness. 'Grandpa sometimes does that so he can eavesdrop on other people's conversations.'

That made Cecilie laugh, but she tried to talk quietly just in case the old man was doing it now.

She asked Rafi where he'd got his perfect American accent from.

'I lived in New York for a while – six years to be precise. My ex-girlfriend was American.' He sighed and stared at the carpet briefly. 'Never thought I'd miss Israel, but when I got back after we'd broken up, I realised that I actually had missed it. A lot.'

She could tell he really meant it.

'What about the political unrest, the danger?' Cecilie asked.

Rafi shrugged. 'That's what you hear on the news, of course. But everyday life is different to that. People just go about their business as they do here or in London or Bangkok or wherever. The outside world often refers to Israel as a "Jewish state", but that's simplistic. The reality is it's a country like any other country in the world, just with mainly Jewish people in it. It's a so-called secular state, where politics and religion are separate from each other. Although having said that, we always have a coalition government consisting of both political parties and religious parties. If that makes any sense to you,' he added with a laugh. 'I could be talking complete bullshit.'

'It's fascinating,' she said. 'There's so much I don't know.'

'Perhaps you'd be interested in knowing more one day.' There was an invitation in his amber eyes that drew her in and she wasn't sure whether they were still talking about his country or something else.

'One day, perhaps,' she hedged.

David woke up. As it was nearly quarter to midnight, Cecilie suggested they go to see the fireworks over the concert hall. Again, David paid the bill, and again he refused to accept a contribution from Cecilie, and they made their way to the lawn in front of the Tivoli Concert Hall, where they managed to find a good vantage point.

Soon the sky burst into in a wealth of pinks, blues, and purples, hot white howlers shooting up into the heavens, dropping down again as gentle silver rain. The crowd ooh'ed and ah'ed as massive green chrysanthemum shapes exploded over the concert building in a finale of blinding lights.

Standing behind David's wheelchair, Rafi rested his hand on his great-grandfather's shoulder affectionately. As she craned her neck watching the fireworks, Cecilie felt him moving closer to her, and soon their fingers found each other.

It was a soft caress, just the tips of their fingers meeting, yet her whole body jolted from the shock, and she ached with a sudden, insane need for him to stroke every curve of her. Her breath grew faster as their eyes met, shining feverishly from the bursts of light above them, as though they could never stop looking at each other.

This is utterly crazy, she thought. So, so crazy. And it was all happening so fast.

But why hold back? Maybe it was time for her to simply enjoy what life had to offer instead of mourning what couldn't be. Like her grandmother had said, it was time to stop being afraid.

Chapter Seventeen

Helsingør

27th September 1943

Bodil met Oskar on the outskirts of Snekkersten. After her experience on the beach with boys throwing stones at her, she wanted to be as discreet as possible, and the only one who knew about the meeting was Aksel.

He'd sent her a worried look, not judgmental, and he hadn't commented. Perhaps he understood what it meant to her to have a suitor for once, even if he was the 'wrong kind'.

But how could anyone fail to like Oskar when they got to know him? Courteous and gentle, he took her arm to help her over uneven ground and made sure to shelter her by letting her walk in the centre of the forest path rather than on the sloping side. No one had ever treated her with this level of consideration, except her mother, and she felt like a duchess.

When he took her hand in his and sent her a look of – what? Longing? – she blushed from head to toe, and had to look away.

As they turned deeper into the forest, she experienced a brief moment of alarm. Was this safe? How much did she really know about this man?

Oskar must have sensed her hesitation for he stopped. 'I mean you no harm, Bodil. But if you wish, we'll go no further. Perhaps we can find somewhere to sit? Is there a bench?'

'There won't be any benches, but I know the perfect log.'

He smiled. 'Everything is perfect when I'm with you.'

'You're just saying that.'

'No, it's the truth.'

Oh, how she wanted it to be true. Maybe it was, maybe it wasn't, but that was for another day to worry about. Right know she just wanted to enjoy every moment in his company, for as long as it lasted.

They found the log and sat down. It was slightly damp moss and moisture in the air, and Oskar spread his uniform jacket out for them to sit on. It was sheltered here away from the breeze on the sea front, but Bodil hoped he wouldn't get cold.

Here they talked about whatever was on their minds. The war, that was hard to avoid, but also Oskar's home in Bavaria. His eyes shone with passion for the place when he spoke of the mountain air, the animals lowing in the pastures, the whitewashed farmhouse with window boxes by every window, teeming with petunias and lobelias, his mother's cooking. He'd done the same when they first met, but Bodil found she couldn't get enough of it. It was exotic and different, like a story from another world.

'It sounds so wonderful,' she sighed.

'We work hard,' he said. 'And it's not always easy in the winter, but yes, it is wonderful. I think about home every single day.'

He clenched her hand, then loosened his grip and stroked her palm instead, caressing the callouses and rough skin.

'See,' he said, showing the palm on his own hand, holding it next to hers, thumbs touching like a mirror image. 'We have the same hands – rough around the edges, soft and pink in the centre, a little bit of dirt under the fingernails. We're alike, you and I.'

Mortified that he'd noticed the dirt she could never quite wash out no matter how hard she scrubbed, Bodil pulled her hand away and placed it in her lap.

'You do realise it's bad luck to compare hands, don't you?' she said, to cover up the embarrassment yet again.

There was something about this man, the lack of guile in his blue eyes, the boyish charm and the slightly awkward attentiveness which had got under her skin. Like the black around her nails.

'No, I didn't realise that. A Danish superstition, perhaps?'

'It might be, I don't know. What I do know is that I need to get back before I'm missed.'

'Of course.' He rose and helped her up. 'But I'll see you again, yes?'

'I'd like that.'

'I'll bring a picnic,' he said.

'A picnic?' Bodil's eyes went wide. 'How will you do that? Wouldn't that be stealing from the army?'

Oskar winked. 'Leave it with me, *Schöne Augen*.'

They agreed to meet again in two days' time after Bodil had finished work, and again at the edge of the forest. Perhaps the log would become their regular meeting place, at least until it became too cold to sit outdoors. What they would do then, Bodil left for the future to decide.

Wednesday the 29th was like any other day for Bodil. Except it was also utterly different. New and full of opportunities. Meeting with Oskar again had had a profound effect on her; whereas he dreamed of home, he said, she dreamed of him – of his voice, of the feel of his hands, of the daring idea that perhaps her future lay with him.

She'd been distracted at home, earning her a clip over the ear from her father, and had made several mistakes at work, to the exasperation of the supervisor. Fortunately, Gudrun had been too wrapped up in her own thoughts to notice, otherwise she would probably have asked her a lot of questions.

Oskar waited for her at the edge of the forest with a khaki satchel slung over his shoulder. The picnic. She'd almost forgotten about that in her eagerness to see him again, and the relief that he'd actually turned up. Did that mean he'd stolen from the Wehrmacht, and what would the consequences be?

'Relax,' he said when he saw her worried frown. 'It's from my mother.'

'What's in it?'

Mischief danced in his eyes. 'A surprise.'

He wouldn't say any more, and Bodil would have to be content with that. The thought of a surprise excited her; it had been a long time since she'd had the pleasure of a nice surprise. They were usually not so nice.

Bodil parked her bicycle and they headed towards the fallen log they had sat on last time. In contrast to the weather two days ago, today the sky was a bright blue with not a cloud in sight, and the log was warm and dry to sit on.

What a beautiful day, she thought.

Oskar told her to close her eyes. She heard the flick of a knife, but instead of inducing fear, the sound filled her with an odd sense of expectation. She felt something cold and firm and smoky on her tongue, obviously a sausage of some kind. She hadn't eaten *spegepølse* in a while, and even though the butcher made her favourite type of sandwich sausage, with work she rarely had time to queue outside with other housewives. At the farm they ate mostly chicken – scrawny old birds past their egg-laying days which her father would behead in the yard and leave for Bodil to pluck. Or sometimes they had herring when she was able to pick up fish fresh from the harbour on her way home.

'Tell me what you can taste,' said Oskar.

Savouring the sausage in her mouth, Bodil thought for a bit. 'I can taste pepper definitely, and mustard, I think. There's something else, a sort of sharp, pungent taste.'

Oskar nodded, or at least she thought he did because she still had her eyes closed. 'That'll be the garlic.'

'Garlic? Never tried it.'

'Anything else?'

'A warm, earthy taste,' she replied.

'Paprika.' Oskar grinned. 'You're very good at this. My mother would be impressed; she makes her own *bierwurst* and takes great pride in creating just the right balance of flavours. Here, try this.' He put some kind of bread in her mouth.

When his fingers touched her lips, heat flashed through her. So, this is what desire feels like, she thought. It was both exhilarating and a terrifying experience because it was as if she had no conscious control over her own body, her knees as weak as beef jelly.

Clearing her throat, she asked, 'Does it have beer in it as well, since it's called "beer sausage"?'

'I don't think so. It's just the name.'

Eventually he allowed her to open her eyes, and Bodil saw that he had placed a cloth across his lap with a large glazed pretzel on it and a curiously-shaped sausage, more like a balloon than the traditional sausage shape.

'That sausage was delicious,' she said. 'And I liked the pretzel too.'

'Mother sent me a food parcel. *And* woollen socks and a scarf because she has this idea that Denmark is near the arctic circle. The irony is that it's actually very cold in the

Bavarian mountains.' He grinned. 'The *bierwurst* needs to be eaten soon, but pretzels last much longer.'

The finished their picnic. Oskar put the last piece of sausage in her mouth, and she enjoyed it for as long as she could before having to swallow it. Had she just been to heaven?

Oskar smiled as she chewed, then he reached out and cupped her cheek in his hand, before placing a gentle kiss on her lips.

This was more than Bodil could bear. She yanked him closer by his uniform jacket and kissed him back passionately, exploring his lips, running her hands over the back of his neck, down his shoulders to his hands, calloused and sinewy, the mark of a man. Then, surprised by her own daring, she placed one of his hands over her breast.

Shocked, Oskar pulled back.

'That would be wrong, *Schöne Augen*. Never before holy matrimony.'

Bodil put her hands in her lap to still them. She wasn't sure whether she was disappointed or relieved that they hadn't gone further. As for further, she was a farm girl; she knew what 'further' entailed, and the image of herself and Oskar in that position was a little disconcerting.

'I respect you,' he said. 'Do you think...?' He looked away, then turned to her again, his face slightly red. 'Do you think you could entertain that idea? I mean, after the war and if we're both still alive? The idea of us. I know we're supposed to be enemies, but I'm not *your* enemy.'

'Yes,' she replied, almost in a whisper. 'I could. But until then we...'

199

We what? She couldn't finish the sentence. So many obstacles and ifs. The dream of a future seemed as fine and insubstantial as a cobweb.

'Dream big, and you'll fall the hardest,' her father had said to Bodil's older sister on her wedding day. Followed by a sneer, of course, what else? But perhaps the old man was right for once.

Oskar finished what she couldn't say. 'Until then we are friends.'

Chapter Eighteen

Helsingør

1st October 1943

K iær had been a little preoccupied most of the week following my encounter with the patrol. Not to do with the patrol, I suspected, but with something else. His face became increasingly careworn, but when I asked him if he was well, he dismissed my concern. One morning he'd arrived late, looking as though he hadn't slept at all.

Rønne began to drop in more frequently, although rarely with a book to be bound. I would find them closeted together, and thought that perhaps they were working on a new edition of the illegal newspaper. But why that should make Kiær look so careworn, I didn't know.

When I arrived at work early on Friday, Kiær was already there, not with Rønne this time, but with the policeman called Thormod, as well as with another man I hadn't met before. Tall with thick, dark hair and hazel eyes, he was dressed in a blue pullover, dark hat, and a camel-hair coat in a classic cut.

When he saw me, he took off his hat and gave a curt nod.

Thormod hesitated, but Kiær assured him that they could talk freely in front of me. 'Frøken Bredahl has been helping me get the paper out.'

The policeman's eyes widened, in contrast to the other man who regarded her with interest and a slightly lopsided grin, much like you might look at a curious specimen in Copenhagen Zoological Gardens.

The smile sent a tingle of awareness down my spine as I suddenly noticed how incredibly attractive he was. This, of course, made me blush – when didn't I? – and I looked down as I felt the heat creeping up into my cheeks.

'This is herr David Nathan,' said Thormod, clearing his throat nervously. 'I was at a party in Copenhagen yesterday. It's an annual thing, with other police officers responsible for foreigners and passport control like I am.' He lowered his voice and looked around him, even though the four of us were the only ones in the workshop at the back of the shop and no one could hear us from the street, or through the back. 'A colleague confided in me that he knew of two people who were hiding from the Nazis, and I offered to take them back to Helsingør with me.'

He held out his hand to indicate the other man. 'Herr Nathan here knew one of the men and came along as well.'

David Nathan shook my hand, and I felt the strength in

his fingers. 'Herr Larsen kindly allowed us to stay the night in his flat and this morning my friends were helped to Sweden.'

'Thormod,' said Thormod. 'No one calls me Larsen.'

David Nathan smiled his lopsided grin again. 'Thormod it is. And please call me David. The reason I didn't go with my friends,' he explained to Kiær, 'is that my mother is in hospital with a mild case of pneumonia, and she's not quite ready to be discharged. Or to be precise, the doctors have officially discharged her and re-admitted her under an assumed name, which means she's safe for now. And I'm also staying behind because I want to help people in the same situation as myself,' he continued. 'I don't want to be just another victim.'

As he spoke, I felt his eyes on me as if he were speaking directly to me.

Helsingør was a small community, and following a sudden influx of travellers since Wednesday outside season, the news that Jews from Copenhagen were fleeing the Nazis in large numbers had quickly spread amongst the locals. I'd been hearing snippets about this for a couple of days now.

It was one thing to listen to gossip though, but quite another to come face to face with one of the people who were being persecuted. To me this man seemed incredibly brave, standing here so calmly when he should have been halfway across the Sound to Sweden by now. And his loyalty to his mother made me warm to him further. I thought of my own parents, of their gentleness and trust in me, and how I'd never leave them behind either if I was in that situation.

'Unfortunately, David can't stay at my flat any longer,' said Thormod. 'My neighbour's son is a volunteer in the Schalburg Corps, and the father is a sympathiser. It's simply too risky.'

I made a face at the mention of the Danish arm of the Germanic SS which had existed under the name Schalburg since April. We'd had active Fascist parties in Denmark before the war, but the Schalburg Corps was highly organised. They used their members as a guard battalion to protect railroads and crossroads from sabotage, and they'd been trying to squash the resistance by murdering various opposition leaders.

'Unfortunately I left my home in a rush and don't have that much money on me,' said David, 'but I'm happy to stay in a shed or a barn.'

'Nonsense,' said Kiær. 'I have relatives with me at the moment, but you can stay here at the workshop. Just remember, please, no lights at night, as the shop has no blackout blinds.'

'Of course. I appreciate it.' David bowed to Kiær.

Emboldened by David Nathan's bravery, I said, 'Perhaps there is another option.'

'Yes, Inger?'

'May I suggest that herr Na— David stays with my family? There should be enough room, and we can easily pretend you're a nephew on my aunt's side. They live in Jutland and rarely visit, so no one would be any the wiser.'

Those hazel eyes gazed at me with sudden intensity. It sent another arrow of awareness shooting through me but I tried to ignore it. 'Will your family not mind?'

I thought about my uncle and his matter-of-fact reaction when I brought home the illegal newspaper, and of my aunt's shrug when she saw it. Then I thought of Gudrun, and was assailed by a niggling doubt that my impetuous cousin might accidentally let the secret out. I'd have to make her swear to keep her mouth shut.

Then it occurred to me that perhaps I was being unfair to Gudrun. On the matter of Bodil's German beau she'd shown herself to be more mature than I'd imagined. Perhaps I owed it to her to have a little faith.

Jens I wasn't worried about.

'No, they won't mind,' I said. 'But to be sure I'll run back and check with them.' I buttoned my coat and dashed back out.

Aunt Marie was in the kitchen preparing vegetables.

'I was expecting that,' she replied to my hurried explanation. 'The word has got around about some folk needing help, which set me thinking about how best to get things ready. I'll ask Jens to put up the camp bed when he gets back from school.'

I returned to the workshop about twenty minutes later, and David accepted the invitation to stay.

Thormod left, visibly relieved. Kiær gave David the task of tidying up materials and organising the bookbinding leathers and patterned papers so it was easy to see where they would need to restock when it became possible.

'This way anyone walking past will just see three people engaged in their job,' he said.

As soon as he could without raising questions, Kiær sent

us home. I took the delivery bike with me as I'd arranged with the girls to go for a bike ride the next day.

'Would it be best if I cancelled?' I asked Kiær.

He shook his head. 'It's best we all carry on with our daily lives. That way everything appears normal.'

David offered to push the bike for me as we walked through the narrow streets, and we chatted about ordinary things like the weather and whatever we saw as we walked. To begin with I was looking over my shoulder several times, but he seemed so calm, and I soon stopped doing it.

Just like any other couple. The thought made my face go hot. Where did that come from? Despite the warmth in his lopsided grin, this man was a complete stranger, and soon he would be gone.

'I was sorry to hear that your mother is in hospital. I hope she'll be all right.'

'As I said, it's just a touch of pneumonia, which she's had before. But she's quite weak and frail. I spoke to the doctor this morning from Thormod's phone, and he told me she probably won't be discharged until Monday. So I'll have to wait.'

'I'm afraid my aunt and uncle don't have a telephone,' I said, 'but the neighbour does, and she's very kind and will allow us to use it. She'll even take messages.'

'Thank you, that's very reassuring.'

I glanced at him briefly as he walked beside me. Despite the terrible situation he found himself in – having to flee his home or face deportation, or worse – the confidence in his stride, which, being a gentleman, he shortened to match mine, exuded calm. In the last week I'd worried what Kiær had been up to and if he was perhaps putting himself in serious danger, but David's composure in the face of adversity acted like a balm to my roiling concern.

Refined and self-possessed, his hazel eyes had sparked with interest when he'd learned that I was distributing the illegal paper, as if he was seeing me as someone equally capable and not a fragile doll or a child who needed mollycoddling.

How different he was to Hans-Peter, even the way he walked. In my mind I pictured Hans-Peter's gait, which was more like that of an impatient and spring-loaded young buck itching to see whatever else was on the horizon, and felt immediately ashamed of my unfair comparison.

In spite of my guilt, David Nathan had stirred something deep inside me which up until now had remained dormant, with the real me reflected in his eyes. I felt it in the way his body warmed the air around us, a private cocoon for only the two of us. In the catch of my own breath when he looked at me, or smiled or spoke, the way his strong, clean hands rested on the handle bars, the brush of his coat sleeve against mine, a demure and involuntary gesture yet wondrously intimate.

I wanted the walk back to the house to last forever.

Aunt Marie shook David's hand brusquely. 'Don't you worry about a thing, young man. You can stay as long as you need.'

'Thank you, fru Bredahl. That's extraordinarily kind of you and your family.'

'Ach.' Aunt Marie waved a hand dismissively as if was nothing, but his plight had clearly touched her and she wiped away a tear.

As promised, Jens had assembled the camp bed in the attic room which he would be sharing with our guest, and Aunt Marie gave me the bedclothes to make up the bed as she rarely went up there due to the rickety steps.

'Make it nice for him. And mind that attic ladder,' she called after us. 'It's lethal.'

'It's all set,' said Jens. Eager as a young gazelle, he ran ahead of us and was already upstairs by the time David and I reached the attic room, where I made up the bed with two pillows and an extra blanket. I noticed Aunt Marie had given David one of her precious hand-stitched sheets to turn over the comforter, and was touched by her thoughtfulness.

'Thank you for letting me share your room,' said David to Jens.

The attic room was dark, aside from one small window in the roof which opened out to the back of the house, but not so dark that I couldn't see that lopsided smile of David's which seemed to send my insides into a spin every time. I drew in a hasty breath to try and compose myself.

'That's no problem,' Jens replied brightly. 'I'm just happy to finally be doing something to get one over on the Fritzes. And because it's the right thing to do,' he added quickly.

'I know what you mean. Let's hope the war will be over soon.'

'I have been doing some stuff,' said Jens. 'Sometimes me and my friend will slash the tyres of the officers' car when they go out for a beer. They're predictable as hell. They often go to Snekkersten Inn, and sometimes the chauffeurs have a drink too. That's when we strike. Wham, like that.' Jens slammed his fist against the palm of his other hand.

'So that's why you've been creeping back home late at night,' I said. 'Don't think I haven't seen you.'

Jens grimaced, which made David laugh. 'Don't tell Mum and Dad, otherwise I'm in for it.'

'And so you should be,' I retorted. 'It might just be horseplay to you, but the Germans aren't known for their sense of humour.'

Jens shrugged. 'David here agrees.'

'Well, I suppose we both do. Just be careful.' And now I sounded like Hans-Peter, I realised. Although to be fair, Jens was only sixteen.

To make everything appear as normal as possible, we had dinner in the kitchen, with Gudrun and Jens seated on the haybox. Aunt Marie had made meatballs, but without the meat as most households tended to have meat-free days due to rationing. Instead she'd used cauliflower, potatoes, and breadcrumbs, and then fried them.

The texture was looser than when made with meat, and I enjoyed the sensation of them almost melting in my mouth. Because of all the excitement today, I'd only just realised how hungry I was. Fortunately there was plenty to go around.

'These are my *grøntsagsfrikadeller*,' Aunt Marie explained. 'Normally I would use a bit of pork – not too much because of rationing – but I presume you don't eat that.'

Wiping his mouth on his cloth napkin, David smiled in response. 'I'm just grateful for whatever you can share. And I'll be very happy to pay, just say what you'd—'

'Nonsense.' Aunt Marie looked almost offended.

'Absolutely not,' said Uncle Poul. 'We can't take your money. You'll be needing that when you get to Sweden. Who knows how long you'll be there?'

'Well, if you're sure… I am indeed eternally grateful.'

'Just get yourself and your dear mother to safety, that's all that matters to us,' Aunt Marie told him. 'For us this is the right thing to do. The Germans have no right to come here and tell us who's a Dane and who isn't. It goes against the grain with us.' She puffed out her chest in indignation.

'It's one of the things in this country that makes me the proudest,' David murmured.

As we were finishing dinner, there was a quiet knock on the door. We all jumped, and I glanced at David, but he seemed to have expected this. I'd overreacted. The Germans would have banged on the door.

Uncle Poul answered and showed a young man into the kitchen. 'It's for you,' he said to David.

'May I?' David asked, indicating the parlour. 'This is my friend from university.'

'Please.'

Apologising for the inconvenience, which was immediately dismissed by my aunt and uncle, the young man followed David into the parlour although he didn't close the door, so it was safe to assume that he didn't mind the family overhearing their conversation.

Respectfully removing his hat, the friend said, 'I'm glad you managed to escape, and thanks for your message through herr Larsen. I was able to track you down from there,' he added, shifting from one foot to the other restlessly.

'Why don't you sit down?' David suggested.

The friend shook his head. 'Can't stay long. I'm off to Gilleleje with some money the student union has collected to help people get to Sweden. Just wanted to share what I've witnessed, so you don't take any chances.' Twisting his hat in his hands, the young man explained how at Langelinie Quay in Copenhagen he'd seen a group of Jews being taken on board a German ship.

'They were pushing and hitting and kicking them. Old men with skullcaps and crouching women clutching their walking sticks. Young women with children too, and all the while the Germans and Danish Nazis were shouting abuse at them. I... I've never seen such lack of humanity and empathy in my life. I...'

Breathless and suddenly overcome, he slumped down on a chair. Uncle Poul who, like the rest of us had heard his account, came into the parlour and placed a glass of *schnapps* in front of him.

'Get this inside you, son. You're shaking like leaf.'

David's friend downed the drink in one, then gasped when he realised how strong it was, but it seemed to revive him.

'Thank you.' He rose and shook Uncle Poul's hand, then he clasped David's hands between his own. 'Take care of yourself, my friend. And your mother.'

After he'd left, David turned to Uncle Poul and once more apologised for the intrusion. 'I understand how distressing this must be for your family, and that it may put you all in further danger. I couldn't possibly have that on my conscience, and if you wish it, I'll find somewhere else to stay.'

My uncle shook his head. 'I think I speak for everyone when I say this makes us even more determined to help. You're still welcome.'

'You were very quiet earlier,' I said to Gudrun. It was later that evening, and we were getting ready for bed. 'Is it because of David being here? Or what his friend told us?'

'Huh?' Gudrun looked up from folding her clothes. 'No, of course not. I want to do everything I can to help these poor people, and stick it to the Germans at the same time.'

'So what is it, then? Something going on between you and Niels?' Perhaps they'd had a lover's tiff, but so far Gudrun had been nothing but open about her feelings, and it worried me that she'd suddenly clammed up. Could she be pregnant? That wouldn't please my aunt and uncle, but it was hardly the end of the world. This was 1943, and Niels clearly loved her. These days, who cared if she was showing while walking up the aisle?

'No, Niels and I are fine.'

'If you say so. But I'm here if you need to talk. All right?'

Gudrun got into bed and turned towards the wall. 'Sure.'

I switched off the light. Gudrun might deny it, but something was clearly bothering her as she hadn't even noticed what must have been glaringly obvious to everyone else in the room earlier. That I couldn't take my eyes off our guest all evening.

I thought of David's respect towards my aunt and uncle, and his humility when, head held high, he'd offered to remove himself from the safety of their home.

And how, in the course of just one day, I had without realising it become deeply fascinated with him.

Chapter Nineteen

Helsingør

2nd October 1943

Hans-Peter dropped Franklin off in the morning. The little dog ran inside the house as if he owned the place, then stopped abruptly at the sight of the stranger helping me with the dishes, his hackles up.

I lifted him up. 'It's all right, silly. This is David. He won't harm you. See?'

David held out his hand gently so Franklin could sniff it, at first tentatively, then the dog proceeded to lick it, and David was accepted.

'You seem to know your way around dogs,' Hans-Peter said, and shook David's hand.

'Not really, but for some reason they usually like me. I'm David. I'm fru Bredahl's—'

Hans Peter held up his hand. 'No explanation necessary. I know why you're here. Anything I can do to help, just let me know.'

'Thank you.'

The men exchanged a few more words, then Hans-Peter left, his eyes resting on me longer than usual.

When Bodil arrived, we got some tea and blankets together. It was too cold for a picnic, and Bodil had to be back early anyway, she'd said, but if we wrapped the blankets around us, we'd be warm enough even when sitting on the sand for a short while.

Again we chose Julebæk, which was the nearest decent beach north of town. I'd been in two minds about going cycling at all; last time we'd been on a bike ride together, Gudrun had practically been assaulted. Nor had I forgotten my near-paralysis from fear, when just over a week ago I'd had a run-in with a patrol on my own. My stomach felt tight at the thought of it happening again.

But I was desperate for fresh air and the open road, and could have cycled much further, although none of us wanted to get too close to Hornbæk with so many German soldiers stationed there at the moment.

'That dog looks like he's the one in charge,' Bodil commented with a laugh. I loved it when she was in good spirits, and for once coming out of her shell a bit. When I'd first met her, she'd been so timid and almost hunched in on herself, and it had pained me to see it. I was a little shy perhaps, but with Bodil it was different; she had been cowed.

I stroked Franklin's hard little head, while I kept my

other hand firmly on the handlebar. The bike was wobbly because the tyres had been patched repeatedly, and I didn't want to end in a ditch. 'He does, doesn't he? Maybe he is. Or at least he thinks so.'

Franklin turned to look at me, and I felt a little shiver run down his tiny body. Excitement perhaps, or maybe he was cold. I stopped the bike and pulled the woollen blanket in the basket around him, and he licked my hand in response, then I rode on.

Gudrun was a little further ahead of us. Frowning, I stared at her rigid back and the tension in her neck. She'd acted the same way this morning, answering monosyllabically whenever anyone asked her a question, averting her eyes and picking at her clothes as if she was ashamed of something. As soon as Bodil got there she rushed out of the house.

Aunt Marie had noticed it too, and we'd exchanged a brief look. I suspected my aunt wanted me to probe. Sometimes it was easier to tell someone your own age what was troubling you rather than your parents. At least initially.

A man was stumbling along the road when we got to the beach. Gudrun was the first to stop her bike, then Bodil and I caught up with her.

Moaning and weeping and unable to keep still, he had a dazed look on his face, and he kept rubbing his wrists as if they were hurting. I noticed he was bleeding from a cut on his throat.

Apprehensively, I grabbed hold of Franklin's collar, but

the dog remained remarkably still, as though his instincts were guiding him.

'What's troubling you, sir?' I asked.

Mumbling, he kept shaking his head as if in disbelief. I put Franklin on the ground and took the blanket out of the basket to wrap around the man, but he hardly seemed to notice, his mind elsewhere, on whatever horror he had witnessed.

'...wife and children...' he murmured. 'Couldn't do it, couldn't do it.'

Gudrun and Bodil persuaded the man to sit down on the grass verge, and Bodil knelt in front of him. 'What was that, sir? What about your wife and children? Can we help?'

'...no help.' He shook his head. 'Sweden...we tried... there *is* no help.'

Rocking back and forth and clutching what appeared to be a child's scarf, the man began crying uncontrollably, loud racking sobs, each one catching in his throat as if he had trouble breathing. The sound sliced through me like a butcher's knife.

'Sir,' Bodil tried again, patting his hand. 'You're bleeding. May we help you?'

As we tried to comfort the man, Franklin suddenly took off. At first I didn't know what to do. I didn't want to lose Hans-Peter's mother's dog. She was devoted to him, according to Hans-Peter, and the only reason she hadn't taken the dog with her to her sister's was because the sister didn't care for pets.

At the same time, here was a distraught and injured man.

'Franklin! Dammit!'

In the end Bodil made the decision for me, nodding that I should follow the dog, while she and Gudrun stayed with the man.

'Franklin,' I called again, this time in a more coaxing manner.

Still the dog didn't respond, but ran in the direction of a public beach cabin. The door was open, and the dog disappeared from view.

'Bother,' I muttered, and walked as fast as I could with my shoes getting heavier from each step I took as they filled with damp sand.

Instinct made me stop just outside the door. Instinct and a strange smell, metallic and sweet.

Then, taking one step further, I went inside.

At first I couldn't see much while my eyes adjusted to the dimness inside, but soon shapes began to take form; Franklin in the far corner of the cabin, standing in front of a dark, amorphous outline on the floor.

My heart lodged in my throat as I went closer, and then I had my answer to the strange smell.

It was blood.

A lot of it.

At first my brain couldn't quite comprehend what my eyes were seeing, then slowly, as if unwilling, my mind caught up. There, on the floor, lay a young woman and two little girls looking as though sleeping soundly, on their backs with theirs arms by the side, eyes closed, slack jaws, peaceful.

Except for the giant slits across their throats like a gaping, angry mouth.

I staggered back, steadying myself against the door jamb, and gasped for breath, but there was none to be had in the thick, syrupy atmosphere inside the cabin. I had to get out, but my legs refused to move.

It was Franklin who pulled me out of my stupor. He started licking the fingers of one of the two girls, gently as a dog might when it's trying to wake its master. Shocked, I grabbed him and stumbled out of the hut, then fell to my knees on the cold sand, clutching Franklin to my chest. The dog was warm and alive – a total contrast to the still figures inside the hut – and I drew comfort from his quivering little body.

The loss of life, the loving arrangement of the bodies, the sudden wailing; everything cut through me as if I were the one who had been slaughtered, and it took a moment for me to register that the keening sound was coming from my own mouth.

My distress attracted Gudrun and a man who hadn't been there when we stopped. They strode across the sand towards me, and Gudrun immediately threw herself down next to me.

'What is it?' she demanded.

I shook my head, unable to speak.

'There's something in there, isn't there?'

The man approached the cabin. Gudrun jumped up to follow him.

'Don't…' I croaked. 'Don't go…in there.'

They didn't listen. How long they were inside I didn't

know. Time stood still as I sat there, the cold and wet creeping into my bones, the listlessly lapping waves, the haunting cry of the seagulls matching the heaviness lodged in my chest.

Dear God, why? If you are there, tell me why.

They came back out, Gudrun pale as a sheet, the man shaking his head.

'We'll need to call the police,' he said grimly.

He started walking back towards the road. I followed, still clutching Franklin who had now begun to squirm against the tight embrace which he had endured stoically until now. Gudrun was slightly behind me.

'We now know what happened,' said Bodil. A woman who turned out to be the wife of the passer-by stood beside her. She told us how they'd managed to coax out of the man that his family were Jews and they had tried to get to Sweden but had failed to find a transport. In the end his wife and daughters had taken poison, and it was left to him to cut their throats afterwards to make sure they were completely dead. There hadn't been enough poison for all of them, and when it came to cutting his own throat, he had faltered and not been able to do it properly.

This harrowing story tallied with the way the bodies had been arranged, beautiful and horrifying at the same time. I wanted to weep, but was too numb.

'I'll run for help,' said the woman. 'The Bundgaard farm is nearby. They have a telephone.'

She set off while her husband stayed with us. It seemed like hours before the police arrived. The distraught man kept muttering to himself and rubbing his skin as if it had been contaminated with something. There was nothing the four of us could do except just sit there with him, but he seemed to find our company soothing. Eventually he put his hand on Franklin's head and began stroking the dog.

When the Helsingør police arrived, they immediately began securing the area and keeping the small cluster of people away who had since stopped their vehicles to ask what had happened.

Kiær's friend, the journalist Børge Rønne, was with them. Recognising me, he gave a quick nod.

A policeman questioned me. 'So, frøken Bredahl, you found the bodies?'

'Yes,' I replied and swallowed back the taste of bile. 'They were already dead, and there was no possible way to…save them.' I tried to keep my voice as level as I could for fear I might break down otherwise. How could I ever get this image out of my head? Those little girls. Their pretty dresses and red bows in their matted hair…

Some things were destined to remain with you, for ever seared on your brain.

Rønne stood nearby, taking notes for the newspaper. Then the policeman turned to Bodil who recounted how we came upon the man wandering in the road, and what she and the wife of the passer-by had managed to glean from his mutterings.

Gudrun still hadn't said a word since she came out of the cabin. I noticed a renewed distance between her and Bodil, and saw the happy chatter last week for what it was, a kind of ceasefire, a gap which couldn't be bridged until

Bodil made the right decision. I was no longer in doubt what the right decision was. Bodil had to stop seeing Oskar.

It's us or them, I wanted to say, but the words wouldn't come.

'Perhaps you and your friends had better go home,' said Rønne. 'This isn't really the place for you to be right now.'

I nodded in agreement. He wasn't patronising us because we were young women, but genuinely seemed to have our wellbeing in mind, and I was grateful for that. I just wanted to go home and forget everything.

'I'll be meeting with Kiær later on today,' he continued, lowering his voice. 'It might be useful if you were able to tell him what happened here, in your own words...'

I nodded again. We got our things together, and an ambulance driver returned my blanket since the man was now safely in the back of the ambulance, where he had received a sedative, the driver explained.

'We'll get him to Sweden and make sure he's treated in a mental institution there.'

'What about the police? Will they not arrest him for having murdered his...' I couldn't bring herself to finish the sentence. 'Or hand him over to the Nazis?'

The ambulance driver shook his head. 'The poor man is ill. And besides, as far as I know, the police have been told not to assist the Germans. The ones I know wouldn't anyway. Don't worry, we'll keep him safe.' He smiled reassuringly.

Instead of coming back to Helsingør with us, Gudrun turned to go in the opposite direction.

'I need to see Niels,' she said in a clipped voice. She

wouldn't look either of us in the eye, and I didn't have the energy for a confrontation so I just nodded. 'Tell Mum I'll be back later.'

'I will.'

Cycling back was arduous, even though we had the wind behind us. My strength had left me, and I pedalled like a mechanical toy someone had wound and wound until it couldn't go any further, even if it had wanted to.

When we said goodbye in Havnegade before Bodil headed south, I put my hand on Bodil's arm, and managed to say what had been playing over and over in my head on the journey back.

'This is what they do, the Nazis. They kill Jews, and in such horrible ways that a person like this poor man we just met will rather end himself and his family instead of falling into their hands. You can't continue going out with Oskar, you just can't,' I pleaded.

'I know,' Bodil replied, a faraway look in her eyes. I had to be satisfied with her answer even though she'd made no actual promise. I really hoped the events of the day had got through to her, but there was nothing more I could say

---

At home I told them what had happened. 'Gudrun has gone to Gilleleje to see Niels. I expect he'll want to help,' I added. I had an inkling there was another reason too, but if it was what I suspected, it was nothing in the big scheme of things.

My uncle just nodded, his mouth a sober line, while

Aunt Marie hid her face in her apron, and Jens slumped on a kitchen chair, tears running down his cheeks openly.

'I want to help!' he shouted, his fists clenched. 'If Gudrun can, so can I.'

His father put a hand on his shoulder. 'I know, Son, and I applaud you for it, but you're too young. You might be more hindrance than help, honestly.'

Jens appeared to accept this, but I couldn't help noticing the determination in his eyes and wondered if it reflected the emotions in my own. I feared he might do something more than slashing tyres, but understood what drove him. It was the same thing that motivated me: a searing hatred, a need to fight against injustice and oppression. The urge to act, and the desire for payback, had nothing to do with a person's age. I'd said the same to Kiær after my mother's letter.

'I'm going to the workshop,' I said. 'Please don't ask me about it.'

Grim-faced and arms crossed, David had been leaning against the wall by the door to the dining room throughout my account, but now he pushed himself away from the wall and fetched his coat from the coat rack in the corner.

'I'll come with you,' he said.

'Oh dear, must you?' Aunt Marie wiped her eyes with her apron, smearing a bit of grate blacking across her cheek. 'Both of you?'

'I believe we must,' David replied and took her hand in his. 'I promise we'll be careful.'

Rønne, Bruhn, and Thormod had already arrived when David and I let ourselves in from the backyard, and a few minutes later Hans-Peter and Dr Winther turned up.

Seething, Kiær was walking up and down the floor like a caged lion, his fists clenched, his jaw tight. I sensed he was only just managing to control his anger and I went to stand beside him, which seemed to calm him down.

'I've heard refugees are hiding in Klostermose Forest,' said Bruhn. 'It's pretty cold at the moment, and I expect they'll be in need of medical help. I could ask my wife. She's a nurse, as you know.'

'Frøken Bredahl and I have just seen a man attempt to cut his own throat.' Rønne placed a hand over his eyes and rubbed them vigorously as though trying to erase the image. I'd tried to do the same, but it hadn't worked. 'These people need urgent help, not just medical assistance,' he added.

Kiær nodded grimly. 'On top of that we have a duty to our country and to everyone in it. It goes without saying. We have to save as many as we can.'

'Let's organise boats,' the journalist added. He and Thormod exchanged a look, and Thormod suppressed a smile.

'Do share it with us,' said Bruhn dryly.

Rønne grinned darkly, and the lines on his forehead smoothed for a moment. 'My first rescue mission, before all of us knew each other, was an author, as well as a colleague of mine at *Helsingør Daily*. My colleague wanted to join the Free Allied forces and had to go via Sweden to get to England. The author was a wanted man. We cycled to

Snekkersten to "organise" a boat. A few days later Thormod questioned me in my office about what my bike was doing at the harbour on the day one of the rowing boats was stolen.'

Leaning back in his chair, Thormod grinned.

'I didn't really know how to handle this interrogation,' Rønne went on, 'but after Thormod had assessed me a bit, he said I'd done right in stealing the boat. We've been friends ever since.'

'I'm still a police officer,' Thormod replied.

'And you knew about my recent transport,' said Kiær.

Thormod nodded. 'I did indeed. So, let's "organise" more boats, liaise with fishermen where we can. One thing is very much on my mind, though,' he remarked. 'I'm willing to join, but on the condition that there's no money involved. In other words, we mustn't profit from the transports. I couldn't defend this as a police officer, and my conscience wouldn't allow it either.'

They were all in agreement with that.

'What can I do?' David asked.

'Perhaps look for people in Klostermose Forest who have nowhere to go,' Bruhn suggested, 'and reassure them that they will receive help. With Kiær's connections we should be able to find them lodgings. All over town people are opening their doors in solidarity to the refugees so it won't be difficult.'

'I can do that. They must be terrified, not knowing who to trust. I'm Jewish myself so that might help. But someone will have to tell me the way.'

'I know where it is,' I said. 'I'll show you.'

'Thank you.'

There was silence for a moment, while we were all deep in our own thoughts. Then David broke it.

'I have to go to Copenhagen on Monday, to fetch my mother,' he said. 'She wasn't well enough to travel when I came to Helsingør with Thormod.'

'You'll need these.' Kiær handed him some documents, which I took to be the false identity papers Kiær had promised. Thanking him, David put them in an inside pocket of his coat.

'Hmm, I wonder what the best way to do that is.' Thormod was thinking out loud. 'The cars we're able to mobilise between us will be needed here to take the refugees to the boats when the boats are ready.'

'An ambulance?' said Bruhn. 'My wife can drive it, and take fru Nathan to the hospital.'

Dr Winther spoke for the first time. 'Sadly none can be spared without arousing suspicion. We already have a number of Jews hiding in the hospital, and they'll need transport soon.'

'Perhaps travelling by train is the best option,' I said, and felt my cheeks heat up as everyone's eyes turned to me. 'I can go with David and pretend to be his fiancée. We can act as if we're going to Copenhagen for a day in the city, perhaps visiting relatives, and when we travel back with David's mother, we can act as if we're going to the coast for a few days' holiday. David already has a new identity, and I know it's out of season, but...' I flushed suddenly, with a feeling that I'd overstepped the mark. Why should they listen to me? Perhaps it was a stupid idea anyway. 'If Thormod could arrange travel documents for us…?'

'That's an excellent idea.' David smiled warmly, making my insides heat up in response. The feeling was followed by shame that I could even entertain such thoughts at a time like this.

Kiær, who had started pacing again stopped abruptly. 'Are you sure about this? It's awfully risky.'

No, I wasn't. I was terrified and would rather just run and hide away for ever. But we'd exhausted all other options and, besides, there were plenty of refugees in town already needing help. It wouldn't be right to divert precious resources away from them.

Rønne had been quiet since sharing his own experience of the tragedy on the beach. Now, sending me an encouraging smile, he spoke again. 'You really are a most extraordinary young lady.'

I blushed again and looked sideways at David. Did he think the same? The look in his eyes told me everything I needed to know. Or maybe I was just imagining things. We hadn't known each other for very long after all.

Only Hans-Peter didn't look too happy about it, but he accepted my decision because it made sense, and I didn't particularly want to discuss it with him anyway.

When David and I were about to leave, Hans-Peter pulled me to one side for a moment.

'Have you actually got the nerve to do this? There's no backing out at the last minute, which I think you know. This is too important. We're talking about the lives of two people, and your own.'

I swallowed hard. He was right; it *was* about other people's lives, and that was exactly why I had to do it. Yes, if I made a mistake, it could cost them dearly, and I was putting myself in danger too. But there had to be some resource inside me, somewhere at least, that I could draw on so I could do what my whole being was screaming at me that I must. My conscience had already made the choice.

'Yes. I can do this,' I said, with more conviction than I felt, 'and I will. It'll be all right.'

He sighed, then exhaled deeply. 'Promise me you'll come back in one piece? You have become very important to me.'

'I promise.'

He looked as though he would have liked to pull me in for a brief embrace, but thought better of it. I was relieved because I didn't want him to do that in front of David. It wasn't as though I'd promised Hans-Peter anything, was it? We'd only been out together a few times.

Earlier I'd noticed Thormod sitting with his head bent as if in silent prayer, which tallied with what Kiær had told me about the policeman – that he was deeply religious.

Now I sent up my own silent prayer, to a god I wasn't sure existed. Because we needed all the help we could get.

Chapter Twenty

Copenhagen

October 2018

'Perhaps it's best if we pause here.'

They were in David's first-floor hotel room overlooking Kongens Nytorv with its view of the Royal Theatre and the entrance to Nyhavn where Cecilie and Rafi had had dinner that first evening. It was a junior suite, David had told her with a certain pride, with deep-cream walls, a parquet floor covered by a plush silver rug, and the comfiest looking twin beds Cecilie had ever seen. David certainly looked comfortable as he rested against the velvet headboard, propped up by several cushions, although he appeared tired and drawn all of a sudden.

'All right,' she said, and closed the diary, even though she was itching to read on. 'So, that's how you came to meet my grandmother. I can't imagine what it must've been like to be in your situation.'

'It was'– David sucked in a breath – 'difficult circumstances.'

He didn't elaborate, nor did he comment on Inger's words, that she'd become fascinated with him. Did he know back then, Cecilie wondered? And would it have changed anything? But she didn't have the heart to ask him right now.

She and Rafi were sitting on a cream sofa, which Rafi had turned around so David could see them while Cecilie read from the diary. He rose now and checked his grandfather's blood pressure, then rested his hand on the old man's forehead.

'Can I get you anything?' he said.

With effort, David shook his head. 'I just need to rest and be alone. A glass of water will suffice.'

Rafi, his face creased with concern, poured a glass of ice water from a jug on the coffee table, then placed it on the bedside table next to David's bed.

'Are you sure, Grandpa? I'm happy to sit here with you. We both are.'

Cecilie nodded in response.

'No, no. I need to be alone with my sorrow. All those lives lost because of…prejudice and religion. Today I feel it keenly.'

Israel's treatment of the Palestinians popped into Cecilie's head, and immediately she felt her cheeks redden with shame that her mind had brought politics into it. This was about individuals.

She tried to imagine the depth of his grief, shared by many people in his country and Jews elsewhere, but knew it was beyond her to completely understand. And she wondered too if Rafi's perception of it was a little different to his great-grandfather's since he belonged to a much younger generation and had also lived abroad.

'Why don't you two spend the rest of the day together?' David suggested innocently enough, although Cecilie sensed a certain mischief behind his tired eyes.

You sly old fox, she thought and smiled to herself.

Rafi glanced at her. 'I'd be happy to if you are. And have the time.'

'I have time,' she replied. 'Normally I prepare for my lessons on Saturdays. But I can do that tomorrow. It makes little difference.'

And what else have I got to go home to?

'That settles it, then.' David indicated that he wanted to take her hand, and she went to stand by his bedside. 'I look forward to seeing you again soon,' he said and squeezed her hand lightly. 'And you,' he added to Rafi, 'I'll WhatsApp you if there's a problem. Now go.'

As they left, Cecilie turned in the doorway, but David seemed to have forgotten about both of them already. Instead he stared out of the tall window to the side of the bed, his lips moving as if talking to someone who was long gone.

'I never knew how you felt.'

Cecilie caught his words as Rafi closed the door quietly behind them. Or at least that's what she thought she'd heard. Who had felt what about whom? Was he referring to

Inger's infatuation with him, or how she'd felt about getting involved? It could have been either, but by the look on his face he was talking about her on a more personal level.

And what did Cecilie feel about the former, that her grandmother may have loved another man before her grandfather? Maybe even loved another man *instead* of her grandfather? Could that be why the jewellery had been hidden in the cellar?

Yet, her grandparents had been happy, she was sure of it.

Pushing the thought aside, she linked her arm with Rafi's. 'So, buy you a coffee?'

'Ooh, I do love a modern woman. Yes, I'd like that.'

'A modern woman, eh? Well, you've come to the right place.'

She took him to a tiny espresso bar overlooking a square which acted like a sort of crossroads between several arms of the pedestrianised area. It was her favourite square in the centre of town; it was like a dial, and if you sat on the edge of the fountain in the middle, with its intricate copper statue offering shade or casting shadows, you could practically see down every single one of the seven streets or passages leading from it.

Before she could point it out, Rafi said, 'We've been here before, I think. I noticed the fountain then. What are those birds on the statue?'

'They're storks. Storks are quite revered in Denmark, but they're very rare these days. Because of modern farming methods.'

Rafi nodded. 'They migrate over Israel, on their way to

Africa, although a few pairs have started nesting in the last decade or so.'

'Really? I didn't know that.'

'Big world out there, Cecilie.' Smiling, he shrugged.

Her neck tingled at the way he pronounced her name. Not 'Cecili-a' as many English speakers did, but with the correct intonation on the ending "e" as in *oeuf*, the French word for *egg*, but without the 'f', which is how she would often explain the pronunciation. Yet Rafi hadn't needed enlightening on this issue.

And what did that mean, exactly? Nothing, surely.

The espresso bar was on two floors. They placed their order for coffee and a sandwich each, and Rafi carried the tray upstairs – despite liking modern women, he was still a gentleman – and they found a table by the window, where they were able to squeeze in on a narrow cushion-covered bench next to each other so they could both look out over the square.

'I'm very impressed that your great-grandfather knows how to use WhatsApp.' Cecilie stirred sugar into her espresso. 'It was well-nigh impossible to drag my grandmother into the twenty-first century when it came to technology.'

'He's a very unusual man in many ways,' said Rafi. 'And in other ways very traditional. Family has always been a big thing for him, and he's forever having people around. What I liked most about him when I was growing up was the way he would talk to everyone the same way, old as well as young. He never patronises anyone.'

Sitting sideways on the bench facing Cecilie, he added, 'I guess he's the one who taught me about equality and treating others how I want to be treated. He sometimes presides over family squabbles, although I'm sure he'll take exception to the word *preside*.' He grinned, then turned serious again. 'It'll be difficult for us all when he goes. Holding us together will probably fall on my grandparents' shoulders, but it'll never be same.'

Cecilie nodded. She'd felt the same after her grandmother died.

His face took on a faraway look as he stared out over the busy square.

'Life changes are not always for the worse,' she said, hoping to reassure him.

Now where did that come from? She'd never looked at it this way before.

Realisation dawned on her that she'd never examined the idea before that perhaps she'd been the one who was afraid of change, that perhaps she and Peter had been stifling each other. Maybe this was another reason they'd split up, not just the lack of children.

'That's not what I was thinking of, actually.' Finishing his coffee, he turned back to look at her. 'It's your grandmother's diary. There's so much I don't understand. I grew up with the knowledge that Denmark was one of the few countries in Europe helping the Jews escape the Nazis. Albania was another country, and here Muslim Albanians rescued the small Jewish population of about two hundred people. It's in our history books. We have memorials like Kikar Denya in Jerusalem, which means Denmark Square, and national heroes like Georg Duckwitz, the German naval attaché to Denmark, who negotiated with Sweden to take the refugees. But why was Denmark different, and how did almost 95% of the Jewish population manage to get away? And why didn't the authorities arrest that man on the beach ? I completely get his desperation. If his fears were right that ending up in a concentration camp was going to be the alternative, who are any of us to say that it wouldn't be better to die quickly and painlessly, together, on our own terms? But the police would regard him as a murderer, surely?'

Cecilie shook her head. 'I don't really know, only that the Danes did help, but I'm sure there's a lot more to it than that. Maybe we should look into it.'

She rummaged for her mobile phone in her bag. 'We could look it up, but it might be useful to print something out or copy it so we can read it more in-depth. Perhaps we might find something about Inger's boss, Erling Kiær, or some of his friends. One of them was a journalist.' Cecilie looked on her phone to check the opening hours of the Central Library.

'The librarians at the Central Library are usually very helpful,' she continued. 'We could go there. It's not far, as you know.'

'Back where we first met. Yes, I remember.' Rafi's smile made her stomach flutter.

They finished their coffee and headed up towards the Central Library, passing The Round Tower which Cecilie had pointed out to him that first day. He'd thought it resembled a prison, and now that she regarded it with a different set of eyes, she could see why. But more like the sort of prison where you'd hold a fairy-tale princess captive, while she waited for her Prince Charming.

Have I found my prince? She bit her lip to stop herself from laughing out loud at the image of Rafi scaling the tower walls.

As if reading her mind, he took her hand in his. There was nothing sexual in his gesture, only comfort and warmth, yet she tingled with awareness of her own desire. And his.

When they reached the library, they were directed to the history section on the fourth floor, which also housed the library's quiet zone. They started at either end of the shelves with World War Two history and researched what they could, given the shortage of time. Rafi managed to find an English language article with a brief summary of events.

'The German decision to deport the Danish Jews,' he read aloud to Cecilie, 'prompted the state church and all political parties, except the pro-Nazi party, immediately to denounce the action and to pledge solidarity with their Jewish fellow citizens.

'For the first time,' he continued, 'they openly opposed the occupation. Denmark's Jewish population had long been thoroughly integrated into society, with some members of the Jewish community having risen to prominence. Because of this, most Danes perceived the

Nazis' action against Denmark's Jews as an affront to all Danes, and rallied to the protection of their countrymen.'

'That would explain a lot,' said Cecilie. 'But I'm thinking, wasn't there something about the king wearing a yellow star on his morning ride through the centre of Copenhagen?'

Rafi grinned. 'That I can answer without looking in history books. As romantic as the idea is, Kind Christian the Tenth did *not* wear a yellow star. This was a bit of spin in an American newspaper, and the American author Leon Uris then ran with it in his novel *Exodus* and made it popular. The book was later made into a film with Paul Newman – did you ever see it?'

'I did. I love old films. It's a bit of a quirk of mine.'

'As quirks go, that's a really cute one,' said Rafi and sent her a smile which made her sizzle inside.

To hide her embarrassment, she returned the book she was holding to the shelf. 'What I'm really curious about,' she said, 'is why Kiær and Rønne decided to call the resistance group "The Helsingør Sewing Club".'

'Yes, I'm intrigued by that too. Did it start as a sewing club perhaps?'

With the librarian's help they found a short memoir written by Erling Kiær himself. 'It was a particularly unique set of circumstances,' said the librarian. He spoke in English for Rafi's benefit, when he overheard them speaking English together. 'The majority of the Jewish population were living in and around Copenhagen at the time, with easy access to the coast and a short distance across the water to Sweden. So, not only did geography play an important role in the rescue, but there was also the Danish mindset. Does your friend know the story of *Fyrtøjet*?' he asked Cecilie.

'What's "furtoit"?' Rafi asked.

'It's a fairy tale. I'll explain.' Cecilie thanked the librarian, and they found a couple of seats next to a tall yucca plant pot where they could read Kiær's memoir together. But first Rafi wanted to know what a fairy tale had to do with anything.

'I know where the librarian was going with this,' Cecilie explained. '*Fyrtøjet* was written by Hans Christian Andersen. The title translates as *The Tinderbox*, and it's a pretty brutal story, as fairy tales often are, but to cut a long story short, a soldier finds a magic tinderbox and uses it to call upon a big dog with massive eyes, asking the dog to bring him the country's princess in the night so he can gaze upon her beauty. Eventually they fall in love, and the princess allows the dog to fetch her in the night. But a sly lady-in-waiting follows them, and puts a cross on the door where the princess is hiding. The dog discovers the cross and puts one on all the doors, so the king's men can't find the princess.'

'Ah, I get it,' said Rafi. 'Because all the doors are the same, nothing stands out. Because most Danes were in open sympathy with their Jewish neighbours, the refugees could be anywhere, and like the king's men in the fairy tale, the Germans didn't have the capacity to search every single house.'

'That's pretty much it.'

He nodded. 'I like it. A fairy tale turned into politics.'

240

'I don't know about politics, but fairy tales contain human wisdom.'

'Can I ask something else about Denmark?' Rafi asked.

'Sure. I'll answer your question if I can.'

'Do all Danes speak perfect English like you and that chap?' Rafi cocked his head at the librarian who was now using a trolley to return books to the shelves.

Cecilie laughed, relieved that it wasn't anything controversial. 'No, but a lot of people speak it quite well, and not just young people.'

'Even when I try to order a coffee in Danish, they switch to English,' Rafi went on with an exasperated sigh. 'Almost as if they know. I never get a chance to practise the few words I've managed to pick up from Grandpa. It's really irritating!'

'Perhaps you'd like to practise with me,' Cecilie suggested, then mentally kicked herself over the unintentional double entendre.

'I'd like that.'

She held his smouldering gaze for as long as her nerve allowed it – which was nowhere near long enough – then she patted the book on her lap. 'Maybe we should read what Kiær has to say first.'

It was dark by the time the library closed, and they were back outside. Kiær's ghostwritten memoir *With the Gestapo in My Wake* had offered another insight into the activities of the group, and the personalities of the four men. It was unclear when they had decided to name the group, but it seemed to have been at an early stage.

It turned out to have been Børge Rønne with his smart journalistic sense who came up with the name, and it was meant as a codeword in case their phones were tapped. The idea was that they would simply be referring to their wives' sewing circle as these were quite common at the time.

'They must have had such fun outsmarting the Germans in this way,' said Cecilie. 'But there was so much other stuff I didn't know.' She huddled into her coat, a much nicer one than her old duffel, and waited for Rafi's reply.

To her surprise, he turned his back on her and kept his face averted.

'Rafi?'

As he turned around, she noticed him wiping his cheeks. 'Yeah, me too,' he replied in a thick voice. 'Sorry, but talk of the Holocaust always has this effect on me. It's the dry way it's sometimes reported in history books and similar sources, rather than emotive accounts that get to me. I can't really explain it. Should be the other way round, shouldn't it?'

'You don't have to apologise. We all react differently and there is no right or wrong way.'

'It has moved me deeply, all these new facts. At home these people are celebrated as heroes, but now that I'm getting an insight into your grandmother's story, it feels more personal. She and Kiær and Rønne, well, they're just ordinary people, and some of them are frightened, but they do it anyway. Without them Grandpa might have died in the gas chambers, and I wouldn't exist. None of my family would.' He pointed to his chest. 'That hits me right here.'

To steer him away from his dark thoughts, Cecilie put her arm through his as they began walking; where to neither of them seemed to know.

Thinking out loud, she said, 'I still wonder how your great-great-grandmother's jewellery came to be in my grandmother's possession. Reading the diary and hearing her voice, I no longer think she stole it, but it's still far from being explained. It seems like a very steep payment to ask in exchange for help, if that's what she did.'

'I'm sure we'll find out,' Rafi replied, and Cecilie detected a note of relief in his voice at the change of subject. 'But I'm sure you'll agree with me that it doesn't seem right to read the rest of the diary without Grandpa. His story is unfolding too, even if it's through the eyes of someone else.'

'I completely agree. And I haven't.'

'It's needs to be soon, though. I don't think he has much time left.'

He was clearly upset by the thought, and Cecilie put her arm around him.

'I know what it's like to lose a beloved grandparent. Make the most of the time you have left – it's precious.'

Rafi stopped and cupped her face in his hands. 'Thank you. That means a lot.'

'Rafi…'

'Will you stay the night with me?'

His words took her by surprise but the sudden flare of heat inside her had already answered his question for her. 'Are you not sharing with David?'

He grinned. 'I have my own room. A few floors further up, and facing the backyard. My choice of room, by the way. I find it difficult to sleep to the sound of the traffic.'

Cecilie smiled. 'Sounds perfect, and the answer is yes.'

'Really?' His dark eyes lit up and then grew heated. He bent to place a featherlight kiss on her lips, but she was suddenly impatient and pulled him closer. She wanted more, so much more, and she sensed he was ready to give it.

She had no idea how long they stood in the street, making out like teenagers, but eventually he leaned his forehead on hers. 'I think maybe we should go indoors now, yes?'

Cecilie could only nod.

'I want to see all of you,' he whispered when they were back at the hotel.

With an uninhibitedness she'd never felt before, Cecilie took off her clothes until she stood completely naked before him. In the soft lighting she felt his gaze, like an artist's brush, explore every single part of her, every bump, mark, and imperfection, and imprinting them on his mind's canvas as uniquely her.

When he removed his own shirt, desire and her newfound confidence took over and she ran her hands over his tanned skin and soft chest hair.

Safe in his strong arms she let him carry her to bed.

Chapter Twenty-One

Helsingør

3rd October 1943

To retain a sense of normality, Aunt Marie hustled us all out of the house for church on Sunday morning. It was briefly debated whether David should go with us and pretend to be her nephew, as someone being home alone in what was known to be a Christian household on a Sunday would be anything but normal, but David had arranged a meeting with Bruhn regarding the possibility that some Jews were still hiding in the local forest and were in need of help.

'If you can find out from Bruhn exactly where he thinks these people might be, I'll come with you after the service,' I promised.

Last night the weather had taken a turn for the worse,

and everyone was buffeted along the cobbled streets which were slippery from rain.

As usual, Aunt Marie huffed during the sermon, and even in the few moments she was quiet, as I sat at the end of the pew, I noticed her rigid back and her tight-lipped demeanour, as though she was still huffing inside.

Normally Gudrun and I would exchange looks and both try to stifle a giggle, but since her return from Niels's yesterday my cousin had hardly spoken, and this morning she'd merely picked at her breakfast. Now she stared straight ahead, at the steps leading up to the pulpit where the minister stood in his black priest robes and white ruff, but she appeared not to be seeing either.

I was wrestling with my own demons. The events at the beach yesterday had imprinted themselves on my mind, like a film reel on a permanent loop; the man stumbling along the road, the wife and children with their gaping wounds. Franklin's small, firm body as I clutched him to my chest so I could feel the life within him. Even when I closed my eyes, the images remained.

Then the meeting at the workshop. Kiær's barely suppressed emotions, Thormod's quiet prayer, the shock and rage and powerlessness which had beset the room for a brief moment. At least until we began to discuss plans. Then the sense that we were doing something came back to me. As long as we were working against the enemy, every setback was just another push towards trying harder.

'I now have here a pastoral letter from the bishop, which has been sent to all of the country's priests, and which I'd like to read aloud,' said the priest. Clearing his throat, he began.

'Wherever Jews are persecuted on racial or religious grounds, it is the duty of the Christian Church to protest against it.'

I thought of David and his mother who'd done nothing to deserve what was happening to them. And other Jews in other countries. Yes, protest we must, and more if it was within our power to do so.

'The Church must protest because the persecution of Jews goes against the view of humanity and neighbourly love that follows from the message that the Church of Jesus Christ is here to profess. Any human life is precious in the eyes of God.'

'Amen to that,' Aunt Marie muttered. Gudrun put her hand over her mother's, either to still her or in sympathy with the sentiment. The latter was more likely.

'Regardless of differences of religious opinions, we will fight for the freedom of our Jewish brothers and sisters, which we value more than life.'

The rage inside which had slowly been building since the beginning of the occupation bubbled up again, but this time with purpose and not helplessness. I *did* value freedom more than anything. Freedom of belief, whether religious or political, freedom of movement, of speech. Freedom to marry whom I chose, to love as I chose.

'The leaders of the Danish Church have a clear understanding of our duty to be law-abiding citizens and not to revolt needlessly against those who exercise authority over us. But at the same time, we're bound by our consciences to assert justice and protest against any violation of rights.'

The priest looked up from the letter as if he had memorised the last part.

'We will therefore unambiguously declare our allegiance to the doctrine that bids us obey God more than man.'

Thanking the congregation, he bowed his head.

Following Communion and the last hymn, the congregation slowly filed out of the church, shaking the hand of the priest on their way out. A sombre, respectful service, but today the congregation hummed with resolve. The pastoral letter from the bishop had added to the feeling that the rounding up of Jewish citizens was directed at the whole of Denmark, that everyone was now potentially exposed to the arbitrary brutality of the Germans.

And as a nation we weren't going to stand for it.

'Beautiful sermon today, Pastor,' said Aunt Marie.

'Thank you, fru Bredahl.' A sad smile tugged at the corners of his mouth. 'That's fine praise indeed. I know we haven't always seen eye to eye.'

'Seems we can agree on something,' Aunt Marie replied tartly.

When we returned, I went to change out of the tweed suit I'd worn for church.

Having walked ahead of the rest of us, Gudrun was already there. She was pulling a thick woollen jumper over her head when I came in, then put her coat on over it, and slipped a knitted hat in her coat pocket. I noticed her pinched face and the deep frown creasing her brow.

'Where are you going?' I asked, although I knew the answer.

'To see Niels.' Gudrun stuffed a pair of mittens in her other coat pocket. 'He's going to help people get across to Sweden, and he needs me.'

'Right.' Perhaps it was more a case that Gudrun needed Niels than the opposite, but I kept that observation to myself. Instead I said, 'I know something has been going on between the two of you, as much as you may deny it. Have you…are you expecting?'

'H-how did you know?' Gudrun froze momentarily, and her voice shook.

'Well, I didn't, not really. I was just trying to find a way of explaining why you've been acting so strange lately. Does that mean you are? In the family way, that is?'

Gudrun gave a brief nod and took a moment before answering. 'Dr Winther says it won't be long before I show.'

'I assume you'll get married soon, then.' I hung up my suit jacket, then unzipped the matching pencil skirt. 'Or are you worried he won't marry you now he's had his way?'

'Of course not,' Gudrun snapped. Then the wind went out of her, and she dropped down onto the edge of the bed, pulling on her coat sleeves as though wanting to disappear inside her coat. 'That's not what worries me.'

'What then?'

'I've been thinking about this for a while, and now more than ever with all these poor people being chased from their homes in fear of their lives. How can I bring a child into this world? How can anyone?' Gudrun's lips trembled.

I felt a jolt in my stomach. 'You're not thinking about... well, surely you wouldn't consider a termination?'

'I don't know.'

'What does Niels say?' I drew in a sharp breath.

'He doesn't know yet. I can't tell him now with all this going on.'

I nodded. 'I agree it's not the right time. I take it Uncle Poul and Aunt Marie don't know yet either.'

Gudrun hugged herself. 'To be honest, I haven't thought that far.'

'And now you're going to Gilleleje.' Just wearing my slip, I sat down beside her and took her hands in mine. 'You can't cycle in this weather. Think about the baby, and yourself. Are you in a fit state?'

'Dr Winther says exercise is healthy.' Gudrun gave a wan smile. 'But no, I won't be cycling. One of the drivers at the brewery is going that way to see some family and is giving me a lift. The sea air will do me good, and, anyway, I've always had good sea legs.'

'Even now you're pregnant?'

Gudrun shrugged, a determined look on her face. 'All right, I haven't been on a boat for a while, but I have to help. These people are terrified. We saw it with that man on the beach. What if it was my family I was trying to save? My child?'

The thought was almost unbearable. *What if it was our family?* I squeezed her hands. 'Just promise me that you won't take any unnecessary risks?'

'If you promise me that you'll do the same,' Gudrun replied. 'That's why you went to the workshop yesterday, wasn't it? Your boss is involved too.'

I rose and put on a pair of slacks and my Fair Isle cardigan. 'David and I are going to the forest. Apparently some people are hiding out there. And Kiær will see to it that they're taken in somewhere. That's the plan so far.'

I didn't tell her about my impending trip to Copenhagen; one thing at a time.

'Tell Mum and Dad that I'll be back late. Cover for me if you have to. No need to worry them too much.'

'They already are,' I said. 'Worried about you.'

'Tell them Niels will look after me.'

And what if Niels is careless?

My mind skipped ahead to possible consequences, none of them able to dispel my fear for her. She seemed so vulnerable all of a sudden. At the same time, the determination in her eyes, which sometimes bordered on stubbornness if you were being unkind, filled me with admiration. Pregnant, and off to defy the Germans.

Exhaling deeply, I sent her an encouraging smile. Despite my misgivings, I knew she'd keep the baby, and the rest of the world be damned. I was sure of it.

Klostermose Forest was about four kilometres southwest of Helsingør town centre. David had borrowed Gudrun's bicycle, and it took us less than half an hour to get there.

Briefly I'd considered asking Hans-Peter if we could

bring Franklin, to make it look like any other Sunday outing, but the weather made it less likely to look like a cycling trip for the sake of it, so I dismissed the idea.

Added to that, he might bark at the wrong moment, and although there was no way he could be mistaken for an Alsatian, a bark was a bark for a person hiding and listening out for German dog patrols.

The forest was exactly as I remembered it from visits with my family five years ago. It was mainly beech trees growing to the top of the long range of hills, with narrow ravines, and deep swampy areas overgrown with tangled roots and stems like floating mats, rendering them almost invisible and treacherous unless you knew they were there.

'Mind where you step,' I said. 'If you're not careful, your shoes will get wet. Or worse, you might slip underneath the vegetation and get caught in the roots.'

'Thanks for the warning.' David grimaced.

We stopped and listened out for signs that people were here, but all I could hear was the wind whistling in the trees and the bare branches creaking and rattling like boys fighting with sticks. A single bird took flight, cawing and wings flapping, flying low over our heads in protest at being disturbed.

My heart leaped into my throat, and I ducked instinctively. 'Lord, I thought it was going to attack me!'

'It's only a crow.' Looking around him, David was frowning. 'So, you know this forest? Where would you hide if it were you?'

I thought for a moment. 'By a ravine, I think. We have to go further in.'

We continued deeper into the forest, carefully keeping track of the direction we were going in. The upward sloping ground was covered in fallen leaves, rust-red and slimy, which made walking difficult. Here and there we found evidence that people had been here recently: cigarette butts, a hair ribbon, a leather glove, but still we saw no one.

I put the ribbon and the partnerless glove in my coat pocket.

Halfway to the top of the hill range, in a small clearing, we stopped.

'Hello-o? Anybody there?'

My voice fell flat in the dense, damp air, and nothing echoed back, only the sense of a watchful forest holding its breath.

'My name is David Nathan,' David tried, in a normal voice instead. 'I live in Adelgade in Copenhagen with my mother Rebecka Nathan, and I'm here to help.'

Still nothing. Then, a quiet rustling, shuffling, low voices.

'David?'

Startled, David turned in the direction of the voice. 'Fru Jakobson? I know this woman. Dear God!'

A heavily pregnant woman in her early thirties came into the clearing carrying a little girl of about five years old and a bag of belongings. Her face was pasty white, her eyes red and raw, and she stumbled slightly under the weight of what she was holding.

Immediately I stepped forward and relieved her of her bag. 'Here, let me help you.'

'Oh, thank you, that's so kind,' fru Jakobson whispered.

'I'd give you Sara to carry but she won't leave my side. And she's so heavy.'

'I understand.' I smiled at the little girl, who regarded me with big round eyes. Hoisting up the bag, the lightness of it surprised me. Was that all this little family's life boiled down to? Hiding in a wet autumn forest, cold, scared, and with scarcely any belongings on them?

Like molten rock, anger stirred inside me like it had since the start of the occupation, and I gritted my teeth.

'Fru Jakobson?' said David again, putting his hand on her shoulder as the woman almost collapsed in his arms. 'Where's your husband?'

'He…' She shook her head as she struggled to find her breath. 'He was taken in Copenhagen. He ran to draw the Germans away, and Sara and I managed to hide behind the outhouses in the backyard. We…heard shots. Sara hasn't said a word since then.'

David explained to me briefly that he and Fru Jakobson used the same stairs in the building they lived in.

'We'll do anything we can to help, fru Jakobson.' I swallowed back a lump in my throat. 'Are you and your daughter alone out here?'

'No, there are others. I'll let them know it's safe.'

It turned out not to be necessary. Slowly other people emerged and entered the clearing; young and old, families, lone travellers, about fifteen of them in total. Some were clearly exhausted, others shook from cold or fear or both, but most of them held their heads high and moved with a sense of purpose and determination. It struck me that these were not the helpless victims I'd expected to find; rather they were playing an active part in getting themselves to safety.

How could such dignity fail to inspire admiration in the onlooker?

They gathered around David who explained that they would receive help, and he gave them Dr Winther's address on the outskirts of town as well as a brief description of how to get there.

'It's not far,' he said, 'but it's best if you divide yourselves into smaller groups and arrive separately, to avoid rousing suspicion.'

It was decided who would go first, and the refugees left in small groups at ten to fifteen-minute intervals.

'I think you'd better walk with us, fru Jakobson,' said David.

'Thank you. I should like that. But first I need to sit for a bit.'

She slumped down on a log as if she were incapable of taking another step, and placed the little girl named Sara on her lap. Sara immediately clung to her mother's neck.

How were we to get this exhausted woman to safety if she could walk no further? One of us would have to support her while the other carried the child, and if the little girl refused to let go, this would be challenging.

Then I noticed Sara clutching a grubby ragdoll, and that one of the straw-coloured yarn plaits was missing a ribbon. Kneeling down in front of her, I reached inside my coat pocket and produced the ribbon I'd found earlier.

'Does this belong to your dolly?'

The girl nodded.

'Would you like me to help you sort her hair out?'

The girl gave another solemn nod. Fru Jakobson smiled gratefully, having sensed what I was trying to do, and gently prised the doll from her daughter's hands. I tied the ribbon around the plait and handed it back to her.

'There. That's a bit better, isn't it?'

Sara nodded again, more vigorously this time.

'What's her name?'

Sara hid her face in the doll's hair.

'She won't answer you,' said fru Jakobson in a flat, monotone voice. 'Others have tried. But the doll's name is Betty.'

'I see,' I said. 'Do you think Betty would like a ride on my bicycle? I have a basket she can sit in. Perhaps you'd like to see my bike for yourself, just to check that she'll like it?'

Sara pondered the question, her large dark-grey eyes never leaving mine, as if she were sizing me up, then she climbed off her mother's lap and took my hand. My body gave a jolt at this simple act of trust. It was as if someone had given me the most wonderful gift imaginable.

While I'd been trying to persuade the little girl to let go of her mother, David had been listening out for sounds around them. Frowning, he said, 'I think we'd better go.'

The walk back down through the woods was slow going as fru Jakobson had to stop several times to catch her breath. Finally we reached the bikes, and Sara allowed me to lift her up so she could sit on the handle bars, with the doll and the bag in the basket in front of her. David pushed

Gudrun's bike with one hand and offered his other arm to fru Jakobson for support.

About an hour later we arrived at Dr Winther's house and entered the forecourt. Hidden behind a tall evergreen hedge and a couple of large oak trees, the house was well-placed for anyone wishing to come and go unseen, and we went around the back as agreed.

Resting my bike against the rendered wall, I lifted Sara down and handed her the doll, then carried fru Jakobson's bag under my arm. Again, Sara slipped her hand into mine as the most natural thing, and I smiled down at her.

Dr Winther's waiting room was heaving with refugees. Kiær was there with Dr Winther, and Hans-Peter too, organising where to house the refugees – overnight in the first instance, and then until it was safe to ferry them across to Sweden.

The doctor inclined her head at me, but Hans-Peter sent me a warm smile, which faltered a little when he spotted David.

'And who have we here?' he said and knelt down in front of Sara.

'This is Sara. She doesn't speak. And this is Betty,' I added and pointed to the doll.

'Betty, eh? That's a very pretty name.' Ruffling Sara's hair, Hans-Peter rose. 'And how are you? Still planning to go tomorrow?' he asked me in a low voice.

I nodded. I still had deep misgivings about the venture, but there was no way I was backing out now.

He sighed heavily. 'Well, you take care. You hear?'

Kiær was explaining things to the refugees. 'The houses along Strandvejen are ideal since they're right on the coast, but in the long run this might become problematic. I don't think the Germans have cottoned on yet, but when they do, this will be the most obvious place for them to place lookouts.'

He handed Hans-Peter a list of names. 'Could you take this small group to Hotel Øresund in Stengade? I've spoken to the manager who will find them rooms.'

'Of course.' Hans-Peter gestured for those people to follow him, but at the door he stopped and sent me one last look before he left. I didn't miss the significance of this. I knew he had feelings for me, had known it the moment he held me close on the dance floor. And I'd liked it as I liked him, but when it came to deeper feelings, I wasn't entirely sure I'd be able to reciprocate them, and now was not the time to think about it.

Bit by bit the waiting room emptied as the refugees were allocated a place to stay, some at the hotel, others in private homes where they had space for families, and others, mainly young men on their own, were given shelter in various attics or basements.

Dr Winther and David helped fru Jakobson into the surgery room where she could rest on the treatment couch, and to distract Sara, I suggested we play with the doll. Sara smiled and made faces to mimic Betty's changing moods , but still no words came out of her mouth.

Shortly after, David joined us again, watching us from a seat opposite. At some point I met his eyes and caught a glimpse of something that looked very much like longing, but it was quickly masked.

Dr Winther returned. 'Fru Jakobson suffers from fatigue, so I've given her an iron supplement, but I think it's best she stays here where I can keep an eye on her.'

'Very good,' Kiær replied. 'I'll let the people know who offered to help. And you, Inger, and David, thank you. Good luck tomorrow.'

When my boss had left, accompanied by the last two men, David and I put on our coats, and I knelt to say goodbye to Sara.

The little girl flung her arms around my neck, almost choking me as she refused to release me, and let out a curious, throaty keening like a small animal in pain.

'But, Sara, darling, I have to go. And you have to stay here with Mummy and this nice lady.' I tried to loosen her grip, but Sara clung even tighter than before.

'Ngnh, ngnh!'

'But sweetheart…'

The sound had attracted fru Jakobson, who came back into to the waiting room with her hand on her lower back for support. 'Stop fossicking, child!' she scolded Sara.

'It's not a problem. I…perhaps…' I lifted Sara up and held her close. 'Perhaps you and Sara could stay with us instead, and Dr Winther can visit you there?'

Chewing her lip, fru Jakobson hesitated. I thought I understood. The woman was tired and scared, and worried about her husband whose fate was yet unknown. But she also had her pride, and didn't want to be a bother.

'It's no trouble, I assure you,' I said. This time I knew for certain that I didn't have to ask my relatives first. If keeping Sara and her mother safe meant that I had to sleep on the floor or in an armchair, then that was what I would do.

'That seems like a sensible option, fru Jakobson,' said Dr Winther, in her soothing, no-nonsense manner.

'David?' Fru Jakobson was obviously finding it difficult to make a decision due to tiredness and she looked to the one person she knew here.

'Inger's family have shown me nothing but kindness,' he replied, and his reassurance seemed to settle the matter.

When we returned to the house with Sara and fru Jakobson, the woman next door was sitting in the kitchen with Aunt Marie. My mouth went dry. Aunt Marie caught my expression and reassured me with a nod.

'This is fru Holm,' she said, 'whom you've met before.'

I forced myself to smile. 'And this is fru Jakobson and her daughter, Sara.'

Sara's eyes lit up at the sight of the cake on the table, a rare Sunday treat when Aunt Marie had saved up enough sugar to make one.

'Jøsses,' said Aunt Marie when she saw the tired woman, and the shabby clothes she and the little girl were wearing. *Sweet Jesus.* She sprang up from her seat and immediately led fru Jakobson to the table, where she poured her a cup of coffee.

'Here, get this inside you. It'll warm you up.'

Fru Jakobson accepted the coffee gratefully, cupping the fine porcelain in her hand like it was the most precious thing she'd ever beheld.

'And I'll cut a slice of cake for the little one, if I may.' Aunt Marie found some extra cake plates and cut a generous slice for both mother and daughter.

'You can cut a slice for all of us,' I said, as tiredness threatened to overwhelm me.

'Cheeky madam.' Aunt Marie shot me a look, but the smile tugging at the corners of her mouth gave away her relief that both David and I were back.

We hung up our coats. The smell of dampness from the forest and the rain earlier spread through the kitchen, to be swallowed up by the more pungent aroma of Rich's coffee substitute.

For the first time since the shortages began I actually craved a cup, and I accepted it gratefully, as well as the cake.

Holding the cup in front of me like a shield, I eyed my aunt and uncle's neighbour, fru Holm. It was true, I'd met her before, but only twice. Could she really be trusted?

'You needn't worry, young Inger,' said fru Holm. 'I already have my nephew's boss and his wife staying with me. You may remember that my nephew works as a tailor'– I didn't but nodded anyway – 'so he says to my nephew, can he look after the tailoring business in his absence, and my nephew says yes, and tells them to look me up, and the next thing I know they're on my doorstep,' she went on, puffing out her chest. 'Anyhow, they're safe and sound now, God willing.'

'All over town people are just opening their doors to help their countrymen,' Aunt Marie put in, 'which is as it should be.'

The tension left my shoulders at the neighbour's assurances, and I relaxed back in the chair, savouring my slice of cake.

When it came to sleeping arrangements, fru Holm offered to take them in. 'I know you're expecting your young man's mother tomorrow, so it'll be a bit cramped here. I live alone and have more room. They can sleep in the parlour, and any sign of trouble, they can hide in the attic.' Fru Holm was looking straight at me when she spoke.

I blushed at the words *your young man* and exchanged a somewhat startled glance with David. His eyes twinkled with mirth, but he didn't comment.

But Sara refused to leave me, and in the end it was arranged that David would move next door, fru Jakobson and Sara would share Gudrun's bedroom with me, and Gudrun would go in the attic with her brother.

Gudrun was in for a surprise when she got home, but I expected Aunt Marie would leave her a note.

———

Later, as I lay listening to their soft breathing, I thought of Gudrun again, hoping that she was safe. She hadn't returned before bedtime, and probably wouldn't now at this hour because of curfew.

Then there was David's mother, and the journey to Copenhagen. I hadn't eaten much at dinner, and not just because of cake at teatime. My stomach was tense with apprehension and the thought of everything that could go wrong, and more besides, but curiously what worried me most was whether fru Nathan would like me or not.

Finally my thoughts settled on David and the way he'd smiled at me when Sara was clinging to me. She was such a pretty child, with the same dark hair and grey eyes as her mother, and despite having scolded the child in her exhaustion, fru Jakobson's face took on a soft expression whenever she looked at her daughter.

Was that what it was like to be a mother? A deep tenderness filling every part of you, so even those who couldn't see into your heart would be able to tell?

And what would my child be like if I ever had one, I wondered? Would he or she have David's lopsided smile and hazel eyes?

Oh, stop it! You're being ridiculous.

One thing I did know. If I ever became a mother, I'd lay down my life to protect my child.

Chapter Twenty-Two

Gilleleje

3rd to 4th October 1943

G udrun met the driver just inside the brewery gates.
Leaning against the wheel arch of the platform truck,
he was smoking a cigarette, but tossed it on the ground and
extinguished it with his boot when he saw her. A family of
four, parents and two youngsters, a boy and a slightly older
girl, stood huddled by the end of the truck.

He nodded at Gudrun, then he said to the small family,
'You lot, jump up and hide beneath that tarp there. Should
keep the worst of the wind off you.'

Without a further glance at his passengers, he climbed
up into the cabin and shut the door. Gudrun waited until
the family were safely aboard the truck, then climbed up

herself and rearranged some of the beer crates in front of the tarpaulin to complete the hiding place.

The father offered to help, but she shook her head. 'I work here so I'm used to it. Just keep your heads down.'

'Does the brewery normally do deliveries on a Sunday?' the man asked, an anxious note in his voice.

'Not usually, no,' Gudrun replied cheerfully as she shifted the last beer crate into place. 'It was actually Parkov's idea. The chairman on the brewery's board. Like everyone else he knows that the Germans love their beer as much as us Danes.'

'Yes, of course,' the man murmured and disappeared behind the tarpaulin.

She'd known that they would have passengers with them today, and she was glad she hadn't mentioned it to Inger because she didn't want to worry her any more than she already had. Sometimes she just wanted to shake her cousin and tell her to stop being so afraid of everything. But then again, they were all taking huge risks and at least Inger was helping now.

When she'd climbed into the cabin next to the driver and they had set off, it occurred to her that the heavy lifting she did in connection with her job would probably have to come to an end soon. Perhaps she could get a job in the office, if only for a few months until she had to give up work completely.

See, baby, I am trying to protect you. Tell my cousin that when you make your appearance. The thought amused her, and she smothered a grin.

The driver was a taciturn chap, which suited Gudrun

fine, and the drive to Gilleleje passed quickly and without incident.

When they arrived, the driver dropped them at their designated place, and drove off on his delivery. It was a house a short walk from the harbour, and although Gudrun didn't know the people living there, Niels had vouched for them.

Other Jewish refugees were waiting in the small back room. Everyone was quiet and appeared patient, yet the air was thick with unease, and Gudrun noticed more than one person clutching their belongings tightly or keeping their family members as close as possible. One young woman was chewing her fingernails almost to the point of drawing blood.

Gudrun wanted to reach out to her and tell her everything would be all right, but her earlier cheerfulness had evaporated, and somehow the words wouldn't come.

Instead she approached the owner of the house. He was in his middle years, with a small moustache and smooth-looking hands, so not a fisherman, she thought. A school teacher, perhaps.

She asked him in a low voice if something had happened.

'The skipper is refusing to sail because it's Confirmation Sunday,' the man replied. 'Apparently he's suddenly got himself an invitation to attend a Confirmation party. We're trying to organise another boat.'

'My fiancé is at the harbour. His cutter is called the *Ofelia*.'

'I know. We'll get these people organised and tell them to come to the harbour later when we're sure it's safe.'

After saying a quick goodbye to the family they'd had as passengers on the truck, Gudrun made her way to the harbour.

She found Niels, his father, and the eldest of Niels's two younger brothers, a lad called Jørgen, in the midst of an argument. Or rather, Niels and his father were arguing heatedly; tidying up a length of rope, Jørgen clearly had enough sense to stay out of it.

She smiled at him. Unlike the other members of the family, who all had fair hair, Jørgen had auburn hair, freckles, and the beginnings of ginger fluff on his chin.

He grinned back. 'They're locking horns, as you can see.'

'What about?'

'Money. Father wants to charge as much as he can, but Niels only wants enough to cover fuel.'

'Well, I'm with Niels on that one,' Gudrun replied firmly.

'So am I.' He regarded her for a moment with an expression in his eyes wise beyond his fifteen years, then continued with his task.

As Gudrun approached them, the wind carried their words towards her.

'…and now I hear Gestapo-Juhl is in town. It's too dangerous!'

The name hit Gudrun mid-chest, and she stopped to steady herself against the side of the boat as the blood left her face, and she felt suddenly cold.

Gestapo-Juhl, or Hans Juhl, as was his real name. Everyone knew who he was. Chief of the security police in Helsingør, the occupant of the Gestapo's headquarters in Villa Wisborg on Søndre Strandvej. Brutal and zealous, he had been born and raised in Schleswig-Holstein, the old border region between Germany and Denmark, and he spoke Danish well enough to understand what people said.

No one could hide from Gestapo-Juhl for long.

'…could just be a rumour,' she heard Niels say.

'Hmm, maybe. That man is damned unpredictable, that's for sure,' the father replied. 'The risk is still too high. We need to get properly paid.'

'Doing the right thing is payment enough for me.' Niels spotted Gudrun and came forward to kiss her on the cheek.

'Didn't raise you to be so damned sentimental,' the older man muttered.

'Am I disturbing anything?' Gudrun sent her most disarming smile in herr Andersen's direction.

'Hmm,' he grumbled, but sounding slightly calmer. 'We were just about to study some maps.' Shrugging, he went into the wheelhouse, and the others followed, but only Niels went inside with his father as the wheelhouse was cramped. Jørgen and Gudrun listened in from outside while Niels and his father discussed which route to take across the Sound in order to avoid running into a German mine.

———————

Later in the afternoon, the relatively quiet harbour became busy as refugees began to arrive, although a lot of the fishermen still stood around with their hands in the pockets of their overalls. To avoid chaos, Danish policemen armed with rifles kept an eye on proceedings and showed the Jews where to go.Gudrun was delighted when the family who had come to Gilleleje earlier on the beer truck were lining up by the *Ofelia*, and they greeted her as though she were an old friend. Although their faces were pinched with tension, especially the adolescent boy, she sensed relief as well that they had come this far.

Most of the fishermen were charging as much as 2,500 Danish kroner per person, and many of the refugees didn't have that much money.

'Oy, oy, oy!' one elderly man exclaimed in Yiddish at the steep price. He and a younger woman who appeared to be his grown-up daughter had lined up by the neighbouring cutter, and were now being refused a space on the boat.

'That's what we should be charging,' Niels's father muttered beside her.

Gudrun flashed him an angry look. This was life and death for these people; how could anyone profit from it? Had they no conscience?

'No,' said Niels curtly.

Muttering to himself, Niels's father jumped onto the deck, cussing and swearing, and began bossing Jørgen about, but the boy endured it with remarkable calm.

As she pondered what she could do to help the old man and his daughter, whether perhaps she could persuade Niels to take another two people – although they probably had as many as the cutter could cope with – the couple were approached by the law student who had visited David the day after Inger had brought him to the house.

What was his name? She couldn't remember, but what she did recall was something about a collection from the student union, and sure enough David's friend handed the couple some money, and they rejoined the queue by their designated boat.

Suddenly there was a cry like a crack from a pistol, where from Gudrun couldn't tell.

'Scatter! The Germans are coming!'

Rooted to the spot with shock, Gudrun watched as terror set in amongst the Jews and they started to run away.

'We're sailing anyway!' Niels shouted but no one heard him in their panic.

Seeing the adolescent boy trip in his desperate attempt at keeping up with his family spurred her into action, and she rushed to his side.

'We're sailing anyway. Tell your family!'

'Mum! Dad!' he cried out.

His parents stopped, and so did other people. Slowly many of those who had run began to return to the harbour. Thankfully there was no sign of the Germans.

'False alarm,' she said to the boy as cheerfully as she could, her pulse still raising

'Y-yes, I guess so.' He gave a nervous laugh.

'What's your name?' Gudrun asked.

The question seemed to put him at ease. At least for now. 'My name is Daniel.'

'How do you do, Daniel. Come on, let's get all these

bags on board.' To take his mind off things, she pointed to the row of suitcases on the pier by the *Ofelia*, which people had left in their panic. The boy turned out to be a willing helper, and soon their passengers, about twelve of them, were on board and hiding in the hold.

Smelling of fish and tar and bilge water, the hold wasn't the most pleasant place to be, but the refugees had to stay out of sight, at least until it was safe for them to come on deck.

Even though it had turned out to be false alarm, the threat of Gestapo was too much for Niels's father, and he refused to sail.

'And you, my boy, are coming with me,' he yelled at Jørgen in his frustration that his eldest son wouldn't obey him.

'I'm staying here,' Jørgen replied calmly.

This resulted in another argument, this time with his younger son, until Niels stepped in and pointed out that they had to go now, and his father could come if he wanted to or not, but Niels would look after the boy.

The older man left, cursing vehemently.

Jørgen sent Gudrun a cheeky grin. 'There'll be hell to pay later.'

'It looks like it.' She grimaced.

They were about to cast off when the sound of rhythmic steps approaching made them turn around. A group of soldiers in the grey-green uniform of the Wehrmacht came out onto the pier, led by a bespectacled man in a lieutenant's uniform, jacket, jodhpur-style trousers, and black knee-length boots, who strode along with his hands behind his back as though he were merely out on an afternoon stroll.

'Good afternoon. Fishing on a Sunday?'

He spoke in broken Danish, and without ever having met the man, Gudrun immediately knew who he was. Gestapo-Juhl.

Bile rose in her throat, and she swallowed hard.

'The fish don't care what day it is,' Niels replied gruffly.

'And these people with you?'

'My younger brother and my fiancée.' Niels casually slung his arm across Gudrun's shoulders.

'I see. So women are fishermen now?'

'A good wife knows her husband's trade.'

'True, true. Can I see some ID, please?'

Keeping up the pretence of being a much beleaguered, working man, Niels flung out his arms. 'Look, I'm just going about my business. I have no such thing on me!'

Gestapo-Juhl gave a dismissive wave. 'Ach, very well. Carry on.'

The soldiers turned on their heels, their trampling boots making the pier sway. A few other boats were moored in the harbour, but since no one was on deck, the Germans didn't bother and left the harbour soon after that.

Gudrun stared after them, her legs shaking. It wasn't until Niels softly guided her towards the wheelhouse that she found the strength to move again.

That had been close.

As they left the harbour, Niels asked Jørgen and Gudrun to check on their passengers. Jørgen lifted the bulkhead to the hold, and Gudrun lit a match so she could see more clearly. Several pairs of anxious eyes stared back up at her, then she heard sighs of relief when they saw who it was.

'I thought we were done for,' said a young man.

Me too, she thought. Then her eyes fell on Daniel, and the young boy's beaming smile made it all worth it.

'You're safe for now,' she said, 'but we're still in Danish waters, so it's best if you stay in the hold for a while longer.'

There was a murmur of assent, then a middle-aged woman approached the opening. She wore an elegant fur coat and a black hat with pheasant feathers.

'Some of us get terribly seasick. Could we have a bucket down here, please?' she pleaded, her face pasty white.

'Of course, I'll see what I can find. Jørgen?'

With Jørgen's help, Gudrun managed to find two buckets, and passed them down to the passengers.

Away from the shelter of the coast, the swells grew, and the cutter was tossed on the waves like a child's toy. Rain began to patter from a grey sky, and the wind lashed in a torrent of its own.

Gudrun and Jørgen stayed in the middle of the boat where it was safest, and she was grateful for the thick jumper she had put on under her coat, as well as her hat. She'd resisted the temptation to join Niels in the wheelhouse because she didn't want to distract him, and she found it easier to follow the movements of the boat on deck. Despite the sea legs she'd boasted to Inger about, a distinct feeling of queasiness had begun to steal up on her, and she kept her eyes fixed on the horizon.

Besides, someone had to make sure the passengers were all right.

They headed north at the beginning and then east to get around a minefield, and after that the sea became a little calmer. Again, Jørgen lifted the bulkhead, and Gudrun stuck her head through the opening.

A strong, sour smell hit her, and she withdrew sharply, gagging and gasping for air to get her roiling stomach under control.

'Is everyone all right down here?' she called down when she was able to.

'No,' came the weak response from a few of the passengers.

Daniel appeared below the opening, and held up one of the buckets. 'We've kept the buckets going from hand to hand, and this one's rather full. The other one got knocked over. And my sister threw up on me.' Despite his sister's accident, he sounded rather pleased with himself.

'Oh dear,' said Gudrun, glad that at least he appeared to be okay. *That boy has got sea legs*, she thought.

She took the bucket from him, and Jørgen took the other slightly less full one, and they emptied them over the side of the cutter. Just then the wind saw an opportunity and threw the smell back in her face, if not the contents. Her carefully controlled nausea, which up till now had been balancing on a knife edge, got the better off her, and she emptied the contents of her own stomach over the side of the boat. Still heaving and retching, she barely noticed Niels's brother holding onto her and preventing her from going overboard.

'I think you're better off in the wheelhouse,' he said. 'I'll stay here. We'll be in Swedish waters soon, and the passengers can come up on deck if they want.'

'I'm sorry,' she mumbled as she wiped her mouth with a handkerchief, repeating the same words to Niels, when she slunk inside the wheelhouse like a dog with its tail between its legs.

'You needn't be,' he replied, staring straight at the sea in front of them. 'Seems like you'll go to the ends of the earth for me, as I will for you. Just as long as you know that I'll tease you about it for the rest of your life.' His eyes crinkled at the corners.

'Hmm.' Gudrun crossed her arms, wanting to be angry, but in the end she had to give in to the laughter which bubbled up inside her. Not vomit this time, thankfully.

After what seemed like ages, lights appeared in the distance. Several of the passengers climbed up on deck, all looking towards the Swedish coast, although some of them were still feeling too weak, Jørgen reported back.

They continued towards the lights, and after another one and a half hours they reached the port of Höganäs. Then they could see the harbour entrance more clearly, and people on land waving their hats. Gudrun stepped out of the wheelhouse and waved back. On deck the passengers all hugged each other.

On the pier Swedish soldiers were standing with bayonets turned towards them, but when they saw the *Ofelia's* cargo, they helped them up and welcomed them.

'*Välkomna, välkomna!*'

As she watched them – these strangers, young and old, rich and poor, who had become so important to her in the last few hours – tears began to run down her cheeks. Many of the passengers were crying too, tears of relief and happiness, that the uncertainty which had plagued them all to the last moment was now replaced by the knowledge that they had made it to safety. Gudrun had never seen anything like it.

I shall always remember this, she thought. *Till my dying day.*

After a refuel and a quick rest, they prepared to leave Sweden. Niels was once more back in the wheelhouse, steering the cutter, and the passengers were still on the pier, as well as many locals. They began to cheer and wave.

Gudrun spotted Daniel with his family as he jumped up and down, waving with both arms, and she sent up a silent prayer that this happy and uncomplicated boy had now been given a second chance.

With one arm around the ship's mast flying the flag, Gudrun whipped off her woollen hat and used it to wave back. Jørgen did the same.

'*Dannebrog,*' she shouted at the top of her lungs over the sound of the cutter's engine as they left the harbour. 'Our flag, our country, our people!'

Eventually they were out of earshot, and the lights of Höganäs dimmed behind them until they completely disappeared from view.

They had done it. There would be other trips, more people to help, but they had done it. They had reclaimed a small part of Denmark's sovereignty.

Not even seasickness could drive away her euphoria.

Chapter Twenty-Three

Copenhagen

4th October 1943

I woke up to discover that Sara had sneaked into my bed during the night. For a moment I lay completely still and breathed in the sweet scent of childhood. Filthy from the forest, Sara had had a bath last night, and the scent of the rationed lavender soap, which Aunt Marie kept in a dish on her bedside table and only used on rare occasions, tickled my nostrils. Then there was Sara's personal smell, warm and milky; it was better than the headiest perfume, and I just wanted to lie here forever.

But I had to get up. Sighing, I extricated myself as carefully as I could, not wanting to disturb the little girl and her exhausted mother, and took my tweed suit into the washroom to get dressed.

Gudrun was back when I came downstairs, tucking into a bowl of porridge with ravenous appetite. Two slices of ryebread with dripping lay on a plate beside her.

'How was—? When did—?'

I stopped mid-sentence. I wanted to ask her how it went last night and what time she got back but didn't want to accidentally say something that Aunt Marie wasn't aware of.

'Oh, Mum knows,' Gudrun replied, her eyes shining with excitement.

She said that she had returned early in the morning, after curfew was lifted, and Aunt Marie, who apparently hadn't slept for most of the night, had already been apprised of events. For my part I explained about fru Jakobson and her daughter. Even so, Gudrun wasted no time in repeating her tale while I ate my own breakfast.

When the name Gestapo-Juhl crept into her account, I clamped my hand over my mouth, and it took a moment before I was able to speak. Him I had heard of.

'That was very admirable of Niels, to keep his head like that.' I couldn't quite disguise the tremor in my voice.

'I'll admit, it was closer than I'd have liked. But we did it.'

'Yes, you did.' I leaned across the table and squeezed Gudrun's hand. 'I admire you. It was very brave.'

'And foolish,' Aunt Marie scolded, but hugged her daughter close. 'My brave, foolish girl. If I'd known...'

'But you didn't. If you had, you'd have stopped me.'

Sighing deeply, Aunt Marie shook her head. 'I realise now that I can't stop you doing anything you've set your mind on doing. You're growing up. Soon you'll be a bride, and one day a mother perhaps.'

Sooner than you realise, I thought.

Gudrun sent me a warning look, and I mouthed back, 'What?' Did Gudrun really think I would tell? At any rate, she'd have to tell her parents herself soon and, like it or not, face the music.

Wiping a small tear from her eye, Aunt Marie changed the subject. 'What time are you leaving today?' she asked me.

'Leaving?' Gudrun frowned. 'Where are you going?'

'I'm going with David to Copenhagen, to fetch his mother. She's in hospital as you know, but being discharged today.'

'You didn't tell me that!'

I shrugged. 'I thought you had enough on your mind.'

'Yes, I suppose so. Anyway…' Leaning back in her chair, Gudrun glanced at the French clock which hung on the wall in the parlour. 'I'll need to change. I'm running late for work. And all I want to do is sleep!'

She left the kitchen, and I answered my aunt's question.

'We're getting the ten o'clock train, and then we'll go to the hospital for two o'clock. David has arranged it with the doctor.'

Aunt Marie got up from the table and began clearing away the breakfast plates. 'I'll make you a packed lunch.'

'That's not ne—'

'Don't argue,' Aunt Marie replied gruffly. 'With all my brave little soldiers going to war like that, of course it's necessary.'

Her choice of words made me smile. I didn't feel much like a soldier, but it was nice to be thought brave. 'Thank you.'

Gudrun returned to the kitchen in her work clothes. 'I was as quiet as a mouse, and our guests didn't wake up. What a sweet child.'

'She is, isn't she?'

'You're in love already.'

I felt my cheeks heat up. 'Maybe.'

Laughing, Gudrun kissed her mother goodbye.

'Oh, be off with you!' Aunt Marie waved the dishcloth at Gudrun who pretended to be terrified and left the house.

When peace had descended, and Aunt Marie had finished making the packed lunch, she sat down opposite me and poured us both a cup of coffee. Her hand wasn't quite steady and the cups rattled in their saucers. 'I do worry for you both. You and Gudrun. And David too. What if someone recognises him in Copenhagen, even in his borrowed clothes?'

'We'll head straight to Bispebjerg on the tram. Then we'll go to the cemetery nearby where we can wait until we can collect his mother.'

For my aunt's sake I spoke with a confidence I didn't feel. The porridge sat heavily in my stomach, and the faint whiff of fried herring rising from the greaseproof paper pack on the table was making me feel queasy. How Gudrun had been able to eat such a large breakfast, I couldn't fathom, but I persuaded myself this stemmed from relief not from lack of fear. Gudrun could be a little heedless sometimes.

Then I remembered: my cousin was pregnant. That would give you a healthy appetite too.

David waited for me outside. He was dressed in Uncle Poul's dark woollen coat and tweed cap with a grey scarf around his neck and I grinned when she saw him.

'You look like one of my uncle's drinking buddies, not a law student.'

'I take it that's a compliment.'

Laughing, I slipped my arm through his. Thus linked, like a normal couple, we walked to the station, where David bought the tickets. I put them in my handbag for safekeeping, then we boarded the train. It was Monday morning, after most people had started work, and the majority of the passengers were mothers with children below the school age, travelling salesmen and well-to-do ladies preferring the more modish shops of the capital as opposed to what the provincial town of Helsingør had to offer.

We found two window seats opposite each other, and David pulled the cap down over his face and pretended to be asleep, just as we'd agreed. Looking out of the window, and the landscape rolling by, I began to feel apprehensive.

Waking up with Sara snuggled next to me had made me forget momentarily about the danger surrounding us, but now a sour taste rose in my throat, and I had to swallow it back hard. If only I'd accepted Aunt Marie's offer of a flask of tea, but it had seemed like too much to bring as I didn't know how much help David's mother was going to need.

After a short while the ticket inspector did his rounds, and I handed over both our tickets.

He nodded in David's direction. 'Tired, is he?'

'Yes,' I replied, hoping that my curt answer would make him focus his attention elsewhere.

But the ticket inspector was in a chatty mood. Clipping their tickets, he asked, 'Doing anything exciting in the big city today?'

'Visiting a relative in hospital.'

'Dearie me. And who, may I ask, is the unfortunate patient?'

Drawing in a deep breath, I exhaled slowly. 'My fiancé's mother.'

'Oh, I see. And you're hoping to make a good first impression, eh?' Handing back our tickets, the ticket inspector winked at me, and a flush crept across my cheeks. This was just a little too close to the truth.

Finally, the man moved on to the next passenger, and I drew a sigh of relief…until I noticed David biting his lip, his shoulders shaking with suppressed laughter. My toes curled from embarrassment, and resolutely I stared out of the window.

Curse him.

The journey continued without problems, and about an hour later we arrived at Copenhagen Central Station. From there we walked a short distance down a less affluent but lively street, teeming with small shops, some of them in the basement below the many apartment blocks: butchers, grocers, clothes shops, fishmongers, florists. On our way to the tram stop we passed the radio shop Stjerne Radio where a group of people were gathered outside, listening to BBC recordings about the Germans. David pulled his cap down, and we crossed to the opposite pavement; it was too dangerous to linger.

The number 10 tram took us to Bispebjerg Cemetery near the hospital where David's mother was staying. I'd been here before as the cemetery wasn't far from the area of Copenhagen where I lived with my parents, and I'd always enjoyed its strict symmetry and long tree-lined avenues.

But today the beauty had no effect on me, and all I could think of was what lay ahead of us, the return journey to Helsingør, and getting David's mother to safety.

We found a bench in the shelter of a golden oak tree, which protected us against the slight drizzle, but at least the weather was calmer than the day before. Even so, it was hardly the perfect day for a picnic, and we attracted a few curious glances.

I shivered slightly in my coat, which I'd put on over my tweed suit, and peeled away the paper from our lunch. As I'd been able to smell earlier, Aunt Marie had packed us some leftover fried herring and cold potatoes, but there were also several slices of rye bread and an apple each. Certainly enough for us both, yet I could hardly get a bite down.

David took my hand. 'You need to eat.'

'You'd think it was me they were after.'

I pulled a face, and he laughed softly. 'You're doing just fine, and no one is paying that much attention to us anyway, except for a few busybodies. So what if we choose to eat lunch in the rain? There's no law against that.'

'You're right.'

His reassuring presence acted like a balm, and I managed to force down a piece of herring and an apple. My thoughts returned to Gudrun and Niels, and how they had evaded the Germans, and I reminded myself sternly that if they could do it, so could I. Especially with David by my side.

I could almost hear Gudrun in my head saying, *stop worrying, just pretend*. Well, I'd do just that. Pretend everything was all right, and then maybe it would be.

At two o'clock we presented ourselves at the hospital. The smells of disinfectant and sickness immediately hit me, and I pushed back the nausea rising in my throat.

Here we were shown into the office of the doctor who was treating David's mother. Fru Nathan was already there, and I got a distinct lump in my throat at the way her face lit up at the sight of her son. Suddenly I missed my own parents so much it ached.

In contrast to my own parents, who were quite robust and could sometimes be a little loud, David's mother appeared gentle and delicate like a bird. I was overcome with a feeling of wanting to protect her.

Once she'd greeted David, fru Nathan turned to me and clasped my hand with both of hers. 'It's so lovely to meet you at last, my dear,' she said, and looked as though she meant it. I had no idea what David had said about me, or how he'd managed to get a message through to her, but was reassured by the friendly expression on her face which was mingled with tiredness and relief.

I let out a breath I didn't know I'd been holding. Last night it had been my main worry that fru Nathan would be a difficult woman, and this turned out to be completely unnecessary. Instead, I could see how silly I'd been.

I really must stop being such a handwringer.

The doctor gave David some medicine for his mother to take. 'We've detected a slight heart murmur, but this should help. When you get to…your destination, you must ensure she seeks further help.'

'Of course. Thank you, doctor.'

David put the pill bottle in his coat pocket, and the doctor opened the door for them.

'Goodbye, fru *Christensen*,' he said pointedly and loud enough for anyone nearby to overhear. 'I wish you a speedy recovery. Herr Christensen, frøken Bredahl, enjoy the rest of your day.'

Fru Nathan was still weak, and David had to support her. I carried the bag the older woman had brought with her to hospital.

'Our downstairs neighbour visited me yesterday. She brought me some personal items.'

'That was kind of her,' David replied.

'She told me the flat had been turned over by…*by the Nazis*,' she added in a low voice. 'Oh, David, what will we be returning to after this dreadful war is over?' She gripped her son's arm as tears began to well up in her eyes.

David patted her hand. 'Let's not think about that now,

Mother. I'm sure she'll look after the place for us. She's always been a good neighbour.'

'Yes, I suppose you're right.' Fru Nathan sighed.

———————

We took the tram back to the central station and boarded the next train to Helsingør. As the train slowly pulled out of the station, and we left the city behind, I leaned back in my seat. My jaw ached from gritting my teeth, and I massaged the back of my neck to loosen it up a little. I felt a flush as I caught David's eye – grim-faced he gave me a brief nod of acknowledgement as he supported his mother who was dozing against him.

I looked away. It shamed me that I'd been so worried for myself when David and his mother scarcely knew what the next day would bring.

Eventually I was able to relax. The journey went well, with a different ticket inspector this time, someone not quite so chatty as the last one.

About twenty minutes before the train was due to pull into Helsingør, we heard the tramping of boots, and a small German patrol marched through the train carriage.

My stomach curled in on itself, and the fried herring I'd eaten earlier threatened to come back up, but I pushed it down when I caught sight of fru Nathan. Her birdlike face had gone grey, and she seemed to crumble inside her dark-blue coat.

'*Ausweis, bitte!*' the soldiers shouted, and there was no

please about it. The passengers frantically reached into their pockets or bags for the required documents.

David calmly handed over the false identity papers belonging to fru Else Christensen and her son, David Christensen, which Kiær had provided them with, as well as the travel documentation, although I noticed his knuckles had turned white as he clasped his mother's shoulder. Sending the soldier a neutral smile, I did the same.

The soldier looked at the papers, then back at us. Narrowing his eyes, he studied fru Nathan's pinched face and David's dark hair and dark eyes. I forced myself to hold the man's gaze with what I hoped was a bland expression. A long silence ensued while he looked from papers to people.

'*Aufstehen!*' he snapped at David. *Get up.*

Although my heart practically stopped beating, I somehow managed to keep calm. With my eyes, I signalled at fru Nathan to stay quiet.

Then a pleasant voice. 'Fräulein Bredahl?'

I turned. It was the officer who'd had a copy of *King Lear* bound at the workshop, and whom I'd met on my first day of doing deliveries. Relief mixed with apprehension rose in me. He'd been friendly towards me then, but you never knew.

'Is there a problem?' he asked in Danish.

I found my voice. 'Well,' I said and tried to sound as relaxed and normal as possible, 'for some reason this soldier here has singled out my fiancé, but we don't understand because our travel documents are in order.'

The soldier said something to the officer in German, which sounded like a question, and even though I didn't understand what he said, I caught the word *Jude*.

Jew.

Although David didn't look like the archetypal Jew, as depicted by Nazi propaganda, his colouring was a great deal darker than most Danes, and so was his mother's. And his nose was different from the characteristic Danish snub nose.

The officer sent me a long look, his eyes resting on my hand, which was adorned by Aunt Marie's modest engagement ring, which I'd borrowed for the day. It was a little loose but not enough for anyone to notice.

'A recent engagement, fräulein? You did not wear a ring last we met.'

I forced myself to smile. 'Yes, we've been to Copenhagen for the day to celebrate. We had tea at D'Angleterre.'

Still considering my answer, he nodded. 'Well, in that case, please allow me to congratulate you.'

'Thank you.'

The soldier said something else, but the officer shook his head.

'*Nein, ich kenne dieses Fräulein.*' *I know this young woman*. 'If she says this is her fiancé and his mother, then it is,' he added, as though being my fiancé and a Jew at the same time were mutually exclusive. Perhaps it was to his mind.

The soldier handed back our papers, gestured for David to sit down again, and moved along the carriage to check other passengers.

Addressing me, the officer said, 'I will visit the workshop soon with another book to be bound.'

'I shall let herr Kiær know,' I replied pleasantly. 'He'll be glad of the business.'

'*Auf wiedersehen. Gute Reise.*' *Have a nice trip.* The officer clicked his heels together, saluted us elegantly, and left.

The last lap of the journey was spent soothing David's mother who was shaking uncontrollably. When we got back to the neighbour's house, fru Holm, who'd been a nurse before her marriage to herr Holm, took charge, and helped fru Nathan to bed. I felt a pang of guilt over my earlier suspicion of fru Holm. Cut from the same cloth as Aunt Marie, the woman was a godsend.

'I'll go and sit with her,' said David when he and I were back outside in the cobbled lane. 'I just wanted to thank you. If you hadn't stayed so composed, we could have been done for. You were wonderful.'

Before I had time to react, he pulled me in for a gentle hug. For a moment I clung to him with a feeling that I'd come home at last, then reluctantly I let him go. Lips parted, he looked at me as if he wanted more, then he smiled and went back inside.

I was left wishing he hadn't been quite so gentlemanly.

Chapter Twenty-Four

Copenhagen

October 2018

'Despite our false papers we still couldn't go to Sweden by legal means,' said David, 'because travel was forbidden unless in very special circumstances, and after the incident on the train my mother was terrified that we'd draw too much attention to ourselves.

'Also, she wasn't able to travel further straight away and neither was the lady from our apartment building, so we had to stay put for a bit. But we were safe for the time being.'

His voice was weak and raspy, almost inaudible, and Cecilie had to lean closer to the bed in order to hear what he was saying.

Rafi had called her that morning to say that David was

in hospital, and asked her to come. Cecilie hadn't hesitated; instead, she'd placed a quick call to the school where she worked, explaining that a relative was seriously ill, and that she had to be there. It hadn't felt like a lie; it was almost as if they were related, not by blood but through shared experiences. And Rafi.

It turned out to be Bispebjerg, a teaching hospital in the northwest quarter of central Copenhagen, and the same place David's mother had been treated before Inger and David brought her to Helsingør. Cecilie didn't think this was a coincidence.

In a single suite with a view over the green area outside, David lay pale and shrunken against the white hospital linen, hooked up to a number of monitors. A nasal cannula delivered oxygen through his nose, and a saline drip was attached to his hand.

The sight of him looking so old and frail made Cecilie feel sad, but she could see he was in good hands with the best possible care, and he was as comfortable as he could be in the circumstances.

'Your grandmother was very brave,' he wheezed, as he tried to catch his breath. 'I knew she didn't think of herself in those terms, that she was terrified, but as the saying goes, "foolish are those who fear nothing". I was afraid too.'

'You had good reason to be,' said Cecilie.

David nodded weakly. 'By then we'd all heard rumours about what was happening to the Jews in the rest of Europe, that they were being exterminated. At the time we didn't really know how bad it actually was. It wasn't—' He started coughing, and Rafi supported him while he managed to drink some water from a cup with a straw. Eventually the coughing subsided.

'It wasn't until the end of the war,' he continued, 'when Allied troops liberated the concentration camps and the most awful images began to appear in the news, that we learned about the extent of the horror. Then there were the stories from those who'd survived...'

David paused as there was no need for him to elaborate further. Anyone who'd ever done history at school, or even those who hadn't, knew at least something about it. Cecilie remember borrowing *The Diary of Anne Frank* from the school library, the story written by the Dutch schoolgirl who had hidden in a loft with her family until they were discovered by the Nazis and sent to a concentration camp. Later she'd read *Night* by the American writer, Elie Wiesel, a harrowing memoir based on his experiences as a prisoner in Auschwitz.

She was pretty certain no Israeli citizen needed educating when it came to the Holocaust.

'Staying at fru Holm's turned out to be soothing for my mother's shredded nerves. Between her and your grandmother's aunt, they did everything they could to make sure she was comfortable.'

David fidgeted with the sheet, and Rafi helped him rearrange it.

'She was never really strong after my father died. He'd left us enough to get by on and for me to study, his dearest wish, but not enough for us to move to a wealthier neighbourhood as she'd always hoped we would.'

David reached for Cecilie's hand. 'You might wonder

why she felt that way, what it was like for her. You see, my mother came from a family of Russian Jews. Back then there was a slight hierarchy between the Jewish families in Copenhagen, between those more established, the "old" families, if you like, and the relatively recent newcomers. Perhaps they looked down upon the newcomers a little, thought they were ill-mannered, although having said that, there was always a strong solidarity with their fellow Jews and countrymen.'

'I never knew that,' Cecilie replied. She was learning so much and, although it was sad, it pleased her to be educated in this way.

Smiling softly, David patted her hand. 'Personally I was glad that we lived in Adelgade where our neighbours were in a similar socio-economic bracket. I didn't bother me. But for my mother…' His watery eyes took on a faraway look. 'This was the second time she'd had to flee; the first time, when she was a teenager, it was from the pogroms in Russia. It affected her deeply to have to leave her life behind once again, and her nerves never really recovered from it.'

Sighing, he lay back against the pillows as if talking had been too much for him.

'Grandpa, why don't you have a little rest?' Rafi suggested, placing his hand gently on his great-grandfather's forehead. 'Cecilie and I will go for a walk, maybe have something to eat in the café, and then be back in about an hour. Or longer if you need it.'

'Take two,' David replied hoarsely. He lay with his eyes closed, then he cocked one eye open, and his mouth curved in a mischievous smirk. 'It pleases me that I was able bring you two together.'

Cecilie felt a rush of heat in her face. How could David possibly know about their night together? Maybe he was just guessing.

'I have no idea what you're talking about.' Grinning, Rafi pressed a kiss to his cheek. 'You old pirate.'

Before they left the ward, Rafi made sure the nurses' station had his contact details. In the café-cum-kiosk they had a quick sandwich, followed by a coffee in a takeaway cup, and then left the hospital building in the direction of the cemetery nearby, essentially retracing Inger and David's steps seventy-five years previously.

In her diary her grandmother had talked about sitting on a bench in the rain, eating fried herring, and as she and Rafi wandered down one of the famous avenues, Cecilie couldn't help wondering which bench it was.

'You know, in spring people flock to the cemetery, to take pictures of the Japanese cherry trees here,' she said. 'The avenue becomes like a long pink tunnel. It's quite a sight.'

Rafi smiled. 'I'd like to see that one day.'

'It'll be in April when they flower.'

'Were there cherry trees back then?' Rafi asked. 'In 1943?'

Cecilie shook her head. 'I don't think so. There would've

been an avenue of poplar trees, but they became diseased and were felled a few years ago.'

They carried on walking, mostly in silence, sipping their coffees, each in their own thoughts. Cecilie had been wondering how to broach the subject of the two of them – if there was a 'them' – but today was not the time.

'This is where David will be laid to rest,' said Rafi after a while. 'This cemetery, I mean. I knew that when I came on this trip with him. It's not a Jewish cemetery, but that doesn't matter to Grandpa. Memories are more important, and now I know why this place is of significance to him.'

Tears welled up in Cecilie's eyes. She finished her coffee and threw the cup in a nearby bin, then dug in her pocket for a tissue.

Rafi put a hand on her shoulder. 'You do know he's dying, right?

'I know.' Cecilie nodded and dried her nose. 'It's hard because I haven't quite come to terms with it yet. I've only just met him.'

'As deaths go, it's a good death,' said Rafi. 'Grandpa has had a long and happy life, with a large family around him. And freedom from oppression. He's had "a good innings", as the British would say. In part, this is due to your grandmother, and I want to thank you.'

Puzzled, Cecilie smiled through her tears. 'You don't need to thank me; I had nothing to do with it.'

'In her absence I'm thanking you, but also for giving us all a chance to hear her story. If you hadn't found that cigar box, and the jewellery…' Rafi shrugged.

'But *you* found the diary,' she pointed out.

'True. But you would've found it sooner or later, I'm sure.'

'Are we actually arguing about this?' Cecilie laughed. 'Joking aside, I'm glad Inger was so brave, that despite her fears she found the strength within herself. I don't think I'd could've done what she did.'

'But you *are* brave. Just think of everything you've been through lately. And you picked yourself up and got on with it. You didn't turn miserable and bitter; instead you're fun and intelligent, and sexy as hell.'

Rafi pulled her in for a passionate kiss, which left her breathless. Then he stood back a little to see her properly, brushing a wayward strand of hair from her face with which the wind had been playing.

'Perhaps *strong* is a better word,' he said. 'Stronger than you think. And I'm not letting you go.'

Searching his face, she saw that he meant it. But that conversation was for another time.

Instead, she said, 'I'm a little surprised, though, that David doesn't want to die in Israel. Can he actually be buried here?'

'Grandpa has dual citizenship, and even though he can't read the language anymore due to his head injury, he's first and foremost a Dane. He always was.'

'Yes,' she replied. 'He was, and he is.'

Hand in hand they walked back to the hospital, and when David was sufficiently rested, Cecilie opened the diary again to read the last few pages.

Chapter Twenty-Five

Helsingør

The same day

Gudrun was late for work, and Bodil had tried to cover for her as best she could. Eventually Gudrun arrived, her face flustered as if she'd been in a rush, although her eyes burned with a curious kind of fire.

'Where have you been?' Bodil hissed. 'The super has been looking for you. I said you'd gone to pass water. If you're not careful, you'll get in trouble.'

Shrugging, Gudrun tied her apron over her work smock and took up her station next to Bodil. Today she and Gudrun were in charge of shaking the last drops of water from the newly rinsed beer bottles, then labelling them and passing them on to the next two women along the assembly line, who would fill and cap them, before they went for inspection and packaging.

'No I won't,' Gudrun answered cockily.

'I wouldn't be too sure about that.' Bodil tossed her head in the direction of the supervisor who hadn't noticed Gudrun slipping in.

Gudrun grinned. 'I'll just tell him to take it up with the man who pays our wages.'

'What's Parkov got to do with it?'

Beckoning Bodil closer, Gudrun told her what she'd been up to in the night. With increasing alarm, she listened as Gudrun spoke of an impromptu beer delivery, sanctioned by the brewery owner, a harbour full of refugees, the Gestapo, and what sounded like the most awful journey in a fishing boat. Her mouth went dry at the thought.

'I thought I was going to die,' Gudrun whispered excitedly, 'although obviously it was worse for those in the hold.'

One of the women filling beer bottles sent them an inquisitive look.

'You need to keep your voice down,' said Bodil. 'You won't want the wrong people to overhear.'

Gudrun lowered her voice, and went on with her tale. 'There were children too, like this kid, Daniel. He was a real trooper, and I'm so happy that he's now getting another chance.'

Shaking her head, Bodil sent her a fond smile. 'You are without a doubt the craziest person I know. But it would seem that under all that bravado of yours lurks a true heart of gold.'

Gudrun frowned. 'The way you say it, somehow makes it sound like less of a compliment.'

'I mean it.'

'Enough chatter, ladies,' the supervisor grumbled. 'This isn't a tea party.'

When he'd left them again, Bodil leaned in and whispered. 'You know, the Nazis are bound to notice all these people in the harbour all of a sudden.'

'Obviously they'll have to hide.'

'Gilleleje is only a village. How can you hide that many people?'

Gudrun shrugged as if this detail didn't need explaining. 'Oh well, private homes, storerooms, the church… There's a big loft up there. No one would think to look, and then—'

'You two, enough!' the supervisor snapped.

He took Gudrun by the shoulders and turned her around to what she was supposed to be concentrating on. Gudrun pulled a face behind his retreating back, and Bodil had to stifle a giggle. It pleased her that they were still friends; after the events at the beach, she'd feared Gudrun would never speak to her again.

Infected with Gudrun's obvious excitement, but also afraid for her, she asked, in a whisper, if she and Niels were planning to go out again.

'We'll go again in a few days. People are lying low today.'

'Promise you'll be careful.' She squeezed Gudrun's arm briefly and returned to her work station before the supervisor blew his top.

After work, Bodil stopped at the grocer's on Havnegade on her way home, where she picked up a bag of oats, some rye flour, as well as a bottle of Atamon preservative for making jams and jellies.

The rowanberries growing on the trees at the edge of the small wood at the bottom of their land had ripened and would need picking soon. By adding preservative to the cooked fruit she could get away with using less than half the normal amount of sugar.

She smiled shyly at the handsome assistant who'd danced with Inger at the inn. It seemed like ages ago now. Usually the assistant would smile back, but today he appeared distracted and gave her the wrong change. When she discovered it and went back inside the shop to point it out, it was the owner's wife who served her this time.

The woman apologised and corrected it. 'I don't know what's the matter with him today. This is the third time.'

As she left, she heard the woman yell for the assistant, which made her feel bad. She hadn't wanted to get him into trouble, but she couldn't afford to be short-changed.

She put her purchases in her bicycle basket and took her usual route out of town. As she passed the inn at Snekkersten, someone called out to her. It was Oskar. Chewing her lip, she hesitated, then gave in and stopped.

He sent her a beaming smile, and her heart skipped a little beat.

'I was hoping you'd come this way today,' he said and offered to push her bike. 'Have you been avoiding me?'

Flushed, she declined. 'No, no. I've, er, been busy at the homestead. Pickling vegetables and the like.'

'May I walk you home?'

'Er, yes, but only to the top of the road.'

'I understand.' Was there a flash of irritation in his eyes? She couldn't be sure.

I must have misread that, she decided shortly after, as Oskar chatted the way he normally would, about his family as well as farm work, which they had in common.

'I see your bump has almost gone.'

'Oh, that.' Automatically her hand flew to her forehead, and he was right, the bump was gone because she couldn't feel it anymore. 'I'd forgotten about that. I'm that used to knocks and scrapes.'

'I hadn't.' His face darkened. 'I don't know why they were picking on you. They should put the blame squarely where it belongs, with the Jews. If it wasn't for them, everything would be running smoothly here, but I've heard they're everywhere along the coast.'

'I haven't seen any,' Bodil replied, as the image of the man on the beach popped into her head. It was an experience she had yet to forget.

'Surely no one can hide that many people,' Oskar went on, as if he hadn't heard her.

'I'm sure there must be places, like village halls or churches,' Bodil said, then immediately regretted it.

Fortunately Oskar still seemed focused on his own thoughts. 'This could be really dangerous for people. Why would they expose themselves to reprisals like that? Oh, and please don't misunderstand me, I have nothing against Jews.'

'A lot of Germans do. They speak of them as though they aren't human.'

'Of course they're human,' Oskar replied. 'It's just a well-known fact that they are a lesser class of humans. *Untermenschen.*'

Bodil stopped as a feeling of cold ran through her. 'I... what? Oskar! You can't say things like that.'

The image of the half-crazed man stumbling along the road came back to her, no less a human than anyone else, just desperate and frightened, and suffering the most terrible grief imaginable.

'The Führer tells us this. And all the scientists.'

'Well, then your precious Führer is wrong!' Bodil snapped.

Oskar stiffened. 'I happen to believe this to be the truth.'

'I-I can't... I don't want to hear you talk like that.' Bodil got back on her bike and pushed off. *How could he?*

'*Bitte*, don't go! *Denk an das Leben das wir haben könnten. Ich li— Du bist mir sehr wichtig, Schöne Augen! Bitte!*' he called after her, his voice rising almost to a cry. *Please, don't go. Think of the life we could have. I lo— You're very important to me! Please!*

'I need to think. I need to think.' Bodil sped off, leaving him behind.

A feeling of emptiness spread inside her, the vacuum left behind from foolish dreams of a happy life. How could he be so...inhuman? Tears running down her cheeks, she pedalled faster and faster, her legs and arms and heart aching because she couldn't accept what he'd just said.

Inger and Gudrun were right. It's us or them.

Chapter Twenty-Six

Gilleleje

6th October 1943

Loitering outside the brewery, Gudrun was hoping to catch Bodil before work. This morning she'd accepted her packed lunch and flask of tea from her mother as usual and headed out of the door without meeting anyone's eyes. She'd sensed a question from Inger, but hadn't given her an opportunity to ask it.

Finally she spotted Bodil turning the corner of Havnegade. Twitching with irritation, she grumbled, 'Who's late now?'

'Actually, I'm bang on time,' Bodil replied tersely.

Which was true, but Gudrun was in no mood to acknowledge that she had been wrong. 'I need you to do something for me.'

'What do you want me to do?' Bodil took off the kerchief which had kept her pale hair in place while cycling and shook it free. It looked flat and a little greasy, Gudrun noticed.

'I need you to tell them I'm off ill.'

'You don't look ill.'

Bodil did, though. There were dark circles under her eyes and she had an air of defeat about her. But Gudrun didn't have time to think about that right now.

'I'm not, but I have to go and help them in Gilleleje.'

'Of course. I'll let them know.'

While Gudrun debated whether perhaps she should ask what was happening with Bodil, one of their colleagues passed them.

'Did you know your friend's going with a German fella? I saw them together a couple of days ago.' Not waiting for an answer, the woman sent Bodil a look of contempt before walking through the gate.

Gudrun glanced at Bodil. 'Is that true? Are you still seeing him?'

Bodil shook her head. 'I'll tell them you're ill,' she said and pushed her bike through the gate to the brewery yard.

———

When she got to the village of Gilleleje an hour later, Gudrun found Niels and Jørgen on the cutter cleaning the boat. Leaning her bike against a bollard, she gave him a chaste kiss on the cheek out of deference to his brother who was watching.

'Have you been out at all?' she asked.

Her fiancé shook his head. 'I wanted to lie low, but the weather on Monday was windy and rainy anyway. More refugees have arrived in town, and I believe the organisers have found them places to hide but it's getting conspicuous.' Niels emptied a bucket of dirty water over the side of the boat. 'I didn't go yesterday either. I've just been checking the engine over, while Jørgen has been repairing nets. And I'm waiting for notification from the people organising it where the refugees are to go. I prefer to sail at night anyway. At any rate, yesterday was too dangerous.'

Niels frowned and stared into the distance. 'When the cutter *Dannebrog* had just left yesterday loaded with about twenty refugees, I think, a car drove down the harbour and three men from the Schalburg Corps jumped out and began firing on the boat.'

Gudrun covered her mouth with her hand. 'Christ!'

'There were several of us here last night, and we didn't know whether the skipper had been hit or not, but the boat began to drift out of control. Gestapo-Juhl was there too, and he shouted that if the skipper didn't stop, they'd fire again. Which they did, about twenty or twenty-five shots, some of them smashing into the wheelhouse. Then the boat ran aground and the skipper and the crew jumped ashore and disappeared.'

Gudrun felt her legs begin to shake and stared at Niels, her heart beating hard. It could have been him.

'What about the Jews? Did they get them?'

Sighing, Niels pulled her close. 'Yes, I'm afraid so.'

'Those poor people.' Gudrun hid her face against his chest and let him stroke her hair. Then she thought of Daniel, now safe in Sweden, and she drew herself up.

'I know.' Niels scratched the back of his neck. 'Here's something that might cheer you up a little. Gestapo seized the cutter and berthed it near the coastal police building. This morning, shortly before you got here, the skipper stole it back and sailed off with it. He's a wanted man now, so I expect he's in Sweden.' He grinned softly.

Gudrun's mouth fell open. 'How did he manage that?'

'The duty officer went to check another boat just arrived, and apparently no one saw or heard anything, not even the engine starting.'

'I don't suppose you or Jørgen saw it either.'

'Can't say that I did.' Niels winked.

Gudrun laughed and threw her arms around him, and he smiled down at her.

'I love it when you're happy.'

A large schooner named the *Flyvbjerg* was moored on the eastern pier. Niels was curious about it, he told Gudrun, because he hadn't seen it at Gilleleje Harbour before, and wanted to investigate. When the skipper appeared on deck with his crew consisting of two young men, and disembarked, Niels and Gudrun introduced themselves.

'Where do you hail from?' Niels asked the captain.

The captain lit a cigarette. 'From the island of Funen. We're taking a cargo from Copenhagen to Jutland, and moored here last night hoping for better weather for the crossing.'

As the men discussed the weather, they were approached by another man pushing his bicycle. Gudrun frowned; there was something vaguely familiar about him. Then she recognised him as an assistant professor at the grammar school in Helsingør, which Jens attended, and relaxed.

'Good morning, herr Schmidt.'

'Good morning. I need to speak with the captain of the schooner.'

Gudrun pointed him out, and herr Schmidt introduced himself. After a brief conversation about the boat and its capacity, and the weather in general, herr Schmidt lowered his voice and sent a sideways glance at Gudrun and Niels. Gudrun understood his intention.

'It's okay, herr Schmidt. My fiancé owns a cutter moored on central pier, and we're also trying to do what we can.'

Taking her meaning, the assistant professor relaxed visibly and asked the captain the question he'd been skirting around. 'Are you able to transport a boatload of Jews?'

Sucking his teeth, the captain hesitated, then he shook his head. 'That's risky business. This isn't just my boat; it's my brother's too. He's not going to be happy if I lose it. Look around you, plenty of other schooners here. Why don't you ask them?'

'They all say you're the right person for the job.'

'Oh, they do, do they?' The captain frowned.

'You'll be paid.'

Still the captain hesitated, but after conferring with his two crew members, he accepted the job and they agreed on a price and a departure time of one o'clock in the afternoon. He and the assistant professor then left to get the coastal police officer's approval.

During their conversation, frustration had been building inside Gudrun. 'I wish there was something I could do to help,' she said to Niels when they were back on the cutter. 'We can't just sit here all day.'

'Why don't you go and see my mother? She's a member of the women's civil defence corps. She'll know, or send you to someone else. I need to stay in the harbour. '

'Fine. I'll see you later?'

He nodded and reluctantly she set off.

As she left the eastern pier, the coastal police officer passed by and gave the ready signal for the *Flyvbjerg* to sail immediately. At first it puzzled her because the skipper and Schmidt had agreed one o'clock, but then she realised it made sense to use the time when the Germans were not around. Fortunately she hadn't seen any soldiers yet.

The message from the harbour that the schooner was setting sail spread almost faster than Gudrun could walk. As she headed up the main street in the direction of the church to the narrow lane where Niels lived with his family, the quiet seaside town, now out of season, suddenly sprang to life.

Around her doors flew open, and refugees streamed out of almost every house. Almost immediately the whole street was full of people: men, women, and children from all walks of life, young and old, rich and poor. Locals were helping them get to the harbour, and those not so light-footed were either carried or rolled off in wheelbarrows and on similar transports.

People with empty, expressionless faces staring ahead of them, all on the run from the Germans simply for being Jews, and intent on one thing only: getting themselves and their loved ones to safety.

Tears welled up in her eyes at this strange and disturbing sight, and a bitter taste filled her mouth. Although much too soon, she automatically placed her hand over her slowly growing belly.

How can this be happening here, in Denmark, in our quiet and peaceful democracy? Is this the world we live in now?

———————

Mogens, the youngest of Niels's brothers, was just setting off on his bike when Gudrun reached the tiny cottage.

He sent her a cheerful grin. 'I'm off with the scouts to sniff out where the Gestapo are lurking.'

'Be careful,' she muttered, but he was already out of earshot. She watched his retreating back. With his blue eyes and blond hair he looked so like Niels it was uncanny, and briefly she wondered who their child was most likely to take after. Hopefully both of them.

But the happy fantasy didn't alleviate the tension in her neck and shoulders, nor her dark mood. It hung over her like a cloud, over the whole town like a boiling cauldron of nervousness, the constant knowledge that the Gestapo could be here any moment, and she looked carefully around her before she ducked inside the cottage.

Niels's mother was in full preparation mode. 'They need young women at the Mission Hotel down on Havnevej to help make food for the refugees.'

With instructions of who to speak to, Gudrun headed back in the direction of the harbour. Passing a house on Main Street where a woman was working in her garden, Gudrun felt an odd tugging at her shoe, and discovered that the laces had come loose on her sensible lace-ups. As she knelt down to tie her shoe laces, a black car with an Helsingør number plate parked in the woman's driveway, and a man got out. Round glasses, no officer's cap, fair short-cropped hair so he appeared almost bald.

Gestapo-Juhl.

A sliver of ice ran down Gudrun's back, and she shuddered. Intent on the woman working in her garden, the man hadn't spotted Gudrun yet, and she didn't move.

'A busy bee today, are we, madam?' he said, his jaw working furiously as though he was barely managing to keep his temper under control.

'No more than usual.'

The woman's neutral reply seemed to incense him. 'I expect you went to the grocer's to warn them about my presence in town. No matter; we'll find out where they're hiding!'

He turned on his heel, sent Gudrun an irritated look, then crossed the road with his men to search a house opposite. Gudrun didn't wait to see what the result of his search was. Instead she ran as fast as she could towards the harbour. Did he know about the refugees boarding the schooner? If he'd been in town long enough for an informer to tell him, he might well.

Those poor souls… Gudrun had to warn them.

Her lungs were burning when she reached the harbour, and she could hardly get a word out. Stopping to catch her breath, she gestured to Niels who appeared on the deck of the cutter moored on centre pier. He sent her a curious look.

'Ge-Gestapo are here!'

His face paled. 'You sure?'

'They're on Main Street. It's Hans Juhl himself. I—'

Niels put his hands around his mouth and bellowed across the harbour, louder than Gudrun had ever heard him. 'The Gestapo are coming! The Gestapo are coming!'

The cry spread like wildfire and created chaos and panic on the eastern pier. The refugees thronged around the schooner, anxious to get on board, and assistant professor Schmidt who had promised a group of Jews hiding at the butcher's that they would get a space on the boat, was now trying to get a message to them.

'Send word to the fifty people at Olsen's that they need to come to the harbour immediately!' he shouted.

Not long after that another group of people came running towards the harbour. All of them managed to get on the boat in time, except one woman who had become separated from her family in the rush.

Still out of breath, Gudrun watched the desperate woman waving to her husband and children, then she hid her face in her hands and sobbed pitifully as the schooner left the harbour.

I must go to her, she thought.

Someone beat her to it. One of the locals led the lone woman away to safety. Gudrun hoped she would find passage on another boat.

And the Gestapo still didn't appear. Where were they?

———————————

She spent the rest of the day in the kitchen at the Mission Hotel, helping prepare food for the refugees, which they couldn't distribute until after dark. Twice during the day they received reports on how many they were catering for, which increased steadily as more and more Jews gathered in places large enough to accommodate such numbers. In the end there were about eighty people hiding in the church loft, and over fifty on the top floor of the parish house.

In the afternoon, Niels dropped by. His mother had told him where Gudrun was, and when he noticed the many large serving dishes covered with paper, waiting to be distributed amongst those hiding, he frowned.

'Wouldn't it be better to carry the food in covered baskets?' he asked.

Gudrun nodded. 'I've already suggested that, but we don't have enough, and those we have just aren't big enough. Any news from the harbour?'

'They're still trying to organise another schooner, but they won't be able to depart until the middle of the night. We now know daylight is too risky.'

Gudrun shuddered, remembering the panic this

morning. It was a miracle the *Flyvbjerg* had managed to get away.

Before he left, he pulled her close and pressed a gentle kiss to her forehead. 'Be careful. There are informants in town.'

'I will,' she said. 'You too.'

A tight knot was forming in her stomach as she watched him leave, and the awful thought that she'd never see him again took hold. Then she pushed it aside. They had a job to do, and then everything would be all right. She had to believe that.

As darkness fell, the women in the hotel kitchen began to leave in small groups, each carrying a covered dish.

'When you get to the church, knock on the door and say the codeword,' said the woman who was in charge of providing the food. She wore a felted uniform hat on her head and a white armband with the initials DKB, which stood for the women's civil defence corps.

Gudrun's group consisted of herself and two other women, both in their mid-thirties, and they were dressed in inconspicuous clothes and sensible shoes like her own.

From Havnevej they turned into the road leading to the church, and then headed towards Main Street, where the entrance to the cemetery and the church was. As they turned the first corner, Gudrun felt a prickling sensation on the back of her neck, but when she looked behind her, there was no one.

But the feeling wouldn't go away, and her hands began to sweat so much she almost dropped the dish she was carrying.

'Careful there,' said one of the other women. 'Hungry people are waiting for us.'

They entered the cemetery through the gate in the low stone wall, and the other woman knocked lightly on the church door, then delivered the codeword *The Hope*. The door to the darkened church opened quietly, and they slipped inside. As the door was closing slowly behind her, Gudrun caught a movement by the cemetery gate and felt a pair of penetrating eyes on her, although she couldn't be sure.

It was almost pitch black in the loft with only the scarcest of light coming through the few small, round windows in the tiled roof. But it was enough to see the scared and hopeful faces turned towards them. The Jews sat mostly quiet, on either the floor or the centre ledge, and one young man sat on the bottom rung of the ladder leading to the bell tower. But even if Gudrun hadn't been able to see them, if only as grey ghostlike figures, she could feel the throng around her, hear the breathing, shuffling, murmuring as though they were one solid mass of tension and unease.

Silently she began taking the dish around, picking her way carefully in the dark to avoid stepping on people or various belongings. Some mumbled a quiet thanks; others were too anxious to speak. One lady suddenly started laughing hysterically, but was promptly told to be quiet by those sitting nearby.

After the dishes were empty, Gudrun and the other two women left the church loft. Gudrun was the last to leave, and just as she was about to set foot on the stairs, an older man stopped her. He pressed a small bag into her hand, which she could tell contained money.

'Why are you—?' she whispered.

'Shh,' he said. 'This is a poor community and yet they help us without thought to themselves. Some of us here are wealthier than others, and we've made a small collection. There is 1270 kroner in the bag. Please give it to the priest, so he may distribute it amongst those in need.'

'That's… Thank you. I will.'

In the dark, Gudrun couldn't really see his face but she heard the quiet dignity in his voice, that despite their own compromised position these people spared a thought for the disadvantaged. He was putting his trust in her to deliver the money, but also trusting a society he believed in.

She slipped the bag in her coat pocket, whispered goodbye, and left the church loft.

Before returning to the Mission Hotel, she had to find the priest, and she asked one of the other women waiting for her outside the gate if they knew where he lived. On her way there she kept looking behind her, but there was no sign of whoever or whatever she thought she'd seen earlier.

The priest wasn't at home.

'I'm afraid I don't know where he is,' said his wife, as her eyes searched the street for signs of the Germans, 'but I'll make sure he gets the money, and the message as well.'

She closed the door as quietly as she'd opened it, and Gudrun headed back in the direction of the hotel, avoiding Main Street and instead choosing a more roundabout route wherever possible. She still wasn't convinced they hadn't been followed from the Mission Hotel to the church earlier.

As she was about to turn the corner into Havnevej, she ran straight into a group of Gestapo soldiers. They had stopped a number of other people who now stood with their hands above their heads facing a wall, and one of the soldiers grabbed Gudrun's shoulder roughly and forced her to do the same.

How long she stood there, unable to communicate with any of the others, she couldn't tell, but after a while she felt the cold creeping up from the ground and her fingers and hands prickling with pins and needles from having to hold them up. She couldn't see what was happening behind her, heard only the soldiers speaking amongst themselves, but because they spoke in their own language, she had no idea what they were talking about. They seemed calm, as if this was merely a routine check, and she persuaded herself everything was all right.

Suddenly there was a rush of activity, shouting and the sound of heavy boots moving away, although a cluster of soldiers remained to guard them. One word she was able to pick out: *Kirche*.

Church.

Had the Germans discovered where the Jews were? Her lungs constricted with fear and she had to swallow down bile, fear rising inside her.

Fifteen minutes later the soldiers let them all go. At least, Gudrun thought it was no more than fifteen; it could have been more. Only one thought kept spinning in her head: *someone has to warn them*.

When the soldiers were no longer watching, Gudrun ran as fast as she could towards the church, down side alleys and through people's gardens and yards, disturbing sleeping chickens and geese. She was out of breath, legs pumping automatically, but she ignored any discomfort and carried on.

It was too late. The church was surrounded. Even knowing the codeword, there was no way she could get inside and warn the refugees.

And there was no way for them to get out, except into the arms of the Gestapo.

Unable to move, she watched in horror as the net tightened around the church. Other people had gathered too, equally unable to prevent what was about to happen.

But the church wasn't the only place in town where a large number of people were in hiding together. The Mission Hotel had catered for at least fifty people at the parish house. Perhaps the Gestapo didn't know about that yet. There was still time to warm them.

Slowly she backed away, when she felt a pair of eyes on her. Gestapo-Juhl was standing beside one of the black cars, and he was looking right at her as though he'd read her mind.

He barked something in German, and before she knew it, two Gestapo men had her in a vice.

Juhl strode right up to her, narrowing his eyes behind his glasses. 'You!' he snapped. 'You were here this morning when that schooner sailed off, and on Sunday! What do you know?'

'N-nothing,' she stuttered.

'I don't believe you.'

'I really don't know anything.'

He put his face close to hers, so close she could smell coffee on his breath. 'Everyone knows something,' he raged, flecks of spittle collecting in the corners of his mouth. 'This piss-pot little town, in this piss-pot little country, how dare you defy the order of the Wehrmacht! Take her away!' he demanded of the two Gestapo men. 'Find out what she knows. Use whatever means necessary. I've had enough of this disobedience.'

Gudrun's pulse started racing, and black spots appeared before her eyes. 'Please, I don't...don't know anything!' Her plea came out like a whimper, and she hated herself for it. And it was untrue; she knew about the refugees in the parish house, and the codeword.

'We'll see about that when they start working on you.'

'No, please, no! I can't... I'm not...'

I'm not brave, she wanted to say. She realised now that she was merely foolhardy. She was afraid of what she might say if they started hurting her, but she knew that she wouldn't be able to withstand the kind of physical pain people could inflict on others when they really wanted to.

The two Gestapo men began to push her towards one of the black cars. She tried resisting, but she was only one woman against two men, and they simply dragged her along, effortlessly, as though she weighed nothing, her shoes scraping against the road.

'No, please,' she called desperately over her shoulder to Gestapo-Juhl. 'I... I have information!'

If she told them what she knew, surely they would let her live. And the baby would live too, hers and Niels's baby. She thought about all the Jews who had managed to get on board the *Flyvbjerg* and sail away because she had warned them before the Gestapo arrived. She'd saved some, hadn't she? She'd done her best. She needed to hold onto that thought.

May God forgive me.

'Yes?' Juhl turned around, one eyebrow raised.

After she'd told him about the Jews in the parish house, Gestapo-Juhl looked at her dispassionately for a moment before giving his men another order.

'Take her to the villa. And set an example.'

Chapter Twenty-Seven

Helsingør

Earlier the same day

I pushed my borrowed bike through the side gate and
parked it under the small lean-to behind the workshop
in Stengade.

Sara and fru Jakobson were still staying with my family
because the pregnant woman was too exhausted to travel at
the moment, and this meant that Gudrun was still sharing
the attic room with Jens. Not that she seemed to mind. After
her exhilaration over the trip to Sweden she'd been a little
preoccupied, and this morning had been no different. She'd
accepted her packed lunch and flask of tea from Aunt Marie
as usual but had studiously avoided eye contact with
anyone.

Uncle Poul had sent her a suspicious look, but said nothing. And well he might because I sensed Gudrun was up to something.

Rønne was in the workshop when I entered through the back door, seated at the large table in the centre with Kiær; Bruhn and Thormód arrived shortly after. They were having a meeting.

'Please join us, frøken Bredahl.' Bruhn smiled and pulled out a chair for her.

'Yes, thank you. I will.' Pleased that they had accepted my involvement now, I insisted on getting them all a soda first, and then joined them.

'It has come to my attention that quite a lot of refugees are staying near me,' said Kiær, who lived with his family in a large villa in the village of Snekkersten. 'It's not so surprising really; we're only a forty-five-minute train ride from Copenhagen, and many of them will know the fishermen from their summer stays in the village. Besides the people from the forest we found shelter for, it's a natural place to go for potential sanctuary.'

Kiær went on to explain that he knew of many locals who had helped hide the refuges in various sheds, cellars, and attics. 'Some are even in Egebæksvang Church just south of town. The question is, how can we help them to get to Sweden?'

Thormod cleared his throat and fiddled with some papers that were lying in front of him on the table. 'A friend of mine in Helsingør, a businessman, has contacted a resistance group in Gilleleje. Apparently, they're organising boats, some of which are big enough to take several hundred passengers. Schooners, I'm told. May I suggest we try to get the refugees in Snekkersten to Gilleleje so they can get on one of these boats?'

'When did you have in mind?' Rønne asked.

'I'd suggest tonight,' Thormod replied. 'The weather is ideal. Cold, foggy, some showers; it's the perfect cover.'

We debated the practicalities, weighing the pros and cons – or rather the men did while I put in a word here and there. In the end it was agreed that Kiær, Rønne, and Bruhn would handle the transport to Gilleleje, while Thormod was to remain at the police station in Helsingør to gain intelligence of the whereabouts of the Germans. Hans-Peter and I would come too; Hans-Peter because he could drive, and me because I'd shown myself adept at dealing with children in distress.

Nodding, I accepted the role, grateful for their confidence in me, although it still irked me a little. Sara was only one child, not children in plural, and it didn't mean I was any better at handling kids than Kiær was, who happened to be the father of two.

'The kids will need to be sedated for the journey to ensure they're quiet,' Kiær added. 'I'll ask a doctor I trust.'

The group dispersed, and Kiær and I continued with the tasks of the day. I went home, as normal, and had dinner with the family. Sara had discovered that if she refused food and only ate if she could sit on my lap, she would bask in everyone's attention, and although she still hadn't spoken a word, she was clearly enjoying it.

The only person missing was Gudrun. I suspected she'd bunked off work and gone to Gilleleje to help Niels again. To make up for her absence, Aunt Marie spoke extra loudly about all and sundry.

Just after nightfall, I cycled to the north end of the road leading to Klostermose Forest and swung into a remote timber yard, where the organisers would meet the refugees.

There, in a number of large garages, several trucks and three cars waited for the Jewish refugees who began to arrive in small groups led by those who had housed them. Kiær asked me to help him keep a tally of what the refugees were paying each.

'We only ask them to pay according to their means,' he explained and handed me a notebook.

In the end he'd collected 60,000 Danish kroner, money which would be used to pay the drivers of the trucks and the crew of the schooner.

Hans-Peter was there, and I was pleased to see him. He'd shown himself to be calm and competent, just what was needed at this time, and I gave him a friendly greeting. He seemed to have accepted my involvement now and smiled back. It was a relief that he'd realised the decision was mine and that I wanted to play my part too.

David was calm and competent too, but his mother needed him by her side, and for him to be here this evening would expose him to unnecessary risk.

Still, I couldn't help wishing he was.

Aside from most of the refugees and the truck drivers, whom I hadn't met, there was only one other person unknown to me. He introduced himself as Dr Jørgen Gersfelt.

'I have a medical practice here in Snekkersten. And because I'm a doctor, I have permission to use my car. Which comes in handy.'

He smiled, shaking my hand. He had a long, straight nose, slightly crooked front teeth, and dimples in his cheeks. I liked him immediately, although I wondered why Dr Winther wasn't with them today.

Gersfelt answered my unspoken question. 'Dr Winther has had a visit from the Gestapo. She's all right,' he added quickly when he saw my reaction. 'They let her go, but she reckons they're watching the house and she's keeping a low profile.'

This was bad news. I worried for the kind, no-nonsense female doctor and hoped she was all right, but there was no time to think about that now.

When all the refugees had arrived, by flashlight, Dr Gersfelt gave the few toddlers tranquilising injections, and I distributed sedatives and seasickness pills to the adults. Whatever worries I'd had began to fall away at how well-organised it was, a far cry from the chaos Gudrun had recounted from her crossing, where most of those onboard, apart from Niels and his brother, had been horribly sick.

The drivers kept their engines running throughout so they could be ready to drive off at any time. In the quiet night, the sound of the engines seemed as loud as rumbling thunder.

'Shouldn't we be worried about the noise?' Hans-Peter whispered in my ear. 'I'm sure it can be heard by the Germans far and wide.'

I nodded, butterflies dancing in my stomach. The thought had occurred to me too.

Finally, the passengers were ready to climb onboard the trucks and hide under tarpaulins, and I got in Gersfelt's car. Hans-Peter went with Rønne, and Kiær and Bruhn shared the last of the three cars. As the cars and trucks left the timberyard, a few curious onlookers had gathered to watch the departure.

Uncertainty crept over me, and I bit my lip. How come the locals knew what was happening? Who had told them, and what might the consequences be for the transport? Neither Kiær nor Gersfelt would have advertised what we were doing.

But getting out of Snekkersten went without a hitch, and I began to relax. The drivers took a route circling around Helsingør, along winding country roads and through the forests of North Zealand, with the trucks staying close together. A couple of times along the way we stopped so Kiær could call Thormod at the police station in Helsingør for news about the Gestapo's whereabouts.

The first time Thormod reported that several Gestapo cars had been seen heading in the direction of Gilleleje. The second time, when Kiær called from Esrum Inn, he was told there was no immediate danger, and the trucks continued as planned.

About three kilometres from the village of Gilleleje the trucks stopped again and drove into the yard of a farm. The increasing sense of unease during the journey had given me a headache, and I didn't catch the name of the farm-owner or that of the farm itself. I was beginning to regret coming along and wondered if I dared ask the doctor if he had something which might help.

What use will I be to anyone if I'm ill?

Hans-Peter squeezed my shoulder briefly. 'Are you feeling unwell?' he asked in a low voice. 'You look a little pale.'

'Just a nervous headache, I think.'

'Perhaps you just need something to eat.'

He turned out to be right. The farmer and his family greeted us all with open arms and arranged for both hot and cold meals and drinks as a matter of course. While the men debated what to do for the last leg of the journey, I and a couple of the Jewish women helped the farmer's wife clear up.

'Thank you for your generosity,' I said to her.

'Ah, that's nothing. It's the least we can do. And it's the *right* thing to do.' The farmer's wife didn't ask if I belonged amongst the refugees or not; it didn't seem to matter to her either way.

It was agreed that Rønne would drive into Gilleleje for a reconnaissance. About an hour later he returned.

'I found one of the contacts. He seemed pretty anxious.' Rønne was biting his lip. 'There are rumours that the Gestapo have learned about the impending transport. Best if we await further notice, I think.'

Well past midnight we still hadn't heard anything. Many of the refugees had fallen asleep where they could, and even Hans-Peter was snoozing in an armchair. Too anxious to sleep, I watched him, his handsome face relaxed and his blond hair sticking out in all directions. He reminded me of a carefree boy, exhausted from a day of mischief.

If only it was merely mischief we were all up to; instead, this was deadly serious. For some reason, this led to me to think about Gudrun. Where was she? Was she safe? I hoped so. The thought of my exuberant cousin in trouble made my stomach harden.

Tired of waiting, Kiær, Rønne, and Bruhn decided it was time to investigate further.

'May I come too?' I asked, although they hardly needed me. 'I find it difficult to just sit here and do nothing. And there is a chance my cousin is there helping too.'

Bruhn drove us to a place north of Gilleleje. We parked the car down a narrow lane beside a thicket of conifers, and walked the last half kilometre along the railway tracks into the small town until we reached the house of one of the contacts.

When we got there, the door was locked, and the house seemed abandoned. Rønne knocked hard on the door, but there was no sign of life. He knocked again, stronger, but there was still no answer. In the end he kicked the door as hard as he could.

'Easy,' said Kiær.

Rønne sent him a resentful look. 'We need to know what's happening, don't we? How else are we going to get all these people on the boats?'

After what seemed like ages a man opened the door. His face was ashen, and his hands trembled. 'I thought you were the bloody Gestapo!' he said in a slightly shrill voice, although his relief was palpable that they weren't.

Kiær explained who we were.

The man shook his head, his eyes suddenly bulging. 'You have to leave immediately!' he hissed. 'The Germans have discovered everything. They've rounded up all the Jews who were hiding in the church loft. God knows what'll happen now!' He slammed the door.

Shocked into silence, we stared at each other, the question forming on everyone's lips. What the hell are we supposed to do now?

Kiær was the first to react. 'Let's go. Now!'

We'd barely got out of the garden gate, when, at breakneck speed, a car came to the house and stopped. The Gestapo jumped out, but we had no time to see what happened next. We ran. Through gardens, jumping over one fence after another and eventually came out on the road we'd initially planned to follow back to the car.

'This isn't safe,' Bruhn said, trying to catch his breath.

Instead, we made a detour across the fields to the town's southern entrance road. Just as we had reached the road, several German patrol vehicles approached, and we had to double back across another field, crawling, and stumbling over the ploughed furrows to get back to the farm.

By now, my lungs felt as though they were on fire. I'd always considered myself fit and healthy, but I'd never had to run like this in my entire life and I was hurting all over. The exertion seemed without end.

It was about four o'clock in the morning when we turned into the farmer's yard. I drew a sigh of relief, and sent up a quiet prayer that we hadn't been caught. Then I added a prayer that Gudrun hadn't been anywhere near the church when the people hiding were rounded up.

'That was devilishly close!' Rønne wiped his forehead with a handkerchief.

'I wasn't particularly eager to meet them either,' said Kiær dryly, relief etched on his face. 'It would have been hard to explain why we were out on the road at this hour, and if the Gestapo had searched me, they'd have found a heck of a lot of money.'

When Kiær broke the news to the anxious refugees, several of the grown-ups became hysterical, and some of the children cried heartbrokenly.

Hans-Peter, who was now wide awake and annoyed he'd 'missed all the action', as he put it, knelt in front of two of the children and tried to calm them, and I lifted up a little boy.

'There, there,' I said, bouncing him gently on my arm. 'It'll be all right, just you wait and see. You just need to be brave for a little bit longer. Can you do that?'

But the child was inconsolable, and all I could do was continue rocking him.

'Will you please strangle that kid!' someone shouted. 'The Germans might hear him!'

I sent the person who had spoken a furious look. 'He can't help it. Just because he's been sedated, that doesn't mean he has no emotions. Anyway, I doubt the Germans can hear us out here in the middle of the countryside.'

But whether the Germans could hear the crying child or not, the question remained what to do now. After the round-up at the church it was too dangerous to stay in the Gilleleje area, but so was driving back to Snekkersten.

In the end, Kiær, Rønne, and Bruhn decided this was the safest option of the two because in Snekkersten the refugees could be dispersed in the houses of the locals again. The truck drivers were reluctant to take the same trip again, and Kiær had to negotiate a new payment with them.

To everyone's relief this wasn't a lot of money. Kiær paid the drivers out of the 60,000 kroner, and the rest was returned to the refugees.

'We need to wait until sun-up,' Bruhn pointed out. 'The lights from the trucks will arouse too much attention.'

We waited until 5.30am, and forty-five minutes later we arrived safely in Snekkersten where the refugees were accommodated in the houses in which they had previously been staying.

Disappointed that the trip had been a failure, I crept back into the house and tried to be as quiet as possible. I could hear my aunt and uncle getting up, and right now I was too tired to answer any questions.

Frozen and dirty from the scramble across the fields, I got into bed with most of my clothes on and barely registered when Sara left her mother's bed and snuggled up to me.

Relishing the child's warm body, I fell into a completely dreamless slumber.

Chapter Twenty-Eight

Helsingør

7th October 1943

I was woken by a loud knocking on the front door. Sitting up abruptly, I disturbed Sara, who was lying next to me. The little girl started whimpering.

'Shh, shh,' I said. 'Stay with Mummy.'

I flung on a robe. Jens was on the landing, dressed for school. 'Get Sara and her mother into the attic and tell them to pull up the ladder. Now!' I urged him in a low voice, then rushed down the stairs.

Uncle Poul and Aunt Marie both sat at the kitchen table, frozen in place, but when Uncle Poul saw me, he rose, hands trembling, and went to open the door.

It wasn't the Gestapo as I'd feared, but a local police

officer, and Uncle Poul stepped aside to let him in. When he took off his cap, I went cold.

Clearing his throat, he looked at each of us in turn. 'I'm afraid I have some bad news.'

Aunt Marie's hand flew to her mouth, stifling a whimper, and Uncle Poul put his hand on her shoulder. I simply stared at the policeman, thinking that soon I must wake from this horrible dream.

It can't be.

'The body of a young woman has been found on Julebæk Beach. Identity papers in her pocket indicate this may be your daughter, Gudrun Bredahl. And we also found this.' He took something out of his pocket.

Gudrun's woollen hat.

'No! No, no, no!'

Aunt Marie sagged against her husband, then her legs gave way and she crumbled to the floor, wailing into her apron.

'Oh, dear God, how could you? Not my child, my beautiful child! How could you?'

Ashen, Uncle Poul sat down beside his wife, cradling her in his arms and whispering terms of endearment repeatedly, tears streaming down his cheeks.

Stunned by the news, and the way my normally strong aunt had come undone like this, I stared at them and saw them shrink and age before my eyes, those wonderful, pragmatic people who'd shared their home and their affection with me and thought nothing of it. Then my own grief hit me with the force of a speeding train, spreading from my chest to my limbs, neck, face. With a stifled sob I took Gudrun's hat from the policeman and pressed it to my heart.

'Where is she?'

'She's at the mortuary. We'll need a member of the family to formally identify the body.'

I nodded. 'I'll go. I'm her cousin.'

Behind me I heard Jens on the stairs. He was leaning against the enclosed banister, his young face a grey mask of pain. Clenching his fist, he banged it against the wood.

'Did you…?'

'I heard,' he replied, his voice breaking. 'Perhaps I should go.'

I took his hands in mine and caressed them with me thumbs. 'I think it's best if I do it. I need you here to take care of your parents. Send for Dr Winther.' Leaning closer, I whispered, 'And I need you to take care of fru Jakobson and Sara. Take them to Kiær's workshop. He'll understand. Can you do that for me?'

If the Gestapo had killed Gudrun, as I feared, there was no way of knowing what she might have told them beforehand. I had to act swiftly. What mattered now was the survival of the rest of the family, as well as those in their care. I couldn't bear to think of anyone else losing their life in this senseless manner.

Jens nodded slowly, the grief in his eyes mixed with relief at not having to perform the gruesome task of identifying a body, as well as a determination to ensure that his sister's death, what she stood for and believed in – what we all believed in – wasn't in vain.

I got dressed as quickly as my trembling hands would

allow. Maybe this was all a mistake, maybe Gudrun's papers and hat had somehow ended up in the pocket of another woman. It was possible, wasn't it? But even as I tried to hold onto hope, deep down I knew that I was fooling myself. The feeling left me hollow and drained.

When I got back downstairs, David was in the kitchen with the policeman. The furrows on his forehead told me that he knew what had happened.

'I've just heard,' he said, and squeezed her arm. 'Would you like me to come with you?'

I nodded. The thought of David beside me, his reassuring presence, the warmth in his voice... Yes, with him there perhaps I might just get through this thing.

Uncle Poul and Aunt Marie were in the parlour, seated on the old-fashioned high-backed sofa with its antimacassars. Silently, with their hands clasped, they were leaning against each other, two dark shadows slowly slipping into history like the sepia-toned family portraits on the wall behind them.

Jens stood in the doorway. 'Dr Winther is on her way.'

'I... I'm off,' I said.

He gave a curt nod. 'I know. It's just the two of us now. And we'll do what we have to do.'

David took my hand as we climbed the few steps to the mortuary. Walking behind the policeman, we didn't speak, and neither did the officer. This was no time for chit-chat.

In a white-tiled room with a sheet-covered gurney in the

centre, my worst fears were confirmed. How I got to the room, and out again, I couldn't remember. It was as if my mind had refused to cooperate at that point.

And how I found myself in the cemetery by St Olai Church – a cemetery of all things – I couldn't remember either. A saving grace perhaps, that all that would ever stand out about that morning was the before and after. David held me in his arms as grief rolled over me, wave after wave, tearing me apart in little chunks at a time. And David was with me when those chunks began to come together again, forming a whole me, a new Inger, like droplets of rain gathering to make a larger puddle.

Finally, the storm raging inside me passed. Practicalities took over. There was work to be done, things to arrange, people to inform. Now, of all times, none of us could afford to stand still.

Chapter Twenty-Nine

Helsingør

The same day

When Bodil arrived at work, Gudrun wasn't there.

Not again, she sighed, wondering what excuse she could come up with for her friend's absence this time, one that the supervisor was likely to accept. It annoyed her that she always took it upon herself to do that.

The factory floor of the brewery was quiet, apart from bottles rattling and the sound of the transporter. She felt her colleagues' eyes on her the moment she took up her station, although no one spoke to her. The woman who had called out to her yesterday when she was with Gudrun sent her a look of loathing, running her eyes over Bodil as though she was dirt.

Stripped and reduced to nothing, Bodil's face flushed.

So, they all knew about Oskar now. Helsingør wasn't a big town, the community was tight, and it was bound to have happened sooner or later. Yet at the same time it pained her.

Did they really not understand what it was like never to be looked at properly, only to be regarded as a source of amusement or pity? Oskar was the first man who'd ever seen her as a beautiful woman. And the first person who'd ever said how much he cared about her.

And it wasn't as if she was with him anymore. She'd said as much to Gudrun although deep inside she still hadn't decided. The things he'd said that she'd found so abhorrent, well surely this was what he'd been told, like a child in school, and maybe if he was shown it for the lies they were, he'd stop believing them. Wouldn't he? She'd thought she might be falling in love with him, and the idea of the life they could have had together still consumed her.

Why was that so hard for the rest of them to comprehend?

Drawing in a deep breath, she raised her chin.

Around midday the supervisor came onto the factory floor. He walked slowly, and when he spoke, he chose his words deliberately.

'I'm sorry to be the bearer of such bad news, but I've just learned that Gudrun Bredahl is dead.'

His words were greeted with a stunned silence. In the normally noisy brewery, you could have heard a pin drop. Then there were gasps of surprise, and one woman started weeping softly, followed by others. Gudrun had been popular.

Bodil found her voice. 'How can that be right? I only saw her yesterday morning, and she was absolutely fine.' Then she remembered that Gudrun had been heading to Gilleleje to help her fiancé transport Jews to Sweden. Had something happened to her there?

'I'm afraid so.' The supervisor lowered his eyes before he continued. 'She was found on the beach. Shot dead. They say the Gestapo did it.'

Bodil paled, and she had to find someone to hold onto.

Dead? By the Gestapo's hand? For helping people. Dear God! It was too much to take in.

All eyes turned on her. Her colleague from yesterday, her hands on her hips, came up to her, pushing her face so close to hers that Bodil instinctively took a step back.

'I wouldn't be surprised if you told your German some filthy lies about her,' she sneered, her face distorted with rage and grief. 'You traitor!'

'Bitch!'

'Syphilis mare!'

'You don't belong here.'

The accusations and hatred came like a spray of bullets from all sides and, covering her ears with her hands, Bodil ran out into the courtyard. She put her hand on the wall and felt the rough brickwork underneath her fingers as she fought against the grief which was crushing her from the inside. Gudrun was dead, and it was her fault. Guilt slammed into her; was it something she'd said to Oskar? But she hadn't told him anything really, had she?

She stood for a moment with her back against the wall, trying to stop hyperventilating, but her lungs wouldn't cooperate and she felt as if she couldn't get enough oxygen into them. It just couldn't be. There couldn't be a world without Gudrun in it. It was impossible.

The supervisor had followed her outside. 'Frøken Frederiksen, I think it might be best if you leave for the day. Maybe don't come back for a while.' He spoke softly, and not unkindly. He knew she and Gudrun had been friends.

Bodil nodded, then dragged herself away from the wall and went to fetch her coat. As she pushed her bike through the brewery gates, the thought came back to her again that maybe it *was* something she'd said to Oskar. Her guard down, they had talked about all sorts of things during their time together. Had she said anything about what Gudrun got up to? She couldn't have; she didn't really know that much about it. Had chosen not to know.

But what if she had, unwittingly, betrayed her best friend?

She needed to speak to him, to ask him if he had passed on anything she might have said. It wouldn't bring Gudrun back, but it might make the hurt and guilt marginally less painful. If it truly was her fault, she'd never be able to forgive herself.

She cycled to the place where she knew he was billeted and asked the soldier guarding the gate if she could speak to him. Realising she didn't know his surname, it took a while before she managed to explain in German which Oskar she was referring to as there turned out to be more than one. For some reason she seemed to have forgotten how to speak the language and had to search for the words.

Eventually someone who knew him appeared by the gate. Bodil recognised him from the first time she'd met Oskar outside the inn; he'd been one of the other soldiers who'd made suggestive comments until Oskar had taken him to task.

The soldier was equally disrespectful today, despite his previous dressing down, and he greeted her with a sneer.

'He's not here anymore,' he said. 'They sent him to the east.'

Bodil stumbled back a step, her stomach hardening. The *east...*

'He begged them not to send him,' the soldier added contemptuously. 'Said he had important information to tell them. Don't know if he did. Maybe the coward just said that to try to stay. *Ihn sehen Sie nicht wieder.' You won't see him again.*

Bodil felt herself crumble inside when he added the final coup de grâce.

'Thank you for your services to the Reich.' He gave a mock salute and turned on his heel.

She got back on her bike and pedalled away as fast as she could. She felt besmirched by his suggestive leer, besmirched by her connection to Oskar, betrayed by her own heart. The awful, gut-wrenching realisation that her desperate need for love and acceptance had made her careless. The possibility that she had, inadvertently, shared some crucial information with Oskar, though what exactly she would never know.

That Gudrun really was dead because of her.

No longer able to cycle, she got off her bike and threw it in the bushes. Why did she need a bike now, or a red skirt, or anything else for that matter? Nothing mattered except this massive hole in her chest which could never heal.

Then, as practical as ever and with a thought to the scarcity of supplies, she picked up the bike again and made her way home on foot, pushing it, the road longer and more agonising than ever before, with each step like a jab to her heart.

Gudrun was gone. Oskar too, for what were the chances of him surviving the fight against the Russians? They were as brutal as the Germans, or worse.

And Inger... How could she ever look her in the eyes again, knowing what she had done?

———

Her father looked up from cleaning out the chicken coop. 'Why are you back so early?' he grumbled.

'I...felt unwell.'

'Hmm. Not so unwell you can't pick them rowanberries before the birds get them all?'

Bodil rounded on him. 'Would it hurt, for once in your life, to say something kind to me? You're the most malicious son of a bitch I've ever known, and everyone fucking hates you! You'll die alone and forgotten!'

His face distorted with rage, her father took a step towards her with his hand raised, but she stood her ground. Perhaps it was something in her eyes, or maybe he had a change of heart, but he lowered his hand again and returned to his task with a growl.

'Just get to it.'

She went upstairs to change. When she had finished, she went into her brother's room and slipped her purse under his pillow. In the barn she found a pail and whatever else she needed, then made her way across the field to the woods at the end.

Chapter Thirty

Helsingør

Later the same day

When I returned to the house, it was like entering a mausoleum. My aunt and uncle had gone to bed, and neither fru Jakobson nor Sara were there – just as I'd become used to the sound of Sara's tiny feet padding on the kitchen floor. I even missed her pushing the increasingly dirty ragdoll in my face so the doll could say hello.

Dejectedly I sat down on the haybox and leaned my head back against the wall, hoping to catch some echo of the family banter and gentle disagreements. *The family might never recover, but would the house? Or did it absorb sad memories like coats of paint?*

Eventually Jens returned, and there was a new determination in the way he came in and sat down across from me. An older Jens, thrust into full adulthood all too soon.

'Fru Jakobson and her daughter are at the workshop as you asked. Kiær agreed that after…what has happened, it's best to get them to safety, and the people staying at fru Holm's as well.' Jens folded his arms over his chest.

'They're all to go to Snekkersten after dark,' he went one. 'Kiær is going to try getting some of the refugees you attempted to move yesterday to Sweden from there instead. He says it'll have to be in small boats, though.'

I nodded. It seemed pointless to ask how he had all this information; he was clearly part of the group now, and if Kiær saw no reason to worry about Jens's young age, neither would I.

Jens took my hand. 'I'll arrange this with David. They must walk in small groups of two people to the designated place. I'll show the way, at a distance. Perhaps you should get some sleep.' A new maturity flashed in his eyes and I wondered where he was finding the strength for this. But perhaps when things were at their lowest ebb, people managed to dredge up the necessary courage. Later, when we had the luxury of time, he could collapse, but for now he was operating on sheer willpower for the sake of his sister's memory.

I shook my head. 'First I need to see Bodil. She and Gudrun were best friends. I want her to hear it from me.'

But Bodil wasn't at work. A couple of women in brewery aprons stood in the courtyard smoking.

'They sacked her,' one of them explained.

The other woman shook her head. 'They didn't sack her, just told her not to come in for a bit after we found out what happened to Gudrun. Though if you ask me, they should jolly well toss her in the nearest dungeon and throw away the bloody key. She's the worst kind of traitor, a *tyskertøs*. And *you* should know better than to get involved with the likes of her.' She jabbed her finger at me then stubbed out her cigarette with a vicious stab and went inside. The other woman shrugged and followed her.

The venom was like a slap in the face, and I stood frozen momentarily while I recovered.

What was the matter with these two? How could they even think that Bodil had anything to do with it? She'd never betray her best friend.

And how must Bodil be feeling? Devastated by the news, no doubt, as we all were.

I got on my bike and headed south of town to Bodil's homestead just outside Snekkersten. I'd never been there and had to ask a man walking along the road for directions. It turned out Bodil's father was well known around here, although judging by the man's expression it wasn't for good reasons.

I could see why. Bodil's father was in the farmyard when I got there. Looking me up and down as if I had some nerve asking after his daughter, he sneered that she had to work, unlike some he could think of.

'She has no time for your girlie nonsense.'

Suddenly, incandescent rage flashed inside me, and I stared him down. First Bodil's workmates, now this odious man who looked as if he thought it cost money to smile.

'I assure you this is not girlie nonsense. Her best friend has died. A best friend who also happens to be my cousin,' I added sharply. 'And I need to talk to her about it.'

He shrugged and turned to walk away, but I blocked his path. 'Where is she?' I demanded.

'Hell and damnation!' he spluttered. 'What's the matter with women today? She went that way, to pick berries. Now get out of my sight!'

He pushed away from me and almost collided with a young man who had just come out of the stables carrying a bucket in either hand.

'Watch where you're going, you clown!'

The young man – Bodil's brother, Aksel, I thought, who'd be a little older than Jens – sent me an apologetic shrug at the older man's rudeness, and I grimaced back. Then I went in the direction Bodil's father had pointed, to a cluster of trees at the end of a field. Stepping over the deep furrows reminded me of the mad scramble across another field in the night. So much had happened since then that it felt as if years had passed.

As I got closer to the small wood, I saw what at first appeared to be the colours red and white, as though someone had raised the national flag in amongst the trees.

How strange, I thought.

Except it wasn't the Dannebrog. It was Bodil in her red skirt and white blouse hanging by her neck from a tree, the rope creaking as her body swung back and forth in the light wind, and her brown shoes, one with a built-up heel, banging against the trunk.

'Oh, Bodil, noooo!'

Immediately I rushed up to her and placed myself under her. She was only hanging two feet off the ground, and I had to create some slack on the rope, but the forest floor was too soft, and I sank under our combined weight. Touching Bodil's wrist I checked for signs of life, but her skin was cold and bluish, her eyes protruding. There was no pulse.

Shocked, I dropped down onto a fallen log. 'What have you done?' I whispered. 'Why didn't you speak to me? I'd never have thought you capable of betrayal.'

As I sat there, Aksel came running. He must have followed me as I went into the woods. 'No, no, no, no!' he yelled. 'Help me get her down!'

Together we lifted Bodil to loosen the noose around her neck and laid her down on the moist vegetation. I watched as Aksel unleashed his grief, collapsed over his sister's body, crying uncontrollably.

Cold and empty inside, I myself lost track of time. Here was yet another young man who had lost a most beloved sister; the reasons were different, but the underlying cause the same.

This damned war. The bloody Nazis.

With the help of two men from the neighbouring farm, who had been working in their field, we carried Bodil back to the farm and laid her gently down on the tattered sofa in the parlour. The two men then left to call for the local doctor to come and officially pronounce the cause of death.

Aksel sat beside the sofa, cradling his sister's hand to his cheek. At a loose end, I didn't know whether to stay or to give the family privacy. In the end, Bodil's father made the decision for me.

He came into the parlour and took one look at his dead daughter. 'I suppose I'll have to get some hired help now.'

Bodil's brother jumped up. 'You bastard!' he shouted. 'This is all your fault. If you'd treated her as you ought, maybe this wouldn't have happened. I hope you rot in hell!'

He planted a large, strong fist in the older man's face, sending him flying. His father landed in a heap against an armchair where he lay groaning. With a look of contempt I left him where he was and sat down next to Bodil's brother. Together we waited for the doctor to arrive.

After what felt like hours, I finally made my way home. Energy had drained out of me like water from a vessel, but I had to find the resources for this evening's rescue attempt. After a cup of coffee and something to eat, which I forced down only because I didn't want to collapse later, I left the house yet again. The cool evening air revived me and, with renewed determination, I cycled to the meeting place in Snekkersten, a set of beach cabins behind a row of tall trees. The day had been so harrowing already that I was numb enough not to even feel afraid.

Hans-Peter was there, and he gave me a brief hug, then left with David to organise a boat from the small harbour at Snekkersten. I stayed behind with the small group consisting of fru Jakobson and Sara, the elderly couple who had been staying with fru Holm, and fru Nathan.

As we waited for David and Hans-Peter to return, David's mother pulled me aside.

'I want to thank you for everything you've done for me and my son, even at such a time as this. The loss of your cousin...' She shook her head in sadness and paused because there was no need to add anything. 'But I must prevail upon you one more time.'

'Of course,' I replied.

She handed me a small beaded velvet bag, tattered from many years of use, a ladies' evening bag from a bygone era. 'In here is my jewellery. I want you to look after it while I'm gone. David would want to sell it when we get to Sweden, I should think, but these are family pieces. I couldn't bear to part with them. Better if they stay here for now.'

'I can't... I mean, you'll want it with you, surely,' I protested.

Fru Nathan insisted. 'I've trusted you with my life. I think I can trust you with my jewellery.'

In the end I agreed, and while no one was looking, I hid it underneath one of the large boulders on the beach. If I was caught and sent to prison, I could get Jens to retrieve it.

Although I hoped none of us would be.

David and Hans-Peter returned with a rowing boat and moored it in the shelter of the jetty. One by one the refugees waded out to the boat and climbed in; walking along the jetty itself would have been too conspicuous, even though it was pitch black.

I got in as the last person, with Sara in my arms, and sat

down next to fru Nathan across from David and Hans-Peter, who began to row. The two men were chuckling quietly amongst themselves.

'What's so funny?' I whispered, but even a whisper seemed incredibly loud in the quiet evening.

'That was easier than I'd thought,' David whispered back. 'No one disturbed us. We just placed the boat in the water, and Hans-Peter found the oars behind one of the fishermen's cottages. Then we rowed past the coastal police officer who was standing at the end of the pier. He didn't even bat an eyelid.'

I grinned at them in the dark. After the trauma of today, seeing two grown men acting like schoolboys was just what I needed. For a little while, at least, it dulled the ache in my heart. So did sitting here with Sara, in the dead calm as the boat silently glided through the water, the only sound the slight groaning of the oars in the rowlocks. There were no lights in the boat, and we steered by the guiding light from the Swedish town of Helsingborg six and a half kilometres across the water. As luck would have it, it was a quiet evening, and the sea was calm, with only gentle waves lapping against the rowing boat.

I'd told Sara that we had to play a game of who could be quiet the longest. 'Quiet like mice,' I'd said, placing a finger over my mouth.

Sara copied me, then placed a finger over the mouth of Betty the doll too, and as she leaned against my chest, she proved to be as good as her promise. Not a sound came from the little girl. Holding her close, my heart swelled with pride.

The tailor's wife, who had stayed with fru Holm, had taken the exhausted fru Jakobson under her wing and sat in the stern while her husband sat in the bow.

Then there was a shout from the beach, loud like cannon fire in the still night.

'*Halt, oder ich schiesse!*' *Stop or I'll shoot!*

I clamped my hand over Sara's mouth as her eyes went so wide the whites were visible in the dark, and everyone ducked down inside the boat except the rowers who now rowed as fast as they could, the need for silence no longer a necessity.

We couldn't be sure the Germans could see us in the dark, but now they would be able to hear us.

Several shots were fired seemingly at random, and David slumped forward with a groan right next me. For a short moment, my heart stopped beating altogether and I had to clamp my lips together not to utter the cry of anguish that welled up in me. I reached out to touch him in the dark and felt the warm, sticky blood from his head on my hand, although I could tell he was still alive.

Knowing her son to be injured, fru Nathan became distressed, but fru Jakobson suddenly found strength within herself, holding the older woman in her arms.

'Shh. He'll be all right,' she whispered. 'We're all going to be all right.'

'Grab the oar!' Hans-Peter hissed in my ear.

Without hesitating, I clumsily changed places with David and took the oar David had been using. From the beach, the soldier, or soldiers, kept shooting, but the bullets landed in the water far away from us, and then eventually they gave up. There wasn't much they could do; by the time they managed to get in touch with a German patrol boat, the rowing boat would be far away and could be anywhere.

For the second time in my life – the first being on an outing with my parents – I rowed, repeatedly pulling and pushing the oars faster than ever before. My arms and legs ached, the palms of my hands rubbed till they were raw, and my chest felt like it was about to explode.

My only thought as tears ran down my cheeks was that Gudrun and Bodil were dead, and now possibly David too if he didn't get help soon. If I could run for my life across a muddy field, I could do this too. I could do it for David, for Sara, for all of them.

I will not let it break me, I will not.

If I do, we have all lost.

Beside me I felt Hans-Peter's presence, knew that his face would look as grim and determined as mine, although I couldn't see him in the dark.

How long we rowed, I couldn't tell, but it would have been several hours. Time stood still; it had no meaning. All that mattered was the rhythmic push-and-pull, push-and-pull.

Just as I thought I could go no further, Hans-Peter stopped rowing, and we allowed the boat to drift on the waves. Glancing behind me, I saw how close the lights of Sweden were.

Or was it a trick of my mind?

Out of nowhere we were suddenly caught in a search light, blinding us. Fru Jakobson and the tailor's wife screamed, and the smell of urine from where Sara sat in the bottom of the boat rose, fear and panic giving it an acrid odour. The little girl had wet herself.

Pulse racing, I covered my face in my hands. We'd come so far, only to lose everything at the very last minute. Then a voice, the sweetest music I'd ever heard, and a greeting I'd always remember.

'*Välkomna till Sverige.*' *Welcome to Sweden.* 'This is the coastguard. We will help you now.'

Friendly hands reached down, and the crew helped us onboard the coastguard vessel. One man tied the rowing boat to the side, then two men climbed down into it so they could bring David up on deck safely.

'This man needs urgent medical attention,' said Hans-Peter.

They brought David into the cabin and out of the cold, where they covered him with blankets. He was deathly pale and had a deep gash on his forehead where one of the bullets had grazed him, but his eyes were open, and he sent me a lopsided smile. I knelt beside him and took his hand.

'David...'

'I know,' he said in a low voice, as if he had trouble speaking. 'You need to get back before sun-up.'

Drinking in his features, the thick, dark hair and those hazel eyes, the colour of a fairy-tale forest, I pressed a kiss on his lips which were cold and tasted slightly of salt. 'If circumstances were different...' I whispered.

He squeezed my hand. 'If circumstances were different, we would never have met. And that I wouldn't have missed for the world.'

Appearing behind me, Hans-Peter placed his hand on my shoulder. 'Inger, we have to go.'

'I know,' I replied, tasting the tears I didn't realise I was shedding. 'Take care of yourself, David.'

'You too.'

As I came back out on deck, Sara ran up to me and flung her arms around me. I knelt to talk to her. 'I have to go now, but you be a good girl for your mummy. And when you get a little brother or little sister, make sure you're the very best big sister in the world.'

Sara nodded solemnly and let me go. As Hans-Peter and I climbed back in the rowing boat, I heard Sara speak for the first time, and my heart filled and broke at the same time at the sound of her unused voice.

'Goodbye, Inger.'

As the lights from the coastguard vessel slowly disappeared behind us, we began the long journey back, but now that the boat was lighter, it wasn't as arduous as before, and we reached the same jetty from where we'd left without any problems. While Hans-Peter secured the boat against the planks below the jetty, I waded ashore and retrieved fru Nathan's jewellery from where I'd hidden it.

I felt no guilt over having stolen the boat, or 'organised' it, as Rønne would say. We hadn't kept it, and the annoyed owner would find it in a day or two. Perhaps he might know that it had been used for a good purpose.

'I'm glad we did this together,' said Hans-Peter, when he'd secured the boat.

'So am I,' I said and closed my hand around the tattered velvet bag in my coat pocket. If I held onto fru Nathan's jewellery tightly, it meant they would come back, didn't it?

It was getting lighter, and we climbed the slope to the villas on the ridge. Here we stopped and looked across the water to Sweden. It was still dark enough to make out the lights of Helsingborg, but dawn was coming and soon they would fade to nothing. Hans-Peter took my hand, and I winced slightly as it was still raw from rowing.

'When the war is over, and Denmark is free again, I'm going to live my life the best way I can,' he said, almost as if to himself. 'I want to be something for other people, for my community. I now realise just how important it is that we have a community. That we stick together.'

I nodded. It was hard to make sense of the loss of those you loved, but perhaps by focusing on those you saved, it might become bearable. About what you gave to the world.

Right now I was having difficulties envisaging the future, but it had to be based on reality, on what was in front of me. Perhaps the future would bring children, soft and sweet like Sara and the little boy; perhaps it wouldn't.

At any rate, there would be other people who needed love and care, and I would do my best to give it all.

Chapter Thirty-One

Copenhagen

October 2018

... I continued to be an active member of the group, and so did Hans-Peter. Jens joined, tentatively at first, but turned out to be a valuable addition. Because of his youth, he could pretend to be out at night seeing a girl (he did eventually find one).

Kiær bought a boat of his own, and we carried on arranging the illegal transports, in the end getting around 700 Jewish refugees to safety, distributed over 143 trips back and forth over the Sound. This was until Kiær was captured and sent to a concentration camp, and Thormod badly injured. The war ended, and I packed my feelings for David away inside, just as I put the jewellery in a safe place in the hope that it would one day be collected. He became a distant memory, and I thought perhaps he had died from his wound.

After all, there was so much life left to live, and I had to live
for three: myself, Gudrun, and Bodil...

C ecilie closed the diary and looked at David as he lay
in his hospital bed, eyes closed. The final diary entry
was dated some years after the war, as if her grandmother
had been tying up loose ends before packing the notebook
away with the jewellery, but for Cecilie something was
missing. What had happened to David in the intervening
years between the war ending in 1945 and him arriving in
Israel in 1948?

It had become clear to her that her grandmother had
been in love with David, although she hadn't expressed it in
so many words. What did David feel? she wondered.

Studying his face – a face she'd come to love in the last
couple of weeks – she noticed how his skin was yellow and
shrunken around the nose, and his rasping breath told her
he didn't have long to go. Was he well enough to fill in the
gaps?

As much as she wanted to, she couldn't ask a dying
man. That would be too selfish.

She took his hand so he'd be able to feel her presence to
the very end, and Rafi held the other.

To Cecilie's surprise he opened his eyes, and she caught
a faint twinkle in them. 'I'm not dead yet,' he said.

Cecilie smiled. 'I'm glad to hear it.'

He chuckled, which led to a coughing fit, and Rafi made
him drink some water. He settled back against the pillows
and sent Cecilie a penetrating look.

'I sense you have some questions. After we arrived in

Sweden, we were told not to send letters back to Denmark. There was some concern that this might expose the delicate network of conspirators and put the lives of other refugees in danger. So I decided to wait.' David squeezed her hand. 'I managed to get a job as a shop assistant in the town of Malmö, so we had something to live on. My mother fell ill again, and between caring for her and holding down a job, I barely had time to think, let alone write to declare my feelings for your grandmother, even if I'd been allowed to. I wanted to do it in person anyway, and I wasn't sure whether my affections were reciprocated. Shortly after, my mother died. She never mentioned the jewellery or Inger, or even our escape, but I suspect that having to flee for the second time in her life meant she chose to repress it.'

David sighed heavily.

'After the war ended, I returned to Copenhagen to find that, despite the best efforts of our excellent downstairs neighbour, our flat in Adelgade had been rented out again, and most of our things were gone, aside from what she'd managed to secure for me. I then lodged with her and her husband for a while. When I finally plucked up the courage to visit Helsingør again, I discovered that your grandmother and Hans-Peter had married.

'I saw her from a distance, although I don't think she saw me, and she looked happy. So I turned my back on Denmark. I had trouble reading the language, as you know, after being shot in the head, but I was still fluent in Yiddish and Hebrew. Palestine, as Israel was called back then, seemed like the only viable option for me.'

Cecilie couldn't help it: a sob escaped her, and she closed

her eyes. The thought of a love lost because of circumstances beyond their control was just so heart-wrenchingly sad and she couldn't bear it.

'Wait,' David murmured. 'I can see that you find this all tragic, and that you wish Inger had known that I came back for her. Well, she did. At least, she knew before her death. You see, sometime after your grandfather died – Hans-Peter – she had a go at finding out what exactly had happened to me. She wanted closure, I suppose, and that's when she found that I was alive and well, living in Israel. Tentatively, she made contact, and for a couple of months we corresponded. I wanted to make plans to meet up, and she pretended to go along with it, although she put me off coming over immediately. I don't know for sure, but I think she knew she was terminally ill and maybe she didn't want me to see her like that. There's something to be said for remembering a person the way they once were. And then…well, you know what happened.'

'Oh!' Cecilie felt relief well up inside her. 'I'm so glad to hear that. It's just a shame that—'

'I know.' David's fingers tightened on hers. 'But I will see her soon, I'm sure of it.'

That was one way of looking at it and she could see he believed it whole-heartedly. It gave her some comfort.

Rafi cleared his throat.

'Rafi?' David gave his grandson a brief nod, and Rafi retrieved something from his bag which he handed to David. 'I'm glad my mother gave her jewellery to Inger for safekeeping. She was right; I probably would've sold it.'

He took Cecilie's hand and dropped something in her

palm, then closed her fingers over it. She opened her hand to reveal a small gold pendant, the one from the cigar box shaped like the Star of David, twinkling with inlaid gems. 'This is for you.'

'But...'

'No "buts",' David croaked, but he looked at her sternly. 'Rafi arranged for it to be restored and cleaned. I want you to have it, in memory of your grandmother and what she did. What they all did. Hans-Peter, Kiær, your grandmother's cousin, the fishermen. Just ordinary people performing extraordinary acts of bravery because they believed in the simple humanitarian principle that we must help those in need. And that we are all equal.'

Staring at the pendant, Cecilie felt the weight of the gold in her hand, a small but substantial and rather unusual piece. Tears welled up in her eyes, sadness for the millions of lives lost, that was hard to avoid. But there was also a glimmer of joy that those who had lost so much had also been able to rebuild their lives. It made the pendant the most precious gift she'd ever received.

'Thank you,' she whispered. 'I'll wear it always.'

'And now I need to rest,' said David, and he lay back in bed.

For the remainder of the day, David dropped in and out of sleep. When he had moments of lucidity, Rafi would read from a Jewish prayer book, but in the end he put the book down and just sat holding the old man's hand while speaking to him softly in Hebrew.

To give them privacy, Cecilie rose and looked out of the

window at the darkening sky as she listened to David's breathing worsening to intermittent rasps.

'It's time,' said Rafi.

Cecilie returned to David's bedside and took his other hand. His skin felt cool and dry, and she cradled it in hers. The three of them held hands until David's chest stopped rising and falling, and his face softened into the features of the young man he'd once been.

Then Rafi pressed the call button for the doctor to come.

Hours later – or was it only minutes? – they found themselves outside the hospital. The sky was a midnight-blue blanket decorated with billions of starry pinpricks, and Cecilie filled her lungs with cold, fresh air, expelling the warm stuffiness from the hospital room.

As she looked up at the stars, Rafi hugged her from behind and pressed a kiss to her hair.

'You were right,' she said, when she was finally able to speak. 'This was a good death. I'm glad I was there; it was an honour to be with him until the end.'

'I'm glad too.' Rafi turned her around to face him. 'But life goes on. It's about what's in front of us, as your grandmother said in her diary, and I'm thinking very much about us right now. Do you think you could, one day perhaps, make the journey and visit me? In the country that my great-grandfather helped build from the ashes of the past?'

'That sounds a bit dramatic,' Cecilie replied.

'It does, doesn't it?' He sent her a cheeky grin. 'But Israel welcomes teachers, you know. Perhaps you could even stay permanently?' His gaze had turned hopeful now, intense as he waited for her answer.

Could she? Her grandmother was gone, her marriage had ended – and good riddance to that – and her parents loved to travel. Could she take this giant step into the unknown?

She thought again why she'd agreed to meet with David rather than just sending the jewellery to him in the post. At first she'd put it down to curiosity that she'd chosen to follow this thread of her grandmother's past, but she understood now that it was because she'd reached a point in her life where it was time to look outward, not inward. To greet each day without fear and stop licking her wounds.

It took courage to live when life didn't pan out as you hoped. Just as her grandmother hadn't allowed loss and disappointment to get in the way of her joy of life, neither would Cecilie.

Chewing her lip, she looked up at him, at his floppy, dark hair and amber eyes, then made a decision.

'I'd like that very much,' she said, and pulled his face down for a kiss.